released

released

Margaret Macpherson

Signature
EDITIONS

Cover design by Terry Gallagher/Doowah Design.
Photo of Margaret Macpherson by Ursula Heller.
Printed and bound in Canada by Marquis Book Printing.

Acknowledgements
This book has been a long time in the making and the author is eternally grateful to those who supported the project through its long gestation. To the Alberta Branch of the Canadian Authors Association and the University of Alberta bookstore for their new Writer-in-Residence program, thank you for time and encouragement. For careful reading of the manuscript in all its various incarnations, thanks to Linda Jennings, Laurel Sproule, Elizabeth Haines, Annie Graham, Sally Ito and Monica MacFadzean — your suggestions and support have been invaluable. To Janet Chotai and Joyce Harries, who saw the baby and did not throw it out with the bathwater, thank you. For fine and careful edits, thanks to Karen and her wonderful team. To Kay, who gave countless cups of tea and sage advice, to Virginia who appeared like an angel when I most needed it, to my original family whose love knows no bounds, and to my spiritual sisters, golden every one, Kathy, Carla, Kelly, Sara and Ann, thank you for believing. And finally, and most importantly, love and gratitude go to my family, William, Freya, Darian and Mark, true hearts all.

We acknowledge the support of The Canada Council for the Arts and the Manitoba Arts Council for our publishing program.

Library and Archives Canada Cataloguing in Publication

Macpherson, M.A. (Margaret A.), 1959-

    Released / Margaret Macpherson.

ISBN 1-897109-14-8

    I. Title.

PS8625.P54R44 2006   C813'.6   C2006-906303-6

Signature Editions
P.O. Box 206, RPO Corydon, Winnipeg, Manitoba, R3M 3S7

for Mark,
patron, lover, friend

He is rolling a smoke in the dunes up above the broad rocky beach when the wave-tousled head goes under. He sees the child struggle briefly, then sink. I can smell the apple he puts in his tobacco pouch, I can see his fingers fumble, the cigarette fall, him shuck the coat from his shoulders, run.

Ian is running, running down the sand, stripping off his sweater, and kicking off his heavy prison issue boots at the shore. Next, he's in the water, its sharp bite stealing the breath from his chest, and headlong, without fear or thought, he plunges into those waves.

There is only murky silence and the stirred-up sea clouds of swirling sand. Nothing. He comes up for air into the bright, loud roar of the sea and goes under again, eyes searching, arms reaching, finding nothing but the endless numbing water flowing fast and cold and weightless through his fingers. His feet can no longer touch the rocky bottom and he is disoriented. Where is the shore? How could a little kid be this far out?

Again, I see Ian pull to the surface, watch him get slapped down by a wave, but somehow I know that gulp of air will sustain him. My own lungs are bursting. I can't breathe. I feel the throb in his unprotected head, and I shout out when the shadow of the boy floats below him, face down, splayed like a spent star. He grabs the body and pulls it up from the water as his own lungs explode.

I dare not exhale as he turns the child onto his back, chin to the sky, and holds him in the crook of one arm, pushing the sea away with the other until he is close enough to feel stones beneath his feet.

There are people now, everywhere. A strong-armed man wades chest deep in the water, pulls the child from Ian, and bundles the small body up onto the shore until it is lost in a circle of concern.

I watch Ian stumble up the slope of the beach. He trips on his own abandoned boots. He cannot distinguish the individual sounds of the siren, a child crying, the screaming seagulls and the hysterical mother, for the waves still pound in his ears. He is chilled and shocked and dripping wet. Someone puts a beach blanket around his shoulders, while someone else breathes air into the boy. Whether the kid is alive or dead, Ian does not know. All he wants now is warmth and solitude, to be left alone long enough to recover.

It is the same thing I wanted, solitude, enough time to recover.

"Ruth? Ruth. Are you okay?" It's my husband, Steve, beside me. His dark eyes are filled with a strange soft light and I know instantly that I am not on that beach; that I am here in the basement with him.

I sway on the balls of my feet, clutching the newspaper clipping in my hand. The smell that I thought was the apple of Ian's tobacco pouch is mildew. The slapping sound is Steve beside me, going through his box of memorabilia; it is not the sea or a dripping Ian patting his soggy shirt pocket looking for a cigarette.

At the same moment I know where I am, I also know that this yellowed paper quaking in my hands is more than an amazing coincidence. It is a gift. It blurs before my eyes and I sink to my knees, afraid, yet wanting so much to believe it is him.

Steve's arms come around me immediately. He knows something is very wrong. I cling to him and shake and shake as though it were me rising from that frigid water, as though it were me dragging the boy back to the stony shore.

I hold the paper in his face and shake it. "You must tell me everything about this. Everything!" I sound deranged, like a crazy woman emerged from the sea. Steve pulls back, sits on his haunches and frowns.

"It was just one of those things. I was at a conference in Halifax. It was just after I met you, before we started dating seriously. Remember I told you about the Dalhousie Lectures? I took the Sunday off and saw this — I don't know? — this rescue on one of the beaches. Some guy pulled a drowning kid out of the water. I took the guy back to my motel room and gave him some clothes. That's about it. I just saw it happen. He came out of nowhere. Saved the kid's life, I'm pretty sure."

"Why are you in the photo? Where is his picture?"

Steve shakes his head. "I took him to my hotel room. I let him shower, to warm up. The guy was blue. After I gave him the clothes he left, just disappeared behind the sand dunes. It was just before the reporter came. Why, Ruth? What is it? What's going on?"

I'm talking fast. My words tumble over each other in their rush to find voice.

"Did he have curly hair and blue eyes, bigger build, huge hands? What was he wearing? What year was this, what time of year?" And even as I speak, I want to drag the words back inside myself. I want to keep this memory in the safe place it has lived for years. This should not surface, not like this. Even though I've asked, I know instantly that I do not want Steve's details. But some protective layer has been punctured and I cannot stop the increasing expansion of this information. I quickly put my hand to his lips.

"It's nothing. I'm sorry. I don't need to know."

But he sits then, cross-legged beside me on the basement floor, and he waits for me to tell.

α

We meet in a bar. It is one of those sponge-wet evenings sometime in early April. The ground underneath my feet feels all squidgy and springy, like a mile below the ground gives way to a liquid centre, hot and shooting rays of fire to the crust. It makes me happy, the softening earth, and the knowledge that grass will be up and green in no time, providing I walk lightly so as not to break through. Winter is gone, its memory as insubstantial as hope.

Kevin walks beside me, but I barely notice him. He is one of my new roommates, tall, thin and gawky. If he were a girl he would be called willowy, but he's a boy and therefore a geek, still carrying his mechanical pencils and blue and red pens in one of those little plastic pocket protectors. I'm sort of embarrassed being with him and I'm glad it is dark so that no one can see us together.

It was me who suggested going for a drink. My last exam had ended that afternoon. Kevin was the only other student living in our house who was also finished for the term. The others were still studying. I almost decided not to go until he showed such enthusiasm. I've never been much of a bar girl, mostly because I don't like the taste of beer. I still think of hard liquor as the stuff that bums and rubbies drink. And fast girls, fast girls in fishnets. I have it fixed in my head somehow that beer and wine are okay and everything else is the devil's potion. So those rare times I do go out, I drink wine. Pink wine, if I can get it. I like the fizzy stuff that goes up your nose and tastes a bit like pop, all sweet and bubbly.

So when it's just Kevin who wants to go, I almost change my mind. I don't want him to get the idea that we're on a date. The guy is nice enough but totally forgettable.

The breeze off the Saint John river is cool and seductive and just being outside, unbundled after the long winter, feels so good. I haven't bothered wearing gloves and my hands float free in the moist night air like they are barely connected to my body. It is so wonderful, this sense of freedom.

We walk past the business district and down toward the water. I inhale deeply, joyfully, and at the same moment a train whistle sounds. It is close, just across the river. I stop and look through the darkness, trying to make out the engine, but it's too dark to see. It is after the whistle dies that we hear the music. The sound of the train far away and then the lonely whine of a blues guitar are exactly right for this spring evening. It is freakishly, uncannily perfect for the way I feel, the train going somewhere in the darkness, and the exams distant and small behind me.

The band is good, too. The lovely floating riff that lures us inside isn't a fluke. When my eyes adjust to the dimness, I see a five-piece combo, two guys, a sax and a trumpet in the brass section, and a paunchy guy working up and down the frets of an electric lead and doing vocals. His face betrays years of straight Scotch and cigarettes, but his voice is huge and strong and he's working really hard, filling that dark tavern with his magnificent throaty songs. The sweat stands out on his brow, and his collar and even the front of his shirt are soaked. The energy feels wild and freeing.

The bar is packed. Kevin hangs back, but I plunge forward into the crowd. Most of the patrons are students, and I recognize a few faces. No one calls out, "Ruth, Ruth, over here," so I just force my way through the throngs of people who are standing, listening. There are a few regulars sitting against the wall, closer to the front. As I look for a place to sit in a crowded bar of happy, spring-fired students, I become infected by the music, by the dark, throbbing tavern and by the wild energy of this April night. I feel magnificently alive.

The chairs in front of Ian, facing him, are empty.

"Can we sit here? Do you mind?" asks Kevin.

I watch Ian's face as he answers. He looks at Kevin quickly, then at me. I see him nod *yes.* I swing my chair halfway around so I can still see the band, but not so I'll have my back towards him. It would be really rude to join someone and then block their view. Besides, he is nice-looking, older, but in a crow's-footed way, a laugh-line way. He looks a lot like my cousin David, with the boyish face denied only by the lined eyes, and that crooked half smile. My half-turned body is an invitation he takes.

"I'm Ian Bowen." He sticks out his hand and I place mine inside his grasp. He holds my hand a split second too long. At the same moment the last lick of the guitar sounds potent and wounded and the drummer takes the band into their break with a final caress of his cymbal.

I smile. "I'm Ruth. This is Kevin. We're roommates." I'm worried that he'll think I'm with Kevin, that we are a couple, so I go on and on about how we all live together, share the same co-op house.

"It's for students, but we each have our own room, our own space."

I want him to know Kevin is incidental. I have my own room. Kevin has his own room. We are very separate, even if circumstances seem to say something else. I tell him about the common space of the house, why I chose to move there.

"It's a cheap place to stay where the food is good and the people are really nice. I like that it's communal. You don't feel so alone."

"You're not from around here, are you?"

I'm pleased he can tell I'm not local. I'm flattered for some reason and I try to make myself sound as worldly as possible. "No, I'm from out west. I've only been here for a few months. I did my first term in residence but there were just too many, you know, rules and things."

I giggle, then. It just comes out like some babbling fake tee-hee. I'm nervous and my hand goes up to my mouth. I still sometimes find myself falling into the old habit of trying to hide my smile. I draw my hand back instantly.

Even as it's happening I feel like I'm trying on a different face. It feels like someone foreign is speaking with my voice. I'm not Ruth Callis, industrious first-year arts student, but instead I'm a lounge lady with the husky cigarette voice and a come-hither look. I want him to see that I am as daring as the bandleader, as sensuous as the night.

Kevin starts talking about our co-op then. He's lived there for three years. *Great parties, man*, he says, like he's really into parties. We exchange looks, Ian and I, as though we both know Kevin is sort of pathetic, just trying to be cool when, in fact, we're pretty sure during a party he spends his time up in the university labs or in his room with the door shut. I roll my eyes when Kevin starts talking about the co-op parties. Just quickly, of course, up and back so Ian will see but not be quite sure if I've actually done it.

"What about you, Ruth, do you like the big house parties?"

I take a drink from the frothing beer glass, aware of his casual use of my name. "I haven't been to any parties," I say, looking right into his eyes. "I just moved into Kevin's co-op house."

"Oh, yeah?"

"I'm staying in town this summer to take some extra classes. The residence I was in last term is being used for Elderhostel, so none of us can stay. The old people take over the campus. You know the type, leisure suits, blue hair. Retired folk."

He laughs at that, and then the band starts again, drowning our words, buoying our mutual interest.

He says a few more things to me across the table while the music plays, and my beer glass is filled again and again, but I only pretend to hear, and smile agreement. The music is very loud.

During the encore, we both order more to drink, neither of us wanting it to be over. Well, actually, he orders two more first and then I do. Kevin doesn't.

When the lights come up, the bouncers start shouting *drink up, drink up*. When they begin taking away our empties before the suds even settle in the bottom of the glass, Ian invites us both back to his place. "I've got a bottle of wine at home. Maybe we could order a pizza."

I think it's really nice he includes Kevin in his invitation. It's a considerate thing to do, the type of thing my cousin David would do.

Kevin declines. Secretly, I'm glad. As he prepares to leave, I tell him I'll just keep Ian company while we finish our beer. My housemate is dubious about leaving me in the company of a stranger, I can tell, but I insist everything is okay and eventually, thank God, he leaves us alone. He looks back at me, once, as he holds the door for a couple of laughing patrons and I think he looks pained, as though he knows something is already out of control.

"He probably feels like he was dumped," says Ian.

"But we're not together."

"You came together."

"Because I wanted to hear the band." I know this is a lie and, mere hours ago, I didn't give a whit about the band but something, or rather someone, has cast a spell on me.

We both drink.

"You could still come over," he says, looking straight at me, the look half challenge, half amusement. "This place is clearing out."

And he is right; the bar is almost empty when I look around. In the bright fluorescent lights, everything looks uglier except him. He looks great.

He has curly hair, just a regular dirty blond colour, and freckles and blue eyes. His mouth is soft, bow shaped with a kind of a pouty lower lip. I have a flash of kissing him, right then, imagining what that lip would feel like between mine.

It's crazy. I'm not the type to fantasize about kissing a stranger but it happens like a brief shock, a pop-up cartoon picture of us kissing, my tongue touching that plump lower lip. I shake my head and wonder briefly how I look in the horrible fluorescent light after all the beer I've consumed.

"Yeah, let's get out of here," I say, standing up, feeling the beer roar in my brain.

His smile is sweet. Or is it more bemused?

The musicians are packing up. I can't believe they are the same people who played such infectious music. They look old now, and drained. The bouncers are hustling people out and the clock over the bar has long since lurched past midnight.

"I'm not sure if I should."

"Are you scared of me?"

"No," I say, knowing it is true. "I'll come, but just for a little while"

"Fine."

Ian picks up our coats, handing me mine across the table like a question. I take it, knowing I am embarking on something new, something that makes the blood quicken in my veins. The beer and this strange man, this man I've just met, who, now that he stands, is larger than I had imagined, is making me feel light-headed and brave. It feels like there is a current between us, something electrical and compelling.

I have a flash of myself as a teenager on my knees, praying zealously, passionately, for something as blurry and ephemeral as this place of smoke and glass. Every word and action between us seems invested with meaning, as though this meeting were ordained. The harsh, ugly bar fades to the potency of spring air smooth on my skin. Does he feel it too? Does he know we are embarking on something special?

His apartment is not far from the tavern. It is near the river, a well-kept turn-of-the-century house, renovated into apartments.

"Oh, I've always liked this place," I say, pleased when we turn off the public sidewalk. "I've walked by here before. Do you live in the tower?"

"No, I wish I did. That's a two-bedroom. There's a couple there, with a kid. She yells a lot. I'm below them."

He holds the main door for me, and I enter and pull open the second set of glass doors. A wide staircase with a curving banister runs up from the central foyer. On either side of the staircase, running into the darkness, are doors with brass number plates on them. I let him go ahead. I've had a lot to drink. A voice inside my head says *Whoa, whoa, Ruth,* but the voice is easy to ignore.

Each movement, and the few words of conversation we've exchanged on the walk to this place, feels staged, as though all I have to do is follow some script. Unwittingly, I have become an actor in an art film. I feel like I am watching myself climb the staircase and I am acutely aware of my legs beneath me. They feel strong, those legs, strong and powerful, and the motion of them climbing the stairs to his apartment feels exactly right. If there is a God, I know He is smiling down on me at this moment, for I know exactly what I am doing.

The apartment is very small; two rooms, with a Formica table and two chairs separating the kitchen from the living area. One starts where the other ends. There is tile for the kitchen and carpet for the living room. There is a pink sofa, and an easy chair, blue. Both are nubby and worn, the old-fashioned furniture you still see in thrift shops once in a while.

The couch is wide in the arms, soft in the seat and backs, with springs stretched loose from age and wear. The chair has no legs and sits directly on the floor, but the sofa stands on concrete blocks. There is a lamp on an end table that is really just an upside-down milk carton and there are books everywhere, stacked, splayed, spine opened and upside down, hung on the window sills, spilling off the couch and poking out from underneath. Oh, yes, and prints on the walls. There are prints of famous paintings. I recognize a Van Gogh, *Starry Night,* and Monet's *Water Lilies.* They seem strangely feminine in this place.

"It's nice," I say, meaning it.

"I wasn't expecting company."

He closes a door, presumably to the bedroom, and takes two candles out of a kitchen cupboard and puts them in candleholders already thick with drippings. The remnants of multi-coloured wax rivulets have hardened on those candleholders in a kaleidoscope of frozen motion. They look beautiful. He lights the wicks with a flourish, holds the flame trembling for a moment between his thumb and forefinger, and then, blowing it out, sets the candles on the coffee table.

"Sit down. I'll get us a drink."

I choose the blue chair even though it's lower. I tuck my feet under myself, hoping to appear small and comfortable.

A marmalade cat comes out of the bathroom.

"Oh," says Ian, his voice thickened by drink and affection. "Hello, Sadie. How's my girl?" and then he stoops to stroke her. The cat rubs up against his hand, an arched orange wave, quivers in delight, and starts to purr loudly. I can't take my eyes off his hands. They are so big and seem so gentle.

He crosses the small room, rummages through a bottom cupboard and brings out a large bottle of wine. It is red, unopened. The top screws off. He pours the wine at the counter with his back to me, and brings it in thick, ceramic coffee mugs that say *Day's Family Cafe*.

"I'm sorry I don't have proper glasses." He hands me the mug.

Ian sits on the pink sofa, across from me, and almost immediately the cat jumps up into his lap. He smiles as he strokes her, but there is something sad about that smile. He lowers his face into the cat's body and speaks with his face in her fur.

"I used to have two cats, but Harry died a couple of days ago."

His voice is shaky and for a moment I think he's going to start crying. I don't know how to respond, and before the correct sympathetic sounds come from my throat, he continues with his story as though he has been waiting all night to say this one thing.

"He drank Drano, Harry did. I was trying to unclog the shower. I never thought for a minute the cats would drink it, but Harry must have been thirsty. I took him to the vet — ran most of the way — but he died before I got there. Sadie really misses him. So do I."

I look into my cup, swirl the wine. What can I say?

We both drink and he puts on a tape to ease the awkwardness. Twelve-bar blues fill the room. Another man with gravel in his throat is singing about losing his baby and how he didn't know how much she meant until she was gone. *Gone.*

The word echoes and falls between the blue chair and the sofa, and then rises again. *Gone.*

"Hurtin' music," he says, putting on a false Southern drawl and smiling at me.

Yet, it is just right with the candles and the wine. There is a lot of wine in that great big bottle with the twist-off cap. He refills my glass before I get anywhere near finishing, and he tops up his own as well. Soon, like the song, the red wine is gone.

I stay the night. It is the wine and the conversation and the candles. We talk about northern lights and blues music and famous artists and fishing. We talk about the police force and careers and choices and chicken noodle soup and favourite books. Hours go by. In the end, he makes up a bed for me on the pink sofa.

"It's too late for you to go," he says simply, smoothing a faded flowered sheet over the rough surface of the couch. "This will be okay."

I agree, but I don't sleep. He kisses me once on the mouth, a soft gentlemanly kiss, before he disappears into the other room, and I lie very still for a while, feeling the kiss, warm and shy, just as I'd imagined, only better for being real. And, with the music in my head, the lingering sadness of that word *gone,* and wild red wine making me crazy and brave, I stand and feel my way into his room, and find him also lying awake and ready in the darkness.

I fall into him, and his arms go around me, just so, like he knew I would come to him. He breathes my name once, *Ruth*, like a groan, and we make love in the dark tangle of his bed, slowly, neither of us speaking.

In the morning, Sunday, I wake, large-headed and groggy. There is a moment of *oh-my-God* panic at first when I open my eyes not knowing where I am or who he is, but details creep back though my foggy, thick head. Ian.

"Was it all right last night?" he asks.

"Yes," I answer. "Wonderful."

He brings us each a glass of water and we make love again, while the light pours in on us. He is more passionate, more forceful, this second time, with a different urgency, but afterwards he is gentle, and he sighs such contentment and pleasure that I bite back my questions about other times, other people. I don't want to ask because the rest of the world feels distant and held at bay by the two of us and the fragility of our fuzzy Sunday morning.

I shower while he makes an omelet and when I come out of the bathroom, barefoot and hungry, I am amazed at the food in the fridge: vegetables, sliced meats and cheese. I turn to him, questioning.

"My mom was here. She always buys groceries." A sheepish smile. My heart leaps again. A guy who loves his mom. Wonderful. Fantastic. I think of the three of us around a table, Ian introducing me proudly. Despite my fogged brain, the future is clear.

He puts green peppers in the eggs after he discovers there are no onions, and we have tinned orange juice out of last night's same thick mugs. After eating, we leave his place and walk together down to the river towards the statue of one of the city founders. I feel I have to say something then, because bare-chested college boys playing football and couples walking dogs are intruding on our intimacy. I look across the river, deep green and slow, and then into the blue of his eyes.

"I don't do this often."

"I know you don't. Me neither." And we kiss out there in that open space under a blue bowl sky like old lovers would kiss, and I set off, happier than I've been in a long time.

I walk the rest of the way home so thrilled that something like this has happened to me. To me! I've met a decent guy, a regular decent guy who likes me. It feels like a flipping miracle has happened, like he was old Moses, holding out his rod and I was the Red Sea. He'd plunged into me, as my Chosen, and I'd parted and held him inside myself like the best secret there was.

α

The meltwater on the Buster Browns made a pleasant slurping sound and it almost overrode the fact that there was some leakage where the leather was stitched to the soles. My socks were already wet and I hated my shoes so much I was almost happy they were getting wrecked, although my mother's wrath played like a tape in my head. *Change after school. Play clothes are different than school clothes. I don't spend money on clothes to see them destroyed in one season.*

My play clothes were usually jeans with holes in the patches or shirts that were too small, cast-offs from the big girls. Sometimes I could get away with wearing something off the floor that had escaped the swooshing mouth of the washer in the basement. I imagined the machine breathing in, and all the dirty clothes being sucked into its rotating black hole. Did a washing machine know the difference between play and school clothes? Did it spit out play clothes if they weren't dirty enough; reject school clothes if they'd been worn only once? There seemed to be a system of clean, once-worn, twice-worn, dirty and too-dirty, but it was a laundry system only Elsie knew. Right now, I was bucking the system.

A warm westerly wind rushing down Main Street had released me from everyday ordinary things. I was on an adventure and my brown clumping oxfords were taking me to a new part of town. I watched where I was walking, careful to avoid the dog poop that had surfaced through the melting snow. I hated my stupid shoes. I wanted to wear running shoes to school, like all the other kids, running shoes and blue jeans, not stupid skirts, with something Elsie called middies, leotards and these stupid Buster Brown orthopedic clodhoppers.

Cutting through the Catholic church parking lot, I avoided looking at the statue at the top of the church roof. Mary was there with her arms outspread in an appeal for me to go back home and change into rubber boots. I crossed up and over the rock cut, across an empty field and, suddenly, I was nearing the back alley that just might be my destination.

Looking up at the fish-scale sky, I could tell it was still early afternoon. I had lots of time. My mission was to find two puppies, Lab/husky-cross puppies, born a few weeks before and now living in one of these backyards near the park. I'd been itching to see those dogs ever since I'd heard about them. It was crazy how much I wanted to see them. And I didn't just want to look at them, no way, I wanted to kneel down and have those little dogs climb onto my lap, whimpering and nuzzling, looking to me for warmth and love. I'd imagined it so many times. I was preparing to adopt those puppies and something in the warm wind felt like it was the right thing to do. It was coaxing me towards them, leading me to their need. I was about to become their human mother. They didn't know it yet, but I did. I'd known it ever since I'd heard Angela Thompson and Patricia McNab talking about them after library.

Abandoned, they'd claimed, *abandoned by their mother.* I could hardly believe my ears when I heard it. How fantastic. How fortunate. I immediately planned to seek them out and care for them. They needed me and their helpless little puppy need far outweighed the discomfort of my wet feet and the nagging anxiety that I was decidedly far from home.

I'd taken a detour, I told myself. I was actually on my way home. I was just going the long way. Besides, I was driven by mercy. This was a mission of mercy.

The alleyway was sloppier than the field, and the car ruts had formed rivers of soupy ice. My book bag thumped against my thigh so my walking sounded like hooves clattering and I imagined I was on a horse, my trusty steed, and he'd taken me into this unknown neck of the woods. That was something my father always said: neck of the woods. I wondered if there was a throat of the woods or a stomach of the woods, and if there was, what it would look like. This area of town was sort of run-down, not exactly the earhole of the woods, but something like that, something you wouldn't want to get too close to, like a kid with nits or, worse, ringworm.

It wasn't scary, though. Not really. It wasn't like the old town where all the Indians lived. It was more normal. The little houses the miners lived in were called wartime fours. That was the type of house we used to live in when Dad was just a regular miner on a regular underground shift. Now he worked nine to five, a shaft manager, and we had a better house, bigger and more like the posh government houses. There were some of those on this street, looking blocky and familiar. But it was the other houses mixed in that made it a strange-looking neighbourhood. They looked homemade and a little junky.

Looking at the houses, I was pretty sure Randy Okatonga lived on this block. He was in my grade and his house was next to Mr. Denver's crazy mother. That was one place I wanted to avoid, so I deked over to the shadowed side of the alley, eyeing the backyards suspiciously.

I'd seen her outside in January once. It must have been thirty below. My dad had been doing errands. The car had been parked and running and I'd been waiting inside, reading an Archie comic. I remembered looking up because of the movement and the colour amid all that winter white and there she was, Mrs. Denver, at the side of her house wearing nothing but a stupid house dress with short sleeves and big ugly purple flowers.

She was holding an Eaton's catalogue in her claw hands, but she wasn't reading it. No, she was just watching the wind whip the pages across her vision. She was laughing, too, that was the scary part. She was laughing at the colours and the pictures of all the different things you could buy if you had all the money in the world, all those things skittering and flipping past. I couldn't hear her laughing because the car was running and the windows were closed, but I could tell by her mouth.

I remembered just watching her, staring really, and feeling a little bit sick, and scared that a human being could be so interested in such a weird thing. The fat on the back of her arms looked all puckered and purple as it hung down like a wattle swaying in the wind.

She held the catalogue at a weird angle, high and out from her horrible fat arms like she was trying to let God read the sale items. I hated seeing her and I wished with all my might that she'd disappear, but I couldn't stop watching and I just stared at her until her grown son banged the back door open and rescued his mother from the cold and her showing her old-age craziness to any old person who came along.

Was theirs the white house with the yellow trim or the brown one next door? I couldn't quite remember. It had been a long time ago but not so long that I'd forgotten that crazy catalogue lady. She could have died by now, I supposed, but it wasn't that long ago I'd seen her and surely I would have heard. In this town you always heard that kind of thing even though it wasn't a real subject, like math or current events. If someone died in the town, the mothers got together and talked in quiet voices that stopped as soon as you came into the room for a snack or something. They must have thought kids were pretty stupid not to notice the talking had stopped.

I didn't tell anyone about her being outside though. I didn't want to speak the craziness so I just stored it away in one of the Do Not Remember files in my brain.

But this neighbourhood was making me remember, for sure. I scanned the houses up ahead and tried to keep my mind on my mission. Those pups had to be around here somewhere. But where? I was going to have to go home soon. It wasn't so light anymore.

Almost like an answer to my doubts, I heard it up ahead, the *yip, yip, yip* sound of small animals. There was no mistaking it.

They were in the backyard of a house I'd never noticed before. It was one of the homemade looking places, which meant the people who lived there didn't work in the mine or for the government like most of the regular people in our town. The house had a sagging back stoop and a clothesline that actually had sheets on it. I liked that. Elsie never put the sheets out, even though they smelled so good when they came in. She said she didn't "air intimates," whatever that meant.

In this yard there was a patch of frozen garden with what looked like the remains of lettuce still in the ground, all veiny and gross. And there was a dog pen.

Just as I was about to squat down at the edge of the fence, I saw her, a kid, maybe my age, maybe a year older. She was hanging off the fence looking down into the puppy pen. How had she gotten here before me?

I looked at her quickly. I'd never seen her before. She was probably a kid from the Catholic school, the one on this side of town. She looked back at me, her eyes narrow and suspicious. The girl spoke.

"You live here?"

"No, I came to see the puppies."

"Well, here they are. You might as well take a look."

She was acting like she owned them, cocking her head towards the dog pound where two scraps of black and golden fur tussled. Who did she think she was, the boss of them?

I crouched down on one knee and put my hand through the fence. The smaller one, yellow with a few blobby tufts of white fur, was adorable. He came right away and laid his cold nose in my open palm. "Awwwww." I couldn't help saying it.

"Com'ere," said the girl. "It's better over here." She had cleared the fence and was actually in the stranger's yard, leaning over a bale of straw placed strategically up against a ratty-looking doghouse. The golden puppy wandered away from me to the place the girl was playing with the other one. I eyeballed the fence and decided I could probably do it. I got one foot up, swung my leg over and I was there. We knelt together on the bale, stroking the squirming puppies. I cooed. They were just so darned sweet.

"They're not going to be pulling dogs, that's for sure."

I looked over at her and noticed her black hair fell like two dark curtains down the sides of her face.

"What do you mean?"

"These are bred all wrong. You don't want sucky dogs like this if they're going to be any good in the bush."

"Oh."

"You gotta take them away from the bitch right away, otherwise they go soft like these guys."

Bitch. I couldn't believe she'd said that word out loud. I didn't say anything.

"You gotta do it if you want a working dog. Stay with the bitch too long, and you get wimpy dogs; can't pull, can't track, can't do nothing. Doesn't mean they ain't cute, just useless." She pulled her hand away and sat partway up. Now I could see her whole face but it was a dark shadow against the sun.

I spoke to the puppies instead of the strange girl. "How do you know so much?"

She crouched beside me again. Bits of straw clung to her running shoes, which I noticed were blown out on the side by the big toe. She sniffed.

"My real dad runs dogs."

Then, "I'm Jax. It's short for Jaxine, like Maxine but with a J. Who are you?"

I looked straight into her black eyes quickly and then away again. "I'm Ruth Callis. I go to the public school. I'm in grade six, Mrs. Dalhousie's class. I'm good at arithmetic."

Her nose was crinkled as she rattled off the rote reminder of spelling: "Arithmetic: A Red Indian Thought He Might Eat Tobacco In Church. Damn right, he can," she added, saying the last part quietly, so I could barely hear.

I took a deep breath. "Are you?"

"What?"

"A red Indian?"

She started to laugh, sat back on her haunches and laughed and laughed. Her teeth were really white and straight and it made me self-conscious. I was thinking she had a pretty face, when all of a sudden she grabbed my shoe and twisted it off my left foot.

"No," she said, still laughing. "I'm a brown Indian."

Before I could stop her, she'd pitched my shoe into the dog pen, and leapt over the fence like it was nothing. She started running up the alley, shouting, "I'll see you here tomorrow, Ruth Callis. You get the wimpy yellow dog, I'm taking the other one."

And she was gone. Just like that, she disappeared down the lane.

My shoe, one of the ones I hated so much, now sat upside down amid the slush, straw and dog poop. If I was going to get it back, I'd have to hop across the pen on one foot. But where was that mother dog? Where was the bitch?

I contemplated leaving the oxford in the pen. Hadn't I just wished to get rid of them? But how would I get home? It was late enough already and there was no way I'd make it through the slush with just one shoe. Besides, what would Elsie do when I got there?

I looked beyond the puppies to the doghouse. If the mother dog was in there, she'd surely have come out by now.

And hadn't the girls at school said the puppies were abandoned? But what if that was wrong? Would the bitch bite me with her big hungry teeth? Didn't mothers protect their young? I was pretty sure I'd read that somewhere. But that Jax kid had said something about removing them from their mother. I'd have to take the chance.

"Here. Here. Here," I called in what I thought was a grown-up dog-owner voice. "Here, momma doggie. Here. Here." I slowly hopped across the pen, aiming for the place where my shoe lay upside down in the muck. The pups skittered around my feet, delighted that I was in the pen with them. They yelped encouragement as I tried to maneuver on one foot, one eye on the door of the doghouse.

One of the pups, the golden one, got underfoot just as I was about to scoop up my shoe and I wobbled and slipped, falling backwards on my bum. The puppies ran to me, leaping and licking at my face. I now had mud all over my school clothes, I still had only one shoe and there was wet gunk soaking into my book bag.

Despite all this, I felt strangely happy. There was no mother dog. These pups had definitely been abandoned. If Jax, the brown Indian girl, wanted to make these puppies tough, I was going to be around to make them gentle.

I picked myself up and stuck my soaking sock into my stupid shoe. Maybe I'd come back tomorrow. Maybe that Jax kid wouldn't come around again. I slung my soggy satchel over my shoulder, petted the black pup one more time and heaved myself over the fence before heading up the alley towards home.

Elsie was mad when I walked through the kitchen door and I could see the table was already set for dinner, usually one of my chores.

"Where have you been?" she asked, sort of hugging me, sort of crushing me. "And look at your outfit! Where have you been, Ruthie?"

"I went to see some dogs."

Now she was really mad. Elsie was allergic to dogs. "Dogs?"

"Yeah, puppies, because we can't have one here at home." Shoot, now it made it sound like it was her fault.

"And I suppose you're all covered in dog hair?" Oops, I hadn't thought about that.

"No, they're just small, almost hairless."

She started swatting at me, brushing the imaginary dog hair off my coat.

"Look at what you're wearing."

The school clothes thing again. I decided to pre-empt.

"Yeah, sorry about not changing."

Elsie softened, cupped my cheek in her hand. "I was worried, Ruthie. You're supposed to come right home after school. I won't have you children wandering about town, ragtag and unsupervised."

"I wasn't ragtag." I indicated my outfit.

"Ruthie, you're to come home right after school. No more doggie business. No more wandering about. And look at those shoes. You'll be polishing those up tonight, my girl, after dishes, homework and piano practice. I won't have you children looking like something the cat dragged in."

"We don't have a cat."

She smacked me on my bum then and I headed towards the room I shared with Jiggs, who was sitting on the top bunk reading *Tiger Beat* magazine.

"You're in trouble, Toothie."

I sat down on the bottom bunk, sighing. "Yeah, I know."

Her head appeared, upside down. "Where were you?"

"Just around."

She was still hanging upside down, looking at me. Her face was getting redder and redder. "Doing what?"

"I found some dogs."

"What do you mean *found*?"

"I'm going to adopt them.

"You can't. Elsie's allergic."

"I'm going to visit them every day."

She rolled her eyes and flipped back up to her own bunk. "You have to clear because I set."

She wasn't interested in the puppies. Before she would have been. Something had happened to her. Even Jiggs felt like one of the others now. She was reading a stupid movie magazine and chewing gum, probably stealing Claire's eyeliner and trying out the Egyptian look. When she'd showed me last time, I'd told her she looked good, when in fact she'd looked like something long dead and dug out of the ground. Like a corpse or a turnip with black rot spots for eyeholes.

"Yeah, sure, whatever."

I had to make a plan to get back to the puppy pen before that girl Jax took over. She'd probably have them hooked up to harnesses dragging firewood around before their bones were even set right. She wanted them to be working dogs, I could tell. I wanted them to be pets, my pets. I had to find a way to have my parents approve of this after-school adventure. Or else I had to tell them I was doing something else, something believable.

Two days slipped by and it wasn't until Friday afternoon that I got back to see the puppies. I brought gumboots and an old pair of jeans in a plastic bag inside my book bag. I told my mother I was staying late to help set up for the library book fair. She knew I liked books.

But, wouldn't you know it, Jax, the Indian kid, was there again, this time inside the pen, sort of mucking it out with a rake. I didn't say anything. She spoke first.

"Hey. You're back."

"Yeah."

"You want to help?" She looked shy all of a sudden, like she'd just remembered the shoe business and added, "I won't do nothing bad."

Somewhat reluctantly, I climbed over the fence. I felt my big bum teetering on the edge of the fence and I wished for a split second that I was little and nimble like Jax. She handed me a rake.

"I'm putting all the poop in that corner. Don't worry if there's straw stuck to it, makes it stink less. Once we get it all separated, they said I could take fresh stuff from this here bale."

"Who are *they*?"

"Them people that live here. They come out and talked to me yesterday. Said I could look after the pups till they're old enough to pull a sled. Then they're going down to the old town. Fella down there's looking to get some new dogs on his team."

"So they *are* sled dogs?" She'd said they weren't. Proved she was just a bossy old cow.

"Yup, just like I said before. Didn't I tell you?" And she thrust her pointy little chin out at me, but I didn't challenge her. She had said something about pulling dogs having to be separated like that.

I started to rake the muck to a corner of the pen and Jax started to pull fresh straw onto the frozen ground. The pups whimpered and whined with excitement.

"Do you think we can take them out once we're done?" I asked. She wanted to be the boss, so I decided I might as well let her.

"Yeah, I'm taking them, but it would be good if you could come too, one of them being yours and all."

So she hadn't forgotten. This Jax kid considered the blond pup mine. I couldn't keep the smile off my face and my teeth almost showed. She smiled back at me.

"Where do you want to go?" I asked, feeling as if I'd follow my new friend anywhere.

"I know a cool spot near the lake," said Jax. "Couple big chunks of rock fell off the face near shore and they made a sort of cave thingy. Sometimes I go there and make a fire." She looked up at the sun as if it could tell her something. "We might have time. I gotta be back in by supper."

"Me, too. You mean home, right?"

Her eyes sort of got squinty. "It's not home. It's where I stay. You know, up at the hall, the hostel."

She meant the residence attached to the Catholic school, a place run by nuns and matrons and a couple of town folk who cooked in the big industrial kitchen. Lots of kids lived there, kids in from the bush, parents still living on trap lines, still living off the land. Jax was one of those kids.

"Why do you live there?"

She shrugged, matter-of-fact. "Got nowhere else to live and government says I gotta go to school. My aunt lived here in town. She was supposed to take me, but she went to the city couple months ago, never came back. Anyways, there are lots of kids there. It's not too bad. We got a pool table and stuff like that."

"Do you ever get to go home?"

Jax spit then, right on the pile of poop and straw. "Yeah, I'm going back soon. I'm going back before they want me to, that's for sure. I think my mom's going to come get me real soon, take me back to the bush, up the East Arm where we live." She paused for a minute, looked around the pen and then over the yards to the houses that fronted onto the street. "I'm tired of this stinkin' place. Let's get outta here." And with that, she scooped the pups out the gate with a nudge of her foot and started heading up the alley towards the bush. "Com'on, Ruth. We don't have all day."

First of all, I wasn't allowed to go to the lake without an adult. The lake was dangerous, especially now with the frost coming out of the ground and the ice getting all soft and brown around the edges. I didn't know what made me disobey the voice in my head but I just thought it was all so cool, this girl and her world of caves and sled dogs and campfires.

And so I went. I followed her and the puppies followed us. It was like the movies. It was like owning a dog and having a best friend and going on an adventure all at the same time.

Jax almost wrecked it once we had cut through the park and gotten the pups away from all the backyard smells and into the bush. "What's wrong with your teeth?" she asked.

I immediately put my hand over my mouth and looked down. Had I been smiling? Had she seen? She didn't sound mean, though, the way she asked, so I decided to tell. I took my hand partway away from my mouth, just enough for the words to slip out but not enough for her to get a really good look inside. I didn't like her *that* much.

"It's an appliance. My real teeth got knocked out. In a fight."

She just looked at me and shrugged. I couldn't believe I'd lied like that. It had just slipped out.

"Do you have to take it out at night?"

I brought my hand away so she could get a better look. I hoped the wires and pink plastic weren't all slimy and covered in spit. Jax looked in my mouth and her eyes narrowed.

"What kind of a fight?"

"Well, it was more of an accident, really, not a fight I guess. Not like I got punched or anything. It was an accident. Of birth. An accident at birth."

"What, your momma drop you, smash out all your teeth?"

"No, not that."

"It's gross."

I felt my face becoming red. "Yeah, I know."

Jax suddenly said something that helped. "My kookum's got no teeth and I think she's the coolest person on the planet."

"Mine will come back. A new set. It's just gonna take some time. What's a kookum?"

"Grandmother."

"No teeth?

"Nope. Smokes a pipe, too." Jax made a sucking sound from her own mouth and I could imagine the stem of the pipe in the kookum's mouth, her crinkly old lips around it like Luke's second-hand catcher's mitt when it was closed. Even though I'd smelled tobacco smoke before when Dad and I visited the cronies, I didn't imagine the kookum's smoke all harsh and blue like theirs. I bet it smelled peaty and pure somehow, like the earth.

Jax and I both started to laugh. It was going to be okay. The relief felt fantastic and whatever weird strangeness was between us suddenly went up like the imagined tobacco smoke. The puppies yipped and ran ahead of us, and in the distance, through the black spruce swamp and the rocks, I could see the blue-rimmed edge of the big white lake. Jax whooped ahead of me and I followed, and it felt like my feet in their clompy rubber boots barely skimmed the ground.

α

The second time I see Ian, three days later, he comes to the co-op house. He must have found the address through the university or maybe by just asking around.

It is dinnertime when he arrives. Everyone is back from the weekend, milling around the living room, and waiting for the meal. It is my turn to cook and I've made cabbage rolls, which haven't quite worked out. There are no toothpicks to hold them together and the cabbage leaves have unraveled in the pot, so supper is a mess of cabbage and rice and hamburger swimming in a soupy tomato sauce.

I hear the doorbell ring but ignore it. My hands are greasy and the cabbage leaves still appear tough and uncooked. Besides, I've just moved in. I'm not expecting anyone.

"For you," says Brian, poking his head into the kitchen, and I go to the door, pushing my hair out of my eyes with my wrist, wiping my hands on the back pockets of my jeans. I am both surprised and pleased to see him. I am also a little bit embarrassed to have him see me in my home clothes, the kind of slouching-around, comfortable, baggy T-shirt and jeans that you wear when everything else is in the wash.

"Ian."

"Oh, hi, Ruth. I thought you might like to come over later." He is speaking quickly. "If you're not busy, that is."

"I'd like to, but I've already made plans."

I have. I am supposed to go to a movie with a girl from one of my English classes. We are going to see *Romeo and Juliet*, Zeffirelli's version, both of us pretending it is research. I watch his face. He seems so disappointed, as though I am lying, as though he thinks I've just plucked an excuse out of thin air.

"Oh, well," he says, casually, as if it doesn't matter anymore, "maybe another time."

He looks out of place on our porch. I notice again how big he is, how thick around the shoulders, neck and chest. He looks like a man. He *is* a man. The roommates look more like boys, like my brother Luke or some of his friends.

"I'll see what I can do. I'll try to come later. Is that okay?" I am anxious for him to be happy.

"Yeah, yeah, sure. Whatever."

He says it quickly, like he doesn't believe me, and it suddenly feels awkward with him on the porch like that, shifting from foot to foot. I can tell he isn't comfortable. He steps back to the street.

"Well, bye."

And he leaves quickly, without looking back. He walks with his shoulders hunched forward, and a slight side-to-side sway, almost a swagger.

Ian becomes a secret so easily, without effort, without thought, as though we both know, and agree without speaking, that's the way it will be.

I do go to his place after the movie, making up a story for my friend about an early morning meeting with a faculty advisor. It is my first lie, the first of many lies I'll tell about

Ian. But Juliet has to lie too, doesn't she? Forbidden love demands deceit.

He is so pleased to see me it is enough to push away the irksome feeling that I have not been honest and that no one knows where I am.

"I thought you wouldn't come," he says, eyes welcoming.

I laugh and touch his arm and feel instant electricity, instant erotic energy. What power. I laugh and at the same time I can hear the sound of that trilling laugher. It bubbles up out of my enormous pleasure, out of his pleasure, out of our mutual happiness.

"I know, but I told you I wanted to and now I'm here."

It feels good to be able to do that, to please him simply with my presence. He is lonely. He really expects so little. It is an incredible feeling to be wanted that way. Not just sexually either. It seems more than that. It is me he wants, not just Ruthie in the body. Me. Myself. Wholly. Yes, and holy, too. Because, let's face it, old habits die hard.

α

I thought of it as the summer of Jax, the summer before the summer of Jesus. It was the summer I crossed the line.

There was a game we all used to play when our family went camping, before we had any money to actually go anywhere. No one had their real friends around and we had to play with each other, so Claire and Theresa showed us a game that just needed a stick and some sand. It was the perfect game for the five of us when there wasn't much to do but swat mosquitoes and wonder what was going on at home. You had to jump over a line, toss a stick, leap to freedom. I thought it was the greatest game in the world, mostly because I hardly ever got to be with the older girls. But Elsie would always call us into the tent trailer when it got dark, just when my line was the farthest away and my legs felt the strongest and I knew, just knew, that I would beat them all. We'd beg to stay out, all of us, but especially me. There was no way. Elsie called the shots. Rules were rules. Her rules ruled and no matter how much I wanted to reach my jumping line, it always had to wait. Even if I marked my place with a pile of stones or a special marker, we would never go back to the game in the morning. The older girls no longer cared; they thought the game was stupid and that I was stupid for wanting to win so badly.

But that summer, the summer of Jax, the rules faded into nothingness. Elsie's constant questions — *Where are you going? With whom? When will you be back?* — started to disappear. In the spring I could feel that the imaginary line of her rules was growing soft, but I was quite surprised when it disappeared completely. Elsie had shepherded all the others through the perils of everyday life and they had all survived, one sibling after another. By the time it got to me, she was worn out and less wary. Maybe she had more faith in my abilities to muddle through, but her faith was my freedom.

The town belonged to Jax and me that summer, and more than the town, the bush and rock from which the town had been blasted. Summer was the key. All our family routines slipped away as the screen door banged in and out, in and out, marking the brief glorious long days of a northern summer.

"Keep it closed. You're letting in the mosquitoes," hollered Elsie from the kitchen as Claire and Theresa invited great crowds of teenagers to hang out in the cool basement rec room. I noticed there were boys now, skinny boys with bad skin and long hair swept over one eye. They didn't speak to me or to anyone really, they just tromped down the stairs like zombies, recklessly following my sashaying sisters into the dark reaches of our basement where Jiggs and I were forbidden entry.

Luke also had a gang. Eight or so thirteen-year-olds would take a cease-fire from their gun battles to invade our kitchen every few hours. They swarmed the fridge in search of snacks. Sometimes, Luke offered peanut butter straight up, licked from a common teaspoon if the bread had run out. Elsie didn't seem to mind, or at least she wasn't there to shout.

Our house was like a drop-in centre or what I imagined a train station must be like, a jumble of strangers' faces amid the familiar until they too become part and parcel of the overall chaos. My choice was always to leave, mostly so I could see Jax.

We had made a sign, so if one or the other was late for a meeting, we'd know where to look. There were no telephones at the hostel, at least none Jax could use. The signal was two rocks set on top of each other, a big one and a smaller one, and an arrow scratched in the dirt beside them. If the arrow pointed away from the rocks it meant we were to meet at our secret spot near the lake; if the arrow pointed towards the rocks it meant check out our hiding places in town — the stands at the baseball field behind the arena, Carr's Drugstore, the steps of the city hall or the reedy beach where upside-down canoes made a perfect hide-out for spying and talking.

The code was always at the dog pens behind the brown bungalow, but mostly Jax just waited for me. Mostly she was there, ready.

"Let's go to the lake," she said, automatically taking the lead, "but we better be careful. I think someone is trying to follow us."

"Who, Jax? Who?" I was thrilled by the information.

She shrugged and whistled for the pups. "Just stay close."

We walked up the alley and crossed over the school grounds, our usual route, but Jax suddenly headed off toward the gravel pit behind the public works building. It was a detour to distract whoever was trying to find our secret cave. Once into the bush, we had to walk though a bog where the bugs were thick. Blackflies, horseflies, mosquitoes, you name it, they swarmed around our heads until we were almost running to get away. On the other side of the swamp was a place where the muskeg was right on the surface. It felt so weird, like walking on a trampoline or, if you were a bug, say, it would be like walking on Saran Wrap with the surface of the liquid leftovers slurping at your little bug feet.

When I told that to Jax, though, it sounded kind of dumb.

"It's the permafrost melt," is all she said. "It ain't no leftovers in some stinking fridge. Get a life."

Jax could be really mean like that. I wondered if it was because she didn't have a fridge, didn't even have a real house, for that matter, and I was about to say something mean back when I thought about what it would be like not to have those things.

Jax liked to think she was really earthy and didn't need much to survive. I was earthy too, I thought, as I followed her poking-out shoulder blades through the bush. I loved to play the game of The-Last-People-in-the-World, our survival game, but I also knew that it wasn't real and I could go home and eat real food and sleep in a real bed and have luxuries like electric lights and a mom and dad and, yeah, even Claire and Theresa and Jiggs and Luke. I wondered if I could play this survival game if it were real and I really did have to survive the way Jax did without Saran Wrap and leftover food in the fridge you could just dig into any old time you wanted and stuff like that.

I didn't tell her what I was thinking though. After a while I just nodded and said, "Yeah, what do I know what a bug would feel like?"

And she stomped down hard on the earth with her running shoe and shouted, "Like that!" and I did the same thing, sort of hoping there were no little creatures in my way.

"Like that! Splat!" And we both laughed like crazy.

There were just big chunks of bedrock now with hardly any soil except for little pockets of bush, so we knew we were getting close. It took longer to get to our spot when you went through the gravel pits and it was scarier because it was trespassing to go on public works property. I thought this detour was worth it, though, because there was definitely no one following us now.

"Hey, Jax, why are all the machines back there yellow?" I was thinking about the graders and the snowploughs and all the other heavy equipment back in the yard. Jax was quiet for a while, just kept on walking, but I knew she liked me asking her tough questions like that.

Finally, when I thought maybe she wasn't going to, she answered. "So they don't blend in, Ruthie. So they don't blend into the woods the way we do."

"Is it a good thing to blend in?"

"Yeah."

"We don't blend in so well, do we, Jax?"

She stopped then and turned towards me. "No, you don't because of, well, mostly because of that weird contraption in your mouth and I don't because I don't want to." She paused for a minute. "I can, though. I can when I got to." Then she turned away and the lake came into sight like a shining blue ribbon and we urged the dogs along by running and shouting, scrambling down the rocks to be first to the secret place. At the cave we told secrets. I told her about my teeth.

I'd heard Elsie and my dad talking about it one morning when they thought I wasn't listening. They wanted to send me away to a specialist to see about my weird teeth. They were still small, baby teeth, really, but they were mine and I liked them.

"It's a developmental thing."

"She's a bit young to travel so far on her own."

"But we have to take care of it, John."

"Isn't there anyone in town?"

"In this town?" Elsie scoffed. There was a long pause in the conversation.

"When will this treatment start?"

"Right away. This summer."

"Ruthie's not going to like it. She doesn't do well with change."

"Well, she'll have to learn, John, won't she? You can't go on coddling that child forever."

"She's ten, for Chrissake, Elsie. Ten."

"John, I know how old she is. Remember, I was the one who bore her. It wasn't you. It was not you."

Silence.

Even the kids a few grades behind me in school were starting to lose their teeth. It was always a big deal, a lot of tongue wiggling and suddenly, pop, like a baby bird out of a nest, the tooth was out. There was often a little bit of blood. I was in the playground with Jennifer Yamamoto when her little sister Sako come running over, crying. The blood freaked her out. Even though I pretended it wasn't a big deal, I was quite interested in teeth, mine being so weird and all, but I didn't want to admit it. Sako was young enough that I could get a good view, faking compassion. What I saw was the new tooth coming down, poking out through the gum. It was no wonder that baby tooth had gotten flipped out on to the playground.

"The tooth fairy, won't co...com...come," she bawled, her already weird slanty eyes getting so small they clean disappeared into her head. "I can't find it," she wailed.

A whole pack of kindergarten kids started swarming the slide, searching for the missing tooth.

I put my arm on her shoulder. "Don't worry, Sako," I said, "Nobody's ever seen the tooth fairy, which means she probably doesn't exist."

That made Sako cry even louder. I was feeling like a real jerk when her big sister Jennifer showed up to take her to the bathroom to clean up. She looked strange for a few weeks with her huge half-grown adult teeth hanging down next to her itty-bitty baby teeth.

Most of the kids in my class had full adult teeth. But it hadn't happened to me. My baby teeth were still there. Always had been and, according to my mother, always would be. She wanted to send me to a specialist. My adult teeth were there but they didn't want to come down. An x-ray machine told Elsie that, but it wasn't good enough. Someone, somewhere had decided my teeth needed fixing and I would have to go away, be flown to the city for the fixing. They wanted me to be normal, have real adult teeth, the proper size, all perfectly in place.

Why me? I wondered. Why had I been selected, when so many of the children in my class had much, much worse teeth than I did? I knew mine were small and strangely spaced out but they were clean and white, not anything like the gross rotten pegs of some of the kids. Why, Robbie Youngblood had brown teeth, brown and silver if you counted the filling, and he didn't have to go away. Why me?

What no one had told me was that this treatment was given to me by my father's employers. The higher he rose in the ranks, the more benefits he received. Specialized medical and dental treatment were part of his union package when he moved from miner to shaft supervisor. My bizarre little ailment, my birth defect, met the criteria for southern treatment.

The first time I made the trip down to Edmonton, I went with my mother. Elsie seemed excited and we both got dressed up. The best thing was I got to wear the special jumper that Jiggs had made in grade seven Home Ec. It was fake leather and looked a bit like a barrel, me being so flat-chested and straight up and down and all, but I thought I looked older and more worldly. The main problem was the brown fake leather didn't breathe, so I was hot and sweaty by the time we got to the airport and even hotter when we got on the plane. In fact, Jiggs' jumper didn't bend so well, either, it was all stiff and upright, so sitting in the big airplane seats was really uncomfortable. Even though I had the little air vent pumping down air on Elsie and me, I could feel my blouse, with the too-tight Peter Pan collar that normally I wouldn't be caught dead in, sticking to my back. My face was really hot and I was so scared when we took off I felt a little pee come out, which made everything worse. Elsie didn't seem to notice, and the ladies who worked on the plane were nice, bringing me Coca-Cola, which normally I wasn't allowed to have.

There was some sort of arrangement made with the airport people, something about unaccompanied minors and an "early morning return" which would be for next time. Elsie told me it would be one of the stewardesses who would take me through the bustling airport, bigger and busier than anything I'd ever seen, to the taxi stand, and from there I would be taken to the shining downtown silver office tower of Dr. Martin Gartenberg.

That first time was the worst and I was glad Elsie was there because she did most of the talking. She liked being in the city, I could tell. She had a list of things to buy that you couldn't get at home, always more sensible school shoes, and piano music from some swanky place called the Royal Conservatory, and some spices and things that made her really happy. It seemed a long way to come to buy spices, but Elsie treated me to a milkshake afterwards at a shop that had stools instead of tables. A man named Donald served us. He was wearing the type of outfit they dress babies in before they can talk enough to say "no way." The man's outfit was striped with a matching hat and shirt and, honestly, a bib, if you could believe it.

After the shopping and the break and stuff, we walked over to the building where the specialist was. His building was almost a skyscraper, although not as big as all the other skyscrapers that blocked out the sun, but I wasn't going to tell Luke that. I was going to tell him I'd gone to the top of the type of building King Kong attacked in comics and he'd think that was really cool. Even though Lukie was a boy, he still played with me.

The dentist's office smelled the same as the dentist's back home, like a swimming pool, like someone had just come and cleaned it with bleach. All the real smells were gone and the people who sat in the waiting room seemed like they were made out of cardboard because they didn't talk much, and the plants were fake, and the lights were really bright. The ladies at the front were nice the same way the stewardesses were nice, like they had to be because it was their job, and one of them even bent down and tried to make me smile. I knew she just wanted to see my little teeth, so I just looked straight back at her, didn't crack a smile at all, and eventually she went back up to adult level and talked to Elsie. They were making some deal about next time too.

There was one girl in the waiting room who looked to be around my age. She was wearing pedal pushers and had her hair in a ponytail and she was reading a magazine. I suddenly wished I were wearing pedal pushers. My hair was scraggly and stuck to my neck and the plastic dress that I'd thought was okay back home suddenly seemed so wrong, wrong, like the perfectly worst thing to be wearing in a specialist's office where everyone had very special things wrong with them. I tried to get a look at pedal pusher's teeth but, like me, she was keeping her lips tight together. I noticed she was also wearing white lip gloss that went with her perky pedal pusher look but also made her seem a little like a vampire got her and sucked all the blood out of her lips. Jiggs would like her, Luke wouldn't, and me, I was trying to pretend I didn't care.

When my name was called, we went in. The specialist talked to Elsie and then she went away. I had to lie in the chair and he sat really close to my head. His hands were soft and puffy. He worked in silence, only saying things like *Open up, wider, wider, close a little.* He seemed to be looking for something in my mouth but I didn't know what it was. Dr. Gartenberg never spoke to me, never asked a question, rarely smiled. I thought it was because with me he didn't have to. I was too young. You only had to be nice to adults and the people with money. It didn't matter that he didn't talk because it was impossible to talk back. He was always poking stuff into my mouth. Terrible stuff: hoses or pointy tools or hooked tools or vacuum things that sloshed and sucked up my spit. All I could do was lie in his chair, and try not to move. He put stuff on my chest like I was a tray. I pretended not to mind as he measured and poked and mumbled under his breath. The tools made terrible sucking and whirring noises. I closed my eyes and pretended to sleep. There was some pain sometimes but I would not allow it in. I pretended nothing was happening.

I pretended that what he was doing was normal. It was only afterwards when I opened my eyes and saw the blood on his bib and allowed my tongue to wander the hills and valleys of the inside of my mouth that I realized what damage has been done inside that private space. He had taken out most of my baby teeth. He had sliced open my gums and filled the valleys with spacers to encourage the big teeth to come down. The spacers were attached to a huge plastic thing that was sucked onto the roof of my mouth and felt like a shield from a plastic toy soldier. In the front of the shield fake teeth hung down, trying to look like they belonged to me. They weren't big like normal teeth but they felt huge in my mouth. I was afraid to talk. I was almost afraid to breath. The retainer made me want to gag. I felt my throat opening and closing as I was trying to get air. I wanted to spit it out, whatever it was, but my mouth was thick and frozen and, for some reason, Elsie was smiling and signing some forms and making plans for me to come back in six weeks.

I was being fixed. My words were gone. My mouth was a swollen mess. My brain was frozen and thick but not so much so that I didn't think somebody should have warned me.

In the lobby of the building afterwards, Elsie was kind. She told me gently that the treatments would continue every six weeks. Now, she said, I needed time to heal. She told me the retainer was temporary, and that Dr. Gartenberg would coax the big teeth down. She told me the treatments, which would be anywhere from forty-five minutes to two hours, would be easier after this. When I came again, Elsie said, I should wait in the lobby of the dental building because Mrs. Andrews, an old friend of the family, had agreed to take me back to the airport.

"You remember Mrs. Andrews," said Elsie absently, and then to herself, "or maybe that was before you were born. Still, Ruthie, she's been friends with our family since forever. You'll like her."

Elsie was being unusually nice. She made little whimpering noises like it would help me feel better. She was not unsympathetic. She told me the worst was over. She told me not to be afraid. And then she hailed a cab. And we flew back home.

I was supposed to be grateful, but I wasn't. Mrs. Andrews was always late. I'd sit on the big rust coloured couch near the window that looked out on the street and drum my fingers, counting down the time until the big glass doors opened and Mrs. Andrews would appear, complaining about traffic or parking or the numerous demands on her time. She'd take me across the street to the restaurant, where Donald would bring me raspberry Jell-O in the summer or cooled-down hot chocolate in the winter. He was nice. Mrs. Andrews had a uni-boob. It was very pointy and weird. She was okay, too, but I wished she wouldn't be late.

For two years I went for treatment every six weeks. I didn't like the dental journeys. I didn't like the second weird slobbery thing they put in my mouth after the gums had healed. It was too large and it made my lips bleed. It also made me talk funny and for two or three days afterward I could eat only soft food like soup or macaroni and cheese. More than that, I didn't like having to go away. I didn't want adventure. I dreaded the taxi ride to the tooth doctor. The strange city was terrible and huge. The man in the cab was going to kill me or kidnap me, surely, something. Even when I arrived safely at the gleaming downtown tower, there was still the horrible elevator ride that separated my stomach from the rest of my body as I was propelled to the fourteenth floor. There was Zelda, who cooed and called me brave and had no idea that her office made me want to throw up.

For days before I was to leave home, I couldn't eat. Food made me feel horrible, it made my mouth water and I had to swallow a lot of excess spit. Often in the mornings just before my next treatment, there would be a wet circle on my sheets. The saliva had escaped in the form of pee. I pulled the bedspread up anyway, hoping Jiggs wouldn't mind the smell. The dark circles underneath my eyes couldn't be as easily disguised, but no one seemed to notice.

"I don't like going," I told Jiggs, one night before I had to travel again, before Elsie pinned the crisp five-dollar bill and the address inside my jacket with instructions not to speak to strangers. "I don't want to go."

"Tell them, then," she whispered from the dark drowsiness above. "Tell Mom and Dad, Toothie. They won't make you go," urged Jiggs, as sensible and supportive as any fourteen-year-old who longed for the city could be.

"I can't"

"Why can't you?"

"They've already paid the money."

"The money doesn't matter."

But in the darkness of our shared room, I knew Jiggs was wrong and the money did matter. Little bits of a conversation between my parents floated back through the darkness.

"There's school clothes yet to buy and car insurance. And, there's Ruth's teeth." A long sigh from Elsie.

"Ahh, yes, the teeth of the Tooth. Poor little thing. It will be worth it, Else. One day that smile will launch a thousand ships…" And then the radio news came on and my father was silenced.

A thousand ships? Was that what my appliance was worth? How much did a ship cost?

The questions preyed on my conscience. A thousand ships.

"It does," I whispered to the darkness, suspecting Jiggs was fast asleep. "I heard them talking. The money matters. I have to go."

Her disembodied voice came from the top bunk. "You'll be beautiful when it's finished."

Jiggs was listening. She knew how scared it made me. "Yeah," I said, without conviction, "when it's finished."

"Jeez, Toothie, I'd love to go. I'd go shopping and go to the movie theatre and get to look at all the big buildings. I think you're lucky. So stop whining. Just think how lucky you are."

"Yeah."

Each time I left for the city, I was forced to swallow the fear of being sent away along with the knowledge that I was not, and never would be, grateful. I didn't smile anymore and when I accidentally let one fly — when Luke was in trouble or Jiggs got yelled at — it was all mixed up with the guilt of being singled out, selected above those who were truly needy. I hated my stupid mouth and my stupid retainer, and my stupid parents who wanted me to be perfect, like the other kids in the family.

I couldn't shake the hate. I didn't care about looking normal, about being beautiful. I wanted to be me and hang out with the neighbour kids.

"It's just the way you were born," said Jax when my story was done. "It's just the way you were born."

"I know."

"It's bull," said Jax. "They shouldn't have done that, tried to change you."

"It was for my own good. That's what they told me. *You'll thank us down the road*, that's what they still say."

"Might be true," says Jax. "But I don't think too much about down the road. What about right now? You're okay now, aren't you?"

"Yeah, once the new ones come in."

"But what about this?" She indicated the lake and the smudge of a fire, our two pups wrestling down by the shore. "What about all of this?"

I smiled at her, forgetting the retainer. "Yeah. I like this. I'm okay. Yeah, forget down the road. I'm okay now."

It was my father who'd nicknamed me Tooth. It rhymed with my real name, Ruth, which I think was chosen by Elsie, hoping against hope that I would spend the rest of my days seeking not a mother, but a mother-in-law with whom I could cast my lot.

I called her Elsie because the older girls did, because she asked us to. She wasn't denying being a mother — the five of us made her role entirely obvious — but once I came along she was very much interested in pursuing anything unmotherly. She was religious, my mother, but United Church religious, an important distinction in the grand scheme of things, although somewhat incidental during the years of my infancy, when herding five children under the age of nine off to church or Sunday school was tantamount to Noah loading the Ark.

My parents went to church sporadically during my formative years. It was high days and holy days — Christmas, Easter and sometimes Thanksgiving — that roused them from their usual Sunday morning lie-in, at which point there would be a lot of shouting and the five of us would be hustled out of the house to experience a mixture of boredom and awe in the squirmy pews of the upper chamber.

My first real memory was of my baptism, which at first seemed unlikely until I found out that, unlike the others, I was almost three by the time they got around to the ceremony. I thought of it like this:

"The gown is too small." That was my father (whom I should call by his name, John, but won't — him bestowing upon me the moniker I took years to shed) shouting at my mother from the upstairs bedroom where he was trying to load me into a yellowing lace number that had the distinct odour of spit-up from some other child, likely my poor brother who had been forced to wear the tatty gown despite the distinction of being born a boy.

My sisters still called him Puke even though he was named Luke, probably in the hope that he would someday become a physician and support us all. Luke was next up the ladder from me. He had just turned four and the only vaguely doctorish thing I'd ever seen him do was poke his fingers down his throat or maul one of the older girls with his skinny flailing arms.

"I have my hands full, John. Full. Full. Full. Full." With each repetition my mother drew out the vowel and raised the word a semi-tone.

Our eyes met as my father manipulated my chubby arm into a decidedly small sleeve hole. "Hang in there, Toothie," he said, smiling down at me on the ratty change table that had become a fixture in the so-called nursery, his breath still smelling of unwashed morning with strong overtones of Saturday night. "Almost ready."

When I was truly trussed up, he scooped me up, slung me across a skinny hip and away we bounded downstairs, him humming some off-key churchy hymn under his breath.

Elsie smiled when she saw me in the gown. She seemed quite unaware of my discomfort, and licked her fingertip to plaster a wisp of curl that had escaped, feather soft, from my christening bonnet.

"You look lovely, Ruthie," she said absently, and then to the others, "Come along, troops. Jesus is waiting to meet Ruthie," and we were bundled into the station wagon. The four older ones sat in the back, where dog hair seemed to sprout on the upholstery despite the fact that we did not own a pet. Jiggs, whose nose was already starting to run, begged for the window seat. Her voice was a rasping wheeze. There was a squabble, some yelling, and then a major reshuffling. I was in the front, propped between two large warm bodies. The gown sat beneath my damp bottom, crumpled like a paper throne. My eyes were level with the radio. Usually I looked at the ashtray. Today *was* an auspicious day, after all.

In the church there was a strange calm. I didn't fuss when the water was poured on my head. I didn't make strange with the minister, a man with a beard, a Reverend Yonkers, who I later learned was a draft dodger who'd come to Canada to avoid the Vietnam war.

During my part of the service, I lay passively in his arms, examining first his nose hairs, which moved when he talked, then, with more delight, his eyes, which shone like bright blue marbles behind a pair of Coke-bottle spectacles. I'd never known he had such eyes. I'm sure no one did, what with the bearded lower jaw, the bristling mustache, and the shaggy blond-brown mop above his prescription-thick, dark-rimmed, eyeball-obliterating glasses.

When I'd think back on that baptismal day, those blue, blue eyes were what I remembered most, eyes filled with the hope of somehow transferring his God into another human vessel. Did he think it was as simple as watering a thirsty plant? I didn't know. But I did know that those beautiful hidden eyes struck me with more force than the shock of water and the ancient incantation of ceremony.

I reached up to his face after the Holy Ghost had been deposited, as he held me up for congregational inspection, and I tried with all my toddler strength to knock those horrible thick black glasses off his face in order to reveal to everyone the stunning treasure I had seen, but at that same moment he sat me upright and I was fully human again.

My dad received me back into his arms while Elsie beamed at the mass of faithful who had welcomed me into their lives with solemn vows.

"Let's get out of here," she whispered under her breath to my father, as they struggled back to their pew. But it was too late. My siblings had answered the call to Sunday school and I, the newly baptized, was trapped in the arms of my sweating father and my increasingly anxious mother. God, it seemed, had mysteriously departed the building. But I knew where He was. I, Ruth-the-Tooth Dolores Callis, named after my unfortunate birth defect and Elsie's older sister, knew exactly where God was. He was hiding inside of me.

The same way Reverend Yonkers kept those blue beauties under wraps, God had chosen my little body as His ugly disguise. The waters of my baptism might or might not have penetrated, but the certainty of God sat like two shining marbles in the centre of my tummy. It felt like a stone, like something shiny and hard and indigestible. My new knowledge would not go away. And even though I looked to my father for a glimpse of reassurance, a tiny glimmer of comfort, I realized that only I knew what had happened.

In the secret cave I asked Jax if she believed in God.

She didn't answer right away, just looked around at the lake, the trees, and finally out and up, to the sky. "Of course," she said, like it was a dumb question. "Who wouldn't?"

"But what about the bad things?" I was thinking of something that I wasn't sure I wanted to tell.

"Oh, there's always bad, Ruth," said Jax, casually. "If we didn't have it, we wouldn't know what was good."

Jax was so right. I looked at her black hair and her brown skin and I was just so glad she was my friend. And friends could tell other friends anything, couldn't they? I took a deep breath.

"Jax?"

"Yeah?"

"There's something I've been thinking about."

"Yeah? You gonna tell me?"

"Yeah."

It was the first September I'd been allowed to walk to school by myself. I could do long division. I was allowed ample time to do quiet reading and we started a new unit called social studies. In Miss Gordon's social studies class just after the snow came for good, we learned about the Jews.

I had known some Jewish people before the class but I hadn't actually realized they were Jewish. Their names were the Cohens, Mr. and Mrs. Cohen and the two Cohen daughters and a son, too, I thought, who was way older than me. They owned the hardware store downtown. In fact, Rachel Cohen, in my homeroom class, had been allowed to be office helper every morning during the Our Father. She took messages around to different teachers each morning. I often heard her shuffle past our doorway and caught a glimpse of her killing time in the hallway while everyone else had to recite the prayer that boomed over the loudspeaker. I wondered if she walked around with her hands over her ears, temples of her thick glasses pressed into her skull so she wouldn't get contaminated with the words.

I'd been to their store dozens of times and once to the Cohen home. Rachel, the hallway girl, didn't invite me to their home; rather I was invited by Miriam Cohen, a year younger, a kid I'd befriended quite by accident in a recess game of Red Rover. We'd found ourselves playing and we'd linked arms spontaneously and in perfect step hurled ourselves breathlessly across the sweep of schoolyard. In that moment of victory, in that instant, we'd become friends.

It was a dimly lit day in mid-December, and after school I walked the extra blocks with Miriam because our friendship felt so new and expansive. She invited me into her home so I could warm up before trudging back to my house and, knowing the inadequacy of Jiggs' hand-me-down winter boots, recognizing the numb feeling in my toes, I accepted.

"We'll have a snack,'" said Miriam. "You can see the candles."

And there they were, in the centre of the table in the dim, wood-paneled Cohen dining room, seven candles burning in an exquisite arch. Miriam said they linked the scattered people to the God of Israel. At first I thought she said *spattered* people and I imagined Jews like bright paint flecks all over a boring white wall.

"It's Hanukkah. Sort of like Christmas, but different," whispered Miriam, as though this was crucial and sacred information. "We get gold coins every night."

"Real gold?"

"Yup."

"Wow." I wondered briefly if my dad made them, doled them out specifically for the Cohen family, sort of like Santa, but Jewish.

"And see those candles? They never go out."

"Never?" I thought about the speckled Jewish wall burning up.

"No."

"What happens at night?"

"They burn."

"Aren't you afraid the house will catch fire?"

"No, Ruthie, I'm not."

"Boy, oh boy," I said, looking at her being all intense and serious in the dark, her saucer-like eyes mirroring the lights. "I sure would be."

"That's 'cause you're not Chosen," said Miriam, suddenly confident in her superiority. "By God, I mean. You're not Chosen by God."

"Oh." And, at that moment the overhead lights of the dining room were snapped on and Mrs. Cohen entered, larger than life in some sort of caftan or flowing muumuu. She was bearing a tray with the snack of pickled herring, still wrapped in the slimy see-through lining of its own silver skin, spreading its fishy juice over a heap of thin crackers and black bread.

Steaming mugs of something that for a moment I thought
might be hot chocolate, revealed its true self in a curious
chalky aroma. Nothing was familiar in the house of the
Chosen, and I wondered how soon I could leave without
appearing rude, as I sipped Ovaltine and tasted, for the first
time, the salty, sharp flavours of the Chosen.

But the Jews we learned about in school were not these
people; they were the Jews of the death camps, and it was
almost unfathomable that the Cohens of the hardware store,
with its mundane buckets of bolts, its shiny new appliances
and coils of green garden hoses, could be even remotely related
to the millions who had suffered under Hitler. Miss Gordon
talked about the Holocaust like everyone had always known
about it. She said the number, six million, like it was nothing,
like it was a fact in a book rather than real flesh and blood
people murdered by a crazy man.

I got more information on the Holocaust from the
public library. Four days in social studies devoted to the rise
and fall of the Third Reich was, in my opinion, not enough
when you thought about what terrible things had happened.
Miss Gordon had already moved on to the fact that women
taking over the jobs of men in gun factories had something
to do with her not getting married, which might have been
true, but didn't satisfy my desire to know more about the
ghettos, the crematoria, about why all those German people
had let murder happen right under their eyeballs. What about
the ordinary people? I wondered. Where were they when the
Jews were being herded onto trains like cattle? Where were
the Bavarian milkmaids with their bare shoulders and their
dairy cows, the ones from my picture books, the ones with
round red faces and blonde braids who merrily went to market
every morning? And the jolly accordion players who paraded
around in their little leather shorts, playing *oompahpah* tunes?
Where were they? Why didn't they stop the torture?

I took out books from the adult section of the library
and, once I was home, smuggled them into our room

underneath my winter coat. Elsie monitored our library books and only let us read what she thought was appropriate. I didn't want her to know that I was really, really interested in something so bad. I even hid the books from Jiggs, which wasn't hard considering the fact that she hardly ever noticed me because she was too busy trying to figure out how to put eyeliner around both her eyes so she could look more like a mysterious Egyptian princess and less like a scared back alley raccoon.

My books were from the non-fiction section so I didn't read even half the words. There were just too many on the page. There were lots of German words, too, words in special squiggly writing, but I didn't bother trying to sound them out. It was the photographs I kept going back to. It was the photographs that really bothered me, one black and white picture in particular. I went back to it time and time again, hating the fact that I did, yet going to that same page over and over until the book fell open at that same horrible picture.

From the photo, I couldn't tell whether the person in the chair was alive or not. But teeth, gold teeth, were being extracted from an open mouth. The teeth of the Jews were being pulled before the bodies were sent off for incineration. There was a pile of teeth on a table beside the doctor, who was grinning into the camera like an escapee from the loony bin. This image, the gaping mouth, the mound of teeth and that ridiculous smile stayed inside my head even after I had closed the cover of the book and vowed never to look again.

At night in our shared room, while Jiggs slept, open-mouthed and innocent, I tried not to conjure these photographs of wartime atrocities. But they kept coming. The pulled teeth and the mounds of gold fillings floated to the top of my mind as the night-light cast weird shadows on the wall, and the bath water ran in the bathroom down the hallway. No matter how hard I tried not to, I felt the tears slip down my cheeks. Night after night I wept bitterly for the chosen

Jews who had gone through the gas chambers, toothless and naked, still hoping for the Promised Land. I wept for the Cohens and I wondered whether, if I had been born at the time, I could have stopped it. I wished I could have. I *hoped* I would have.

Somehow I saw my own small suffering, my dental odyssey, as equal. I knew that it wasn't a cattle car that took me, but an airplane, yet somehow, this unwanted separation amounted to the same thing. Hadn't they taken my teeth, too? Without asking? At night I sometimes thought that if my teeth came in time, everything would be different. I would be okay. Every night I ran my tongue over my gums, hoping for a breakthrough. I could feel the teeth below the surface of skin and I could tell they were dropping down. The crematorium faded away and I was almost able to believe in good again.

"Whoa, Ruthie. That's pretty weird," said Jax.

"Yeah, I know." I wondered if I should have told her.

"Do you talk to other people about this stuff?"

"No. You're the first one."

Jax half smiled. "Whoa," she breathed out again. "Heavy."

"Do you have anything, you know, heavy?" I really wanted to even the score. Telling her the story of the Jews had made me feel strange, like suddenly Jax had something she could use against me.

She seemed to think a minute. "Yup."

I brightened. "Really? You gonna tell?"

"Nope."

"Ah, come on, Jax. It's not fair."

"It wasn't fair for them either, those Jewish people, Ruthie. Just because it's not fair. doesn't mean it ain't going to happen. Shit happens all the time. You gotta let it go."

I didn't want to let Jax off the hook on this one. I'd told her my story and now it was her turn. "You're still going to tell me your heavy thing, aren't you?"

"I just did," she said and then she whistled low for Kassie and Skaw. "Let's go back. You coming?"

And back we went and for the first time in a long time I felt as light and fast and as nimble as Jax as we scrambled up and over those lichen-covered rocks toward town.

α

I love everything about Ian, his blue eyes, that smattering of freckles, his curls, those broad shoulders, big ham hock arms and hands made specifically for holding me. I even love the worry lines playing across the forehead, the hint of a scar on his chin. I want to memorize every part of him. I drink him in, until his image is burned on my mind.

I am totally, irrefutably in love. We hold hands when we walk. The sun seems to be perpetually shining. We visit junk stores and laugh at unusual items, a set of false teeth, a clown clock, an old papier mâché moon winking from its dusty wall bracket. He takes it down, turns it over in his great gentle hands. "Imagine making this," he says. "It must have been a lot of work for somebody to mould this and paint it. Look at the eyes, Ruth. They look like they're really smiling."

And I love him for thinking of the labour of a stranger and, more, for saying it out loud. He buys it for me, this crazy purple moon woman and I hang her over his bed so she can watch us through the night after our lovemaking has subsided to gentle snores.

We go for walks, long walks in the countryside. One day he tells me we are going to find food, forage for fiddleheads in the woods. I think it is all a wild adventure, but then we do find them, deep in a gully, near a glade of trees. There in the damp ravine, the sunlight is dappled, falling like freshness through a canopy of green and Ian calls out and crouches and there they are, fiddleheads, as though they are waiting for us. They are a specialty, he tells me, ferns with the most delicate tips, looped in on themselves, curled tightly like a baby in the womb.

We pick buckets of them and take them back to his apartment and steam them bright green and eat them with salt and butter. We lick our lips and watch each other eat and beam great green grins at each other across the Formica table because together we can do no wrong. It is love and it is everything I imagined.

α

Jax and I hung out all summer. She never came to my house; I never went to the hostel. As if by agreement, our friendship was private. We watched the puppies grow, taught them rudimentary commands, readied them for their life ahead as sled dogs.

Jax knew a secret language: she called her pup Kaskitewâw and mine Wâpiskâw. It was Cree, a language Jax's grandmother had taught her when she was little. Even though Kaskitewâw meant black and Wâpiskâw meant yellow, and in my mind naming dogs after the colour of their fur was pretty lame, I thought it was cool they had Indian names. But because the words didn't roll off my tongue the same way they did hers, I dubbed them Kassie and Skaw. When I asked Jax what my name meant in Cree she said there was no word for Ruth.

The people who had given us the care of the dogs reminded us the pups were going to the old town at the end of summer, as soon as they were big enough to work. A man wearing only an undershirt, the gross singlet kind where you could see the armpit hair, growled: "Don't you girls get too attached to them pups. They're spoken for. They're not meant to get all lovey-dovey with people, mind. Working dogs, those." And then he huffed back into the brown bungalow before we could say anything back. But we were still allowed to walk them every day and we did, rambling miles and miles into the bush. Usually we went to the big lake, but after we'd memorized most of its shoreline, we sometimes went inland, forging through the bush until we found a place far enough away to rest and make a camp.

That's when we started playing our game. It had evolved without too much being said. We pretended we were the last people on earth and we were left to survive on the land. Jax was always the leader in the game. I was Tonto to her Lone Ranger. Or, actually I was more like Franklin, the explorer, to her Akatico. He was the guy who knew everything about the bush and taught Franklin. Old Franklin would have frozen a half dozen times or got eaten by a bear or something without Akatico. We'd never learned about *him* in school, but Jax knew. She knew a lot about the bush, and even though she didn't talk much, she showed me things, like the way spring shoots had been nipped off by deer. She poked at bear scat, a fancy word for poop, to determine freshness, and she knew where to find high bush cranberries and even tiny wild blueberries if there'd been a fire through the bush.

I always felt safe with her and Kassie and Skaw. We were a team. One of my jobs was to get us food for the day, which wasn't hard because Elsie didn't mind that I packed a huge picnic in the morning and that I was gone all day. They were good in the summer, my parents. My dad still had to work at the mine, and Elsie spent a lot of time trying to get things to grow in the backyard, which was a bit of a joke. After the snow went in late May, it always looked like a moonscape back there, but it kept her busy. The only rule was that we had to be back home for supper, but because the sun stayed up so long, we were often allowed to go back out afterwards. Sometimes I smuggled more food out to Jax after supper.

In the mornings we met at the brown bungalow. Whoever got there first just hung out with the dogs until the other one came. Then we headed out. Once we got to the outskirts of town, things changed. We started to talk like we were going to hunt, like we were tracking game. That was part of the pretending, but, in fact, I always carried a thermos of soup or a stack of cheese or peanut butter and honey sandwiches. For one thing, we didn't have anything to hunt with. Jax had made us a couple of slingshots, but we mostly used these for target practice and pretending. Jax was a good shot. She used to kill ptarmigan all the time, she told me, but only in the early winter when they were fat. Otherwise the blood on the snow wasn't worth it, she said, the birds were all blood and bones, no meat.

Jax couldn't get food from the hostel. In fact, she said she wasn't even supposed to be living there. They liked the kids to go home for the summer and most of them had. Some had gone up to the Arctic, some had gone back to their communities up the Mackenzie, some had gone with their parents, some had been boarded with family members in town for the summer. Jax hadn't gone anywhere yet. She said they were trying to find something for her, but she wasn't sure what that meant. She was waiting for her mom. I guessed her mom hadn't been into town since school let out, so old Jax was kind of high and dry. She told me one of the supervisors was even talking about her staying at the hostel all summer. Welfare would pay. Part of me wished her mom would come, because I knew that was what she wanted, but part of me was glad she was still here. I thought it must be lonely in the hostel with only one or two other loser kids left behind.

Jax said the people at the hostel were mean, and one day, while we were talking in the cave, she'd showed me the marks on her bottom and the backs of her legs. They were red marks from a strap, not cuts, but painful-looking welts, still visible from the night before.

"What did you do?" I asked, marveling at the six ribbons of red reaching out the back end of her cut-offs and running down the tops of her long brown legs.

"I told the dorm supervisor to fuck off.'"

"Yeah, I guess that would do it."

Jax's looked at me then, her eyes slitty and narrow, like I'd seen her look so many times before.

"Don't you want to know why, Ruth?"

"Why what?'

"Why I told him to fuck off."

She was mad, so I had to talk really slowly, figure out what I was going to say: "I'm not allowed to say that word. Maybe they hit you because you said a bad word."

"No, Ruth. That's not why. *He* did it because he wanted to, because he liked it."

"So you didn't really tell him, you know, the F word."

"No. I really told him to leave us alone. To just leave us alone."

The wind had come up and I could hear something in Jax's voice I hadn't heard before. It was thick and low and there were tears behind her words.

The cave was quiet, and other than the wind, the only sound was the waves outside, the weird kind of heartbeat sound of them washing up on the big rocks. Skaw and Kassie were sleeping together in a single ball of fur. The only movement was their bellies going in and out and the little puffs of dust where their breath came out their noses. It was comforting and I almost hoped she wouldn't speak, wouldn't wreck it by talking more.

Jax poked a stick into the dying embers of our fire. "They're mean. One kid was speaking Cree, just this new kid, younger than me. She didn't know and she got hit. I told the dorm supervisor to fuckin' lay off or I'd break his face."

"And what happened?"

"He pushed back so I gave him a shot in the gut."

I couldn't believe what she was saying. "No way. You slugged an adult?"

Jax sort of smiled. "One of the white boys, hired to keep us in line."

"What happened after that?"

"I got a good licking. But the chickenshit got one of the matrons to do it. More official." She touched the backs of her thighs again and I imagined other markings, other times.

"Jax," I said urgently, "we have to tell someone."

Out went her chin again, that pointy little chin that could make her voice mocking and mean. "You're not allowed to tell, Ruthie. Don't you get it? If you tell, they'll hurt you worse. There's a system and you better shut up about it or I'll really get it."

I was totally stunned. The people who looked after Jax were hurting her! I just looked at her blankly. I couldn't believe she wasn't going to tell.

She kept poking the stick into the fire, even though there were just a few smoking embers left. Suddenly she held up the end of the stick, bright red, and brought it down to her leg. I could smell the hair burning and I knew that it had to hurt. The hot coal hovered just above her flesh and she looked me right in the eye.

"Don't," I pleaded. "Please don't."

She held my stare, defiantly, and then dropped the hot stick onto her calf, held it there for a split second and flung it out onto the choppy surface of the lake. I winced, afraid to look at the horrible self-inflicted white-ringed red mark already showing on her skin.

"Wh...wh...what... did you do that for?" I stuttered, almost hysterical. "Are you crazy? You didn't have to do that! Only a crazy person would burn their own skin! What are you doing? Why, Jax? Why?"

She didn't say anything right away, but she scooped up some of the ash and dirt from the circle outside the ring of rocks we'd built. She spit into the ash, making a thick goo, like a paste, and started applying it to the burn mark. I watched with a horrible fascination.

Jax started to mumble. At first I could hardly hear her, but if I leaned forward to where she was hunched, looking after her burn, I could make out her soft speaking voice. It was almost like a chant, a private incantation. "They can't hurt us. We know the earth. She is our mother and our mother cares for us." Round and round went Jax's hand, smoothing the gunk into her leg. I could see other marks on her leg and I was pretty sure she'd done this before.

"Jax," I whispered, "you're scaring me."

She looked up then, like she'd just realized someone else was with her. There was something burning in her eyes below the film of tears, but her mouth smiled. "My grandmother taught me that," she said giving her leg and its ash poultice a final pat. "If you burn yourself, you mix spit and ash and say those words."

"But you did it on purpose."

"Did what?" She looked at me square on, blankly and unabashedly, until I had to look away.

"I've got to go home."

And indeed, I did. It was dark in our cave and almost twilight outside. It was summer and the sun stayed in the sky so late it was an unreliable clock and I was afraid it was way past the time I was supposed to be home. The lake was still, the way it is just before it snuffs out the sinking sun, and the rocks were shadows looming up from black pits of darkness. We played a hopscotch game on the way back, Jax and I, leaping between the shadows until the lights of our town came to show us the rest of the way home.

α

Ian says he wants to know everything about me, and asks endless questions. He is so interested in me. In everything. In his small room overlooking that lazy serpentine river, while the elm trees leaf out into summer, and the days get warmer and longer, I tell Ian about my childhood, my family, my classmates, my studies.

"It's all about the words," I say. "The way they sound together, the way they complement each other."

"Like us." As he strokes my shoulder, his hand finds the little hollow of my neck, the ridge of bone and pulse.

"I know which poets I like because of the way their words go straight into my heart, the way they make me feel."

"Like this?" His hand dips under the scooped neck of my T-shirt. I want to talk, but I can't. My body responds to his touch.

I want to tell him which poets I admire and why, about the novels I've read, the ones I love, the ones that move me so much I weep, but every time I begin to tell he gathers me up, calls me his baby, his poet baby, and we make love to stop my words.

There. That's it. *Stop my words.* I want to tell him things, but slowly my story is being silenced. And his, the one that hardly has any words, is taking over. After all, what are my pithy little experiences, my religious and literary contemplations, compared to the horrors he's suffered?

While I think I am telling Ian about me, he, in turn, reveals things about himself. He claims he doesn't like to talk about himself. "What's there to tell?" he says, grinning, but then he tells, anyway.

I think at first he's just shy. But in fact, right from the beginning, he is always able to bring the conversation back to himself. I am too consumed with the voice of my own stories. I am his sole focus. I am his only interest. Nothing I do or say is considered trivial or stupid, it's just that the very same thing has happened to him also. But tenfold. It isn't so much what he tells me, as how he tells it. I'm in awe. He seems so learned, so experienced. It's not until we have been together for three weeks that I see his driver's licence and learn that he's nearly thirty-six, a full sixteen years older than me.

One night, very late, after we've been out to the bar, and the candles are lit once again, he tells me about his twin brother. The child died at birth, choked on the way out of the womb, Ian's umbilical cord wrapped tight around his neck.

"He was as blue as I was pink," says Ian, staring deep into a glass of beer. "My birth caused his death." I take his hand then, wondering how he knows this. Who would tell him?

Tell him about your teeth, how you clamped down on Elsie, my brain screams. But another part tells me how ridiculous that would sound. *You bit somebody, he killed somebody,* and so I let it be. I don't pursue the dead blue brother. I am afraid to ask too much, afraid it will hurt him more, afraid, I guess, he'll react.

α

"They thought you were a reptile when you were born."

"How do you know?"

"Everyone knows. How do you think you got that name?"

"Don't reptiles have flaky skin?"

"And teeth. They're born with teeth."

Jiggs was on the top bunk, a platform for stuffed animals and unattainable knowledge. I was below, piecing together the bits and pieces I'd heard, the strange story of my birth.

I didn't remember it, of course, but there had always been something that had marked me as different from the four siblings born before. It wasn't that I was the last, although there had always been a low rumble about my brother Luke not having a proper playmate. I guess after the first three daughters it made sense they would want another boy, so when I came along, just eleven months after Lukie, the largest girl of the lot, it may have been a disappointment. But there was something else and Jiggs, who was afraid of nothing, had said it out loud.

I wasn't a reptile, but I was born with teeth. At birth I had protruding dental buds, six in all, including incisors, with the sure sign of molars bubbling to the service. I knew this because they had always been there and I had always been able to feel them. And I'd been told. Over and over, I'd been told.

I knew my mother Elsie had balked at my condition. I'd heard the story many times. I couldn't be sure of this, but from somewhere in my child's mind I imagined my birth being met with a high-pitched, piercing shriek. After the fluids were flushed from my scrunched-up infant orifices and I breathed in that first grateful gasp of air, I had latched on to the great giving warmth of the soft creature that had expelled me. But my teeth got in the way.

"You screamed all the time. And then she'd scream. You. Her. You. Her. Scream. Scream. Scream. It was madness. We wished she'd take you back to the hospital," whispered Jiggs.

I imagined the scream going on and on, high-pitched, piercing, eardrum-shrinking, eye-popping. I imagined it peeling the institutional grey-green paint off the hallways in the hospital and rattling the flimsy curtain rods around the beds. I was my mother's agony, I'd always heard. Who could blame her for pushing me away?

"What kind of teeth were they, Jiggs? Like the ones I still got?"

"Yeah. Baby teeth but, like, tons of them. Not exactly a whole set of them but probably enough to eat a steak, anyways. And Ruth, you couldn't even hold up your own head because you had one of those scrawny wobbling necks. Oh, Toothie, you were something else."

"Did I only bite Mom?"

"Oh, no, you bit everyone who came to see you. Don't you remember Dad's stories?" Jiggs was on a roll now, chuckling in her warm nest, recalling the torturous tales told around the dining room table. Even though I was the subject of the drama, I saw it unfold like a television show.

"I can't feed her, John," my mother hissed. "I can't feed this one the way I fed the others." Her voice rose two decibels. "You have no idea!"

And of course, he didn't. I could just imagine Dad, John Wesley Callis, shrinking back into those dreary hospital walls, trying to blend into their algae green despite his floral and probably hideous Hawaiian shirt, afraid of too much maternal information coming his way. Breasts he could deal with. In fact, breasts he adored. But feeding, mammary fluids, these were not within his ken.

"What can we do? We have to feed her. She has to eat. Why, the others ate all the time. Day and night. All day and all night."

My mother fixed him with her unblinking emerald eyes.

"Yes, John, all the time. Day and night." He heard the rawhide in the voice, felt the steel cross those jeweled eyes, cutting them smooth and sharp as their gemstone colour. Her green gaze never wavered from my father's stunned face.

"I'll teach you about bottles, John," she said, and then added under her breath, "Unless this one chews the bloody nipples to shreds. To hell with it. I'm off the hook. And John," she added warily, "You're in charge. She's all yours."

I imagined my mother passing me off to him and me being received, albeit awkwardly, into his skinny, concave chest.

When he told the story, he always added voices and smiled fondly at me. It was like he was proud of it, proud that his youngest daughter became so pudgy and plump under his care.

It was around the dinner table, between clearing and dessert, that the stories came out. "Tell us the part about when the guests came to see Ruthie," the older girls clamoured. "When she bit everybody with her huge chompers. Tell us that part, Dad."

And he'd push his chair back from the table and, barely glancing at me, go on with the story as though simple baby teeth were the same as having a child born with a tail or, like Jiggs said, prehistoric scales.

Guests came, relatives mostly, but also some old family friends from across town, to marvel at my parents' propensity to procreate and to shake their heads in wonderment at our numbers. "I wonder how in heaven's name all these Callis kids are going to get a decent education?" they'd murmur while exchanging bemused glances.

"Number five, John?" blustered Dad's colleague Mr. Lapinski, former miner turned management, his snout already deep in a tumbler of Scotch after the requisite gawk in the cradle. "You might want to think about getting out of the shafts, with all these mouths to feed. You think the money is below, glittering like gold, but turns out it's on the surface, boy. The gold is for the ones who walk the office floor."

And Hans Neumann, from up the street: "Hope for elope, Johnny Boy. Hope for elope."

My mother, at the time of my birth, likely thought conception beyond her. She was teetering on the heated cusp of menopausal madness and another baby was the last thing she wanted when I announced my very real presence by clamping down on her tender drooping nipple with my unfortunate teeth. She didn't want another baby and she certainly didn't want a monster baby with exterior incisors.

The teeth weren't that obvious, according to Dad. I couldn't, after all, smile (not that I had any good reason to do so), and solid foods were still a good six months down the tedious road of infant triumphs. "But there they were," he'd exclaim to whoever wanted to listen, "marching top and bottom across the front of my little Ruthie's gums.

But it was my mother who pointed them out to strangers, or, at the very least, the parade of people who popped in with casseroles.

"This one had a real surprise in store," she'd groan with a hollow ha-ha. "The last thing I expected," or "You're just not going to believe this!"

My father recounted: "Little Ruthie, you had your mouth forced open by these gigantic prodding fingers, too often stained yellow by Kools menthols, and the inside examined and exclaimed over by mortified and frightened mothers who'd coo and cluck and pat your mother on the back."

"And what did the people say, Dad, when they felt the teeth?" asked Luke, totally oblivious to the discomfort the story was causing me.

Dad put on the voices: "'My word!' or 'Poor thing,' but they always said it to your mother, not to baby Ruth." His voice went obviously British: "'Why, I never!'"

"Gotta hand it to you, kid. You almost never chomped down on one of those probing fingers. You were a good baby, Ruth, different, it's true, but as good as gold. Better. And you know your old mining papa knows a thing or two about gold. Why, you just let them gawk. You'd open your little mouth — and Sugar, it wasn't much bigger than a lollipop back then — and you'd let every one of them, every last one of them, mind, look at those itty-bitty baby teeth. Well, your momma might have been a little embarrassed at the time, Shug, but, take it from your old man, I was nothing short of peacock proud."

He'd raise an eyebrow then, or give me a wide-eyed look.

"Advanced, that's what you were, born ahead of your time. Why, evolutionary theory has it that all our baby toes will be falling off over the next few eons. Imagine, Toothie, baby toes littered across the landscape, shucked off in gutters and alleys and closets. Tasty morsels for the dogs. No longer needed. Survival of the fittest. The evolution of the species at its most advanced."

And he would go on and on, mimicking holding me in the crook of his arm, rubber nipple firmly in place between my reptilian teeth, and tell us about Darwin's theory, the Galapagos Islands and the splendour of finch on the wing.

In the cave of the lower bunk, I ran my tongue over my gums, wondering about teeth. What were they for if you couldn't chew, couldn't smile, and knew nothing about grimacing or protecting territorial rights? Why had I been born with premature baby teeth? I felt like a different species, a freak, someone set apart. The very first thing I did in my life, mere moments after drawing my first breath, was to hurt someone. I had hurt my own mother.

α

Ian loves cats. I can tell by the way he treats his marmalade cat, Sadie. He strokes her all the time, his large calloused hand nestling in her neck ruff, behind her ear, talking in a soft sing-song voice. I want to be that cat.

One night, we are lying in his bed, and he begins to tell me a story. I want to do something else, romp, frolic, and have wild, happy, sloppy sweaty sex, but Ian turns away, reaches for his beer on the floor. "I don't have it in me, Ruth," he says.

"What? What do you mean?" I'm injured but I pretend it's okay. I lie still and I listen, with my head against his shoulder, watching his chest rise and fall. It is the first time he refuses to make love to me.

He tells me there aren't too many good memories after his mother got the phone call. "I had a ton of babysitters, different ones all the time. I don't think I saw the same person two days running." He drinks long, the foam at the corners of his mouth dribbling into day-old stubble, and he readjusts the pillows. It's like a bedtime story in the morning.

"I rode my bike a lot in the alley and I couldn't figure out why none of my friends would come out. When they did come, they were with their parents and dressed all wrong for playing. I felt like I had the bloody plague, the way those guys ignored me. I guess they didn't know what to say, but, Jesus Christ, they could have at least tried to act normal.

"People brought weird casseroles, one, I remember, with potato chips and cheese on top, and salads, lots of jellied salads." His voice trails off and is replaced by the beer bottle, quickly drained. Ian laughs, more like a snort than a laugh, quite disdainful. "Someone even brought a whole roasted turkey to the door like it was a celebration — fucking Christmas or Thanksgiving — instead of a wake." He throws back the covers and pads out of the bedroom. I hear the long sound of him peeing, the toilet flush, and then the fridge opening.

A wake. It's a strange word. It's wrong somehow. I wonder if anyone is really awake at those things. A friend of Elsie and Dad's died and Elsie came back red and angry because Dad didn't want to leave the corpse alone. He was sentimental and rheumy-eyed when he did come back home, much, much later, and he made me hot chocolate and drank his nightcap while we sat up, late, on the porch watching the stars. I remember asking him why he didn't want to leave his friend's body and he said something about the crossing taking a few days.

Ian climbs back into bed. Opens another beer. It's not quite noon, but I know this is a hard tale to tell. Ian says his father's wake was like a dream. But when the Captain started to come around, promising to take care of legal and financial matters, it changed from a dream to a nightmare.

He seemed to be there almost from the beginning, according to Ian's memory, a hovering malevolent presence. Ian is sure the first time he saw him he was standing at the back of the gravesite, part of the dark outer ring of trench coats that surrounded the uniformed men on sombre navy blue parade. They, in turn, encircled Ian and his mother and a few others, a priest, a smattering of cousins and, of course, the perfectly rectangular hole waiting to receive the box.

"The coffin was draped," he says, looking at something I can't see. I imagine a flag, the maple leaf, a stylized splotch of red lying over the place where his father's heart used to be. Ian's dad was a cop on duty when his chest was blown open by a shotgun discharged at close range in a drunken domestic dispute.

"The Captain came almost right away," says Ian, kicking the blanket away and pulling on the beer. I lie beside him and will him to tell, imagine the boogeyman materializing like a spectre through the fog in order to offer brief words of condolence to Ian's mother.

He continues, "He had great clothes, like, I mean really different than what the guys wore. They were regular and he was fuckin' Mr. Fancy-pants right from the get-go. You know, Italian suits, those stupid shoes with the faggy penny in the little proper pouch. Oh my God, Ruthie, and the way he talked."

His voice goes lower as he mimics. "'I'm so terribly sorry for this, your great loss,' and he looks me up and down and then shakes my hand like I'm one of the goddamn troops he's just inspected."

I don't want to say anything, but I don't understand what's offensive about the words he's just spit out. It sounds to me like the sort of thing I would say at a funeral. I need to understand. "What did the other people do? What did they say to you?"

"The boys? Oh, forget it. They were — I don't know — humble? Sad? Like they really meant it. They worked with my dad. They knew him. They weren't like this pompous fuckin' Captain from the other side of town, all hoity-toity and fancy in a three-piece show-off suit. Shit, most of the boys went to the officers' club afterwards. That's where you really talk. Hoist a few of these and, you know, talk about the service and the good times. They'd remember Dad. Really remember him. That's the difference."

"Did your stepfather hurt you?"

I'm so sure of the answer I'm afraid to ask, but I want to cut to the heart of it and find out what the heck happened. I want this story out in the open. I want it gone.

"Not at first. Not until I started to hate him."

"Didn't your mom do anything?"

"She was weak. A traitor." His lips press together. "Still is."

The way he says it, I feel something change. It's like a candle being blown out, a window being closed to a storm, or sudden sunlight falling on an empty room. There's no going back. My heart aches for him. It won't be easy, this healing. He's holding the hurt.

"It was like she crossed the line into an enemy camp," he says, remembering. "I can't really blame her, though. The fat old Captain had money."

According to him, it was by degrees his mother pledged allegiance to this new regime. First the dinner dates, the gifts arriving at the house, gradually the smell of the Captain's cologne in the morning. Ian remembers the wedding and the move happening almost simultaneously. He claims he was not consulted. He remembers his mother being euphoric, realizing she need never worry about money again. I imagine her ripping up bills with a small, enigmatic smile playing on her mouth. *Paid. Paid.*

"She suddenly started kissing me all the time, without notice, and she shelved her plans to open a boarding house. Instead she started buying new clothes. Not from department stores either, but from women's dress shops. Places I'd never heard of. You should have seen it, Ruth," he says, heading to the fridge to get another cold beer. "Cardboard boxes with these fancy names of boutiques — Elaine's or Chez Moi, shit like that. It was crazy. Not the way we lived at all."

"How old were you?"

"Grade six, maybe. Seven. I hated those boxes. My mom used to save the bags, slick, dark plastic carrying bags with small handles. She'd fold them and stuff them — the bags and you know, the tissue paper — between the counter and the fridge, until the friggin' Captain demanded we clean up. He always said if we needed something we'd buy it." Ian's voice is high and hostile. "What an asshole. At first he called my mom his thrifty little miffkin, or frugal Frieda-used-to-living-like-a-church-mouse. Can you fuckin' believe that? The guy had no respect for my dad."

"Maybe he was in love with her. Maybe he felt like we do."

He pulls away then, angry. "No, Ruth. It wasn't like us, at all. The guy was a prick, okay? A royal, A-1 prick."

"Okay, sorry. I just thought it was such a long time ago."

He's out of bed now, pulling at the tangle of sheets and blankets, looking for his pants. "It wasn't that long ago."

I call him back, trying to assuage this unreasonable anger. "Look, I'm really sorry. What about the story? Come back to bed and tell me what happened with the Captain."

He does come back, but again he's got a full beer in his hand. The pain is written all over his face.

"It was like the fucking Cinderella story for my mom, man. Suddenly she started looking younger, prettier, and I even noticed the lines across her forehead started to ease up. It's just having money, I guess. I was still willing to give him a chance. She quit her job, and we moved, just like that, away from the neighbourhood, from all our old friends. Man, it was brutal."

Things settled down after the move. Ian tells me how he stayed at his best friend Paul McGuinley's house while his mother and the Captain took their honeymoon in Bermuda. Everything at the McGuinley place was the way things used to be, he explains, the food was familiar — like hamburger noodle casserole — and while the family ate, talk at the dinner table turned to men on the beat, conversations of B & E's, the drunk tank and all the petty crime of that hardcore harbour town. After dinner, Paul's parents would go down to the officers' club, to throw some darts and have a few. "It was the way they talked I liked so much," he explains, almost choking with what was so yearningly familiar. Then his eyes get hard again. "That was before they packed me off for good to a fucking Frog boarding school in Quebec."

I don't say anything. I just put my hand on his thigh, and try to bring him out of his anger memories by rubbing my hand in small circles. It works.

"Things were okay for the first few months. I didn't make any new friends, but at least I could see my friends at school. One weekend, the Captain asked me if I wanted to go for a drive."

They'd gone, just the two of them, down to the river. It wasn't long after the wedding and the move to River Heights. His mom encouraged him to go, really pushing the male bonding thing. She didn't know why they were going. "Neither did I," says Ian, closing his eyes briefly, and taking a long pull from the bottle.

Suddenly, I'm not sure if I want to hear this story. Sadie jumps up and plunks herself down between us. I think it's going to be okay when she starts purring and Ian gets a faraway look in his eyes. He's seeing the cat but he's seeing something else, too. I grab his hand. The big red mitt of a hand that has stroked the cat has stroked me. It's all I can do.

The day was bright and warm. Ian says he remembers being absorbed by the electric windows of the Captain's new Monte Carlo. He'd push a lever one way, and with an electric hum the window would go up. Pull backwards, same hum, and the window would go down. "It was pretty radical, considering my dad's old Chev only had the standard crank handles. Those crazy windows kept me occupied most of the trip. I thought of them like a sort of space age adventure game, you know? But it also meant I didn't have to talk to the old bastard behind the wheel."

I can imagine him in that car. A scared little eleven-year-old kid lost in a space fantasy "Three, two, one ... blast off," my imaginary Ian mutters under his breath, pulling at his imaginary control panel. It reminds me of Luke when he was little. Even I can see the spacecraft ascending, slow motion, towards another galaxy. With the window up, the sudden quiet in the car becomes the hush of the space capsule hurtling through the silent void of outer space. And then, the Captain's presence interferes as he starts to slow down and look for a place to pull over. I hear the little boy whisper, "Prepare for touchdown," as the rocket descends to a world where alien winds and probably poisonous gases blow an icy chill into the bones of all brave astronauts.

"Were you scared?" I ask.

"No," he says, shaking his head. "It's like I say, I didn't know where we were going. Or why."

They were suddenly there, he says, at a wide spot on a narrow dirt track. Ian remembers getting out of the car and smelling the river, green and rank, not far off.

"It was late summer and the woods were damp and thick with mushrooms and fiddleheads, like the ones we picked, but already gone to seed. The Captain opened the trunk. That's when I heard the baby crying. But it wasn't a baby at all. It was Mitzy's kittens in a burlap sack. I was confused. They were too young to be taken from their mother. My mom said six weeks at the very earliest. You can't do that, Ruth. You can't take babies from their mothers."

He says this with such conviction, I just nod, remembering Jax and the pups, remembering Jax and her mother and the hostel. The little blond and dark faces of Skaw and Kassie push their cold noses into my memory, and I'm scared of what's going to happen next in the story. Ian continues.

"My friend Paul had already picked out the one he wanted, a grey tabby with white-tipped ears. So I asked the Captain what he was doing. He said, 'Wait here. I don't think you should come with me.' I was suspicious, so I asked, 'What's in the sack?' But I already knew.

The Captain walked to the water, gathering rocks. I wasn't supposed to, but I followed. The sack was wriggling in the old bastard's hand until he smashed it down hard, on the side of this rickety pier." Ian brings his hand down on the mattress. Again and again. His face is a mask.

"Before I could stop him, he threw it underhand into the wider part of the river. I can still hear it now," he says, turning my chin up so I'm looking into his eyes. "The noise was mewing — pathetic mewing — this sort of muffled, shrill sound from the kittens the few seconds they were airborne. Can you imagine what kind of person would do something like that?"

I put my hand to his face, hoping to wipe out that terrible memory, but he continues talking, almost not noticing me. He is staring out into the bedroom, into space. I try to see what he is seeing, feel the way he must be feeling. I try to possess this terrible memory with him. At last he speaks in a very quiet voice.

"The worst thing is we both get into the car and pretend like nothing's happened."

"What after that?" I whisper. "What happened on the way home?"

He tightens his arm around my shoulder and I feel him plant a kiss in my hair, just above my ear. "That's when I started to hate him."

It is like he's said he loves me, in that moment. He's told me his story. He trusts me enough. I am dizzy with it and when we go back down between the covers to block out the light, I am convinced he has spoken about love. I want to heal him. I want to turn all his darkness into light.

Later that week, we go to visit his mother. I don't meet the despised Captain. I start to think he might not even be real. I've studied psychology and I start to think of the Captain as Ian's darkness, the brooding part that he deadens with drink.

His mother is definitely real. We go to Saint John, on the coast. We hitchhike because neither of us can afford the bus. We have no money, and no money means Ian doesn't have anything to pour down his throat; he has no antidote for the memories.

After the meeting with her we go into the city to get a drink. We head to a bar called The Bosun's Chair. It's dark in there even though it's still daylight outside and before I can see the little round tables and the patrons leaning up against the bar, I can smell draught beer, cigarette smoke and that old man smell. It feels dank, like the sea is still there, in the rafters and the planks and in all the crusty old men shambling around the place navigating a soggy carpet and the seaweed tables, covered with horrible, stained green terry cloth to sop up their spilled drinks and later, their spit and their tears. *They still think they're on the deck of some long-forgotten, and, by now, submerged and rotten ship,* I think. I say nothing.

We go to the bar because the visit with his mother has gone badly.

Gone badly. In River Heights, there on the porch, beside him, I know something is wrong. His mother looks flustered when we arrive, unannounced. She is uncomfortable, and holds us out on the back deck, her body blocking the doorway. We don't stay long.

As we walk away, I look back at the house, a nice house, in a nice part of town. But it has nothing to do with Ian. When the Captain bought this house, he'd sent Ian away to school. He's already briefed me on the situation. The house belongs to this man, this Captain, who, fortunately, isn't there. Ian's mother gives him money, although he doesn't ask.

"I'm sorry. I've only got a hundred in cash," she says, counting the twenties into his hand. "I can't write a cheque, or he'll know." She barely looks at me, only nods once, not meeting my eyes. I watch a strand of her hair play in the wind. She's pretty in an older sort of way. Sure, she's got those lines around her eyes and a couple of deadly ones between her eyebrows, but she doesn't look mean or anything. It's more like she's scared. I figure she must be afraid of her new husband, the tyrant, but I also think it's really weird that she doesn't invite us in. And Ian doesn't even bother to introduce me. Who does she think I am? Just this chick, this kid her son has hooked up with? It's not how I want it to be. It's not how I imagined our first meeting .

"She pays you to stay away?" I'm confused and I voice my confusion as we walk back to the highway, before thinking about how it will make him feel. He doesn't answer, only stands, thumb out, heading to town, to a drink.

I'm learning other things about Ian. He writes poems. He shows me some of them after we've spent a few weeks together. I like the fact that he writes. He can only really express himself in poetry, I decide. It explains his reticence, his inability to open up. He's a poet, just like the poets I admire, those dark, tortured ones, Ted Hughes, Dylan Thomas, Earl Birney. *I don't understand yet,* I tell myself. *I don't know real pain.* Ian, of course, does. That's what defines him. That what draws me in.

The poems are kept in a blue binder and each has been carefully typed and copyrighted. He wants to sell them to a band or to someone already famous, Bob Dylan or Leonard Cohen. They are lyrics more than poems, he explains, reading them aloud to me when he's having a good day, when we're sitting around drinking a beer or a bottle of wine and there's more in the fridge. They are lyrics. Each poem has a chorus, a sort of sing-song chorus with rhyming words. "There are extra copies in a safety deposit box in the Bank of Montreal," he says. "If anything happens, you'll have to know where to get the key."

"Happens? What do you mean? Happens?"

Silence.

I read:
>Dark boy outside
>Always looking in
>Even though you say it's gold
>I know your heart is made of tin
>Dark boy outside
>Knows the truth of hate
>There's a dark boy
>Outside
>He won't stay outside your gate
>He's coming in
>He's coming in
>You can't stop him coming in
>And the dark boy
>From outside
>Will stamp out your wicked grin

"Wow, this stuff is really good," I say, although I'm not actually sure if it is. My opinion matters to him because I am an English major. I don't really know how the rhyme scheme works in songs, but because he cares so much about the poems, I care too. It is like that. I can't say specifically what any single poem means and I don't try to, but there is a common theme that I keep to myself.

Every one of his poems is about people who have been done wrong, somehow. They are about good people who become victims of the world's bad judgment. They are laments — poems full of pain and pity — about unfairness, injustice and inequality. This is Ian's vision, but it's a world I can't see. It is foreign to me and I remember the sanctimonious youth of the One True Church and I realize how little I know.

One of the poems is called "Bitch." In brackets Ian has written *for Susan B.* She's the woman he used to live with, a sessional lecturer at the university. Her name has come up a few times, but I've never felt like I could ask too much. Susan B. Bitch. Susan Brightstaff. I say it in my mind, over and over.

Susan. Susan Brightstaff. I wonder about her. How she looked. Where she is now.

"I used to write all her lectures the night before she'd give them," he says, and then as though he can read my mind, "She's in Montreal, on some fucking research fellowship."

That and no more. When he talks like that, I know there is no room for questions.

Ian is intelligent. I love the way his mind works. He seems to be able to see inside people and know their true motive. He says that I am pure light and all that shines from me is goodness. I like that. Who wouldn't? I like the way he thinks about me all the time, and his crooked smile, his tenderness. These are the things that draw me. And his honesty. He tells me almost right away about the therapy.

"I'm seeing someone," is how he puts it, when he casually mentions the weekly sessions. "It's a shrink I see at the university counseling centre. I've got Susan's ID number, so I don't have to pay. His name is Reg. We talk."

"About what? "

"About things. Things that bother me."

"You could talk to me," I say, moving to where he sits on the pink sofa, wanting to help. "You could talk to me about things that bother you."

I don't like to think he withholds the painful parts of his history. Doesn't he know that I could heal those too? I touch the back of his neck where his hair still curls like a little boy's and I vow to never stop loving him.

"It's not as bad now that you're with me," he reassures me.

"What isn't?"

"Oh, the shit in my life. There's been a lot of it, Ruth, but, who knows, with you around maybe it's over. Maybe it doesn't matter so much anymore."

That pleases me. I am making him feel better about himself. *He's been hurt*, I decide. *Maybe by that woman, maybe farther back still, by the Captain.* It's one of the things I love most, his vulnerability, his neediness.

I have my own secrets, too. There are small lies of omission right from the beginning. We never talk about God. I just allude to Him in the most vague arbitrary manner. I don't tell him about the Fellowship of the One True Church or the Blood of the Supreme Sacrifice. My own doubts are enough to keep it down. Or maybe it is shame. Perhaps I am ashamed of my former fervour, my joyous, youthful zealousness when I was one of Jesus' foot soldiers and, by God, we, the Chosen, were going to beat sin and death and live forever.

I'm vaguely troubled by the fact that Ian doesn't want to meet my friends and we hardly ever spend time at the co-op. My room in the house is unoccupied for days; my bed remains smooth and straight and made with the proper hospital corners of Elsie's training. I only come home on nights I am scheduled to cook, and when I stay to eat, the people I share the house with feel like strangers. I hardly know my roommates because I am not there. I am with Ian. He doesn't like the co-op. He calls it the coop. The chicken coop.

"There are so many people, and they seem so young compared to you," he says, back at his place. "And less mature. I just feel funny around them. Like an old man."

He grins then, and draws me close. "I don't mind being *your* old man, but that's it. Why do you want to see other people, anyway? Are you getting sick of me?"

"No, but I have to go back to school soon. The September term is starting. I'll have to spend more time studying, less time, well, you know, hanging out with you."

Going to bars is what I mean. We spend a lot of time drinking together. Not always in a bar, either. Ian wants me to buy booze when my scholarship money comes, and I do, but never, it seems, enough. He drinks a lot, nurses beer after beer, all day, every day. But he isn't an alcoholic. He doesn't fall down drunk. He doesn't slur his words, he doesn't get massive hangovers that incapacitate him. He doesn't have a red bulbous nose, or unkempt clothes. He just drinks. He drinks often, all the time, but never gets really body-swaying, word-slurring drunk. Just more mellow, more gentle and sad and withdrawn, and even if he does pass out some nights, oblivious to me lying beside him, I know he'll wake up in the morning wanting me.

Those late mornings, when we wake with Sadie snuggled between us, and then stay in bed until late in the afternoon, are wonderful. It is easy in the summer, easy to forget about everything else. *I deserve this break*, I think as I watch the summer days drain away and the leaves of the river valley turn from green to gold. *I work hard in school*.

α

For a long time Jax hadn't mentioned anything to me about what was going on at the hostel. With only a few kids, the hitting must have stopped. I noticed her skinny legs looked brown and tanned in her short pants.

Today we were going down to the old town to check out the man who was going to be running Kassie and Skaw the coming winter. Mr. Anderson lived on the shore in the part of the old town we called Willow Flats. For some reason, Jax knew which shack was his and she wanted to make sure he treated his dogs okay.

"Some of them are kept on islands all summer, just thrown fish once in a while," she said and I knew it was true. I'd seen that before, the summer-starved skinny huskies pacing around the bits of bedrock that poked up in the middle of the bay. The dogs, fretting and whining, without a lick of shade, seemed to know they were too far out to swim to shore.

If you were in a boat and you got close enough, you could count their ribs. I pressed my hand between Skaw's ears, rubbed her neck and back. "He can't do that to our dogs."

Jax pressed her lips together. "That's what we're going to find out. Come on."

We cut through the school grounds and headed to the old town over the rocks. It would be too weird to go down by road. People were always driving on that road and they'd see me and report back to my parents. *Saw your youngest, Ruthie, with a pack of mongrel dogs heading down to the float base with some Indian girl. You okay with that?* It was best that my parents didn't know. We didn't play any pretending games on this outing. This was serious. We weren't trying to live off the land, we were just trying to find out the fate of our faithful friends.

The Anderson place wasn't fenced. It was a small kind of bomb shelter house made out of cinder block with at least three or four additions. The front part had old pink paint on it, which was flaking off, and I was pretty sure it used to be a gas station. It made the house look ugly, like the skin colour of an old lady. There were six or seven dogs tied to posts in the front yard, which was worse than our yard, all mud and dog shit and old Ski-Doos and other bits and pieces of machines rusting in the ditches where there was still meltwater. The dogs looked pretty healthy, just dirty and tired. They whomped their tails against the mucky earth as we approached. Two or three of them mustered enough energy to rise, their faces alive with the expectation of food.

"Don't touch them, Ruthie," muttered Jax. "They look wormy to me."

She could be so bossy. Always the expert. "I wasn't planning on petting them. Anyone can see these are working dogs." Jax tossed me a backwards glance. Together we walked towards the front door. Jax knocked.

We'd planned out in advance what we were going to say. I was supposed to ask about puppies. Mr. Anderson was then going to either tell us about his team or he was going to tell us to get lost. Nothing happened. Jax knocked again, harder. One of the huskies started to whine. I felt a little bit sick but I knew it was just nerves.

"Not home. Let's look around."

"No, let's get out of here. This is private property."

"Not in the Flats, it ain't," she said derisively. "This is Indian land."

Before I could ask her what she meant, Jax had jumped off the stoop and was heading around the side of the bunker. Two of the three dogs on their feet followed to the ends of their chains but were brought up quickly by choke collars. The other had curled down again, and seemed to be licking poop off his paw. I heard Jax whistle, low and long. She'd found something.

When I came around the corner I saw it. Up against a corrugated tin wall was a sled, half covered by a blue tarp. Sun was glinting off the steel runners and the sides were made of canvas or maybe hides, I couldn't tell. Jax was crouched down, peeling back the tarp.

"Let's get out of here," I hissed at her. "What if someone comes?"

It was like I wasn't even there. Jax was spellbound. Her face reminded me of Lukie, opening his Santa gift on Christmas morning. "This is it. This is just like my kookum's. She had one just like this. I think this is hers." She slid her open palm down the hook of the runner. I was starting to sweat.

"Com'ere."

"Jax…"

"This is what they'll pull, Ruth. This is where they'll train."

"What is it?"

"It's called a kamik. It's real, too. Not like some Kabloona sled, all for show. How did he get this? It's ours. I'm sure of it."

Just as I was about to hunker down beside Jax to check out the kamik, a whole bunch of the dogs started barking and we saw a green pickup pull into the yard. In front of us were the chained dogs, behind us was the truck. The only escape route would be toward the water, and the shore was at least fifty yards away. We were caught red-handed.

Jax rose to her feet, took a few steps back from the sled and gave me the look. *Play innocent. Ask about puppies for sale.* We were back to Plan A.

Two men got out of the mud-spackled truck. Both of them were big, red-faced, unshaven. The taller, skinnier one had black hair falling across his forehead, so you couldn't see his eyes. Neither of them had seen us. The darker guy kicked at the nearest dog, his boot landing squarely in her ribs. I heard the air go out of Jax's lungs and I wondered if the whine was from the hurt dog or from my own throat.

"What are you kids doing here?" the red-faced man growled. He had a huge beer belly and a pathetic comb-over, just wisps of stringy grey hair, really, crossing a sun-burnt dome. Jax pushed me forward.

"We came to see Mr. Anderson," I stammered. "I …er…we think he's selling puppies."

"Puppies?" He looked at me but didn't seem to see me at all.

"Yeah, like these." I indicated the yard with the tethered dogs. "Only smaller."

The taller guy grinned and spoke to Mr. Anderson: "Baby dogs. She means baby dogs." They both started to laugh like I'd made a joke. I felt like I'd said a bad word, a swear, and I could feel the colour creep up the side of my neck.

Anderson looked over me to Jax. "Whose kid are you?"

"Nobody's. I'm from the hall, the hostel, in town."

"What about your people? Where are your people?"

Jax looked over her shoulder to the Lake. "East," she said.

"On the Arm?"

"Maybe."

I couldn't tell what they were talking about. I just knew Jax looked mean. Mr. Anderson looked meaner. "We have to go. Come on, Jax."

But she stood her ground. Mr. Anderson started to move towards her, crossing the yard with a menacing stride. I was between them and I didn't know what was going on. What was he going to do? I stepped to the side to get out of the way. This was not what was supposed to happen.

"We got some of your pups."

What? What was she doing? Why was she telling him the truth? That wasn't Plan A. That wasn't part of our adventure.

Mr. Anderson was standing so close to Jax and me, I could smell his sweat. He was leaning into her and I wondered if I should start to run or scream. I did neither.

"You do, do you?"

"Yeah, we're wondering when you'll take them."

"You are, are you?"

That chin again. "Yeah."

Suddenly the man with the raven wing across his eyes came forward, and looked directly at me. "How old?"

"Going on fourteen." It wasn't quite true, but it sounded so much better than just turned twelve.

"Fourteen months?" The man looked baffled. It suddenly dawned on me he was asking about Kassie and Skaw. "No, they're only four months, four-and-a-half, outside."

Mr. Anderson turned to me: "Bring them back at six months. They ain't no good to us before that." He scowled at Jax. "You don't know an East End Bessie, do you? Heavy, about twenty-eight, thirty years old?'

"Nope."

He narrowed his eyes then, and going back to the truck, pulled a case of beer from the box. "Don't know how a couple of damn kids get my dogs, but I don't want to see you round here again. You understand? Now, scram."

His words kind of set us free and we ran down the deeply rutted driveway while the dogs tugged and bayed, excited by our escape. All the way home, Jax didn't talk, just walked with her head down, eyes on the ground. I tried to strike up a conversation a few times but there didn't seem to be much point. When we got to my street, we both stopped.

"We've still got two months," I said hopefully. "He seems okay."

"I know who that prick is. He's a bastard. He's got our sled." She spit on the ground, barely missing my foot, and then turned on her heel and started walking towards the hostel.

"Who is he, Jax? How does he know you?" and when she didn't answer, I called after her, "I'll see you tomorrow." Jax didn't even turn around. I watched her getting smaller and smaller down the street until she vanished into that blurry place where the sky and the road meet.

That was it. Somehow, I must have known. She didn't come to the brown bungalow the next day or the next. I cleaned the pen, played with Skaw and Kassie, and hung around waiting. It didn't seem worthwhile going on a walk without her. She made it fun. It wouldn't be an adventure without her. It would just be a dumb walk. Without Jax, taking the gangly-legged puppies out was just another chore. And chores I had at home, most of them undone.

There was only one thing left to do. I had to go to the hostel to find out what had happened.

They only confirmed what I already knew. She was gone. Her mother must have come back from the bush at last. Come to take her home. At least, I hoped it was her. The secretary lady at the front office said someone had taken her. *Someone came yesterday and took her. She's gone.*

Poof, just like that. I guessed I thought she would come and say good-bye. To the dogs, at least. Or maybe even to me. I guessed I thought Jax would come and say good-bye to me.

I plodded slowly across the field, past the flagpole where the ragged Canadian flag hung in the syrupy summer heat, and headed back towards the brown bungalow. I didn't know what else to do, where else to go. I didn't want my house, with all the proper people who knew how to act and carry on like it didn't even matter when someone disappeared, so I went back to the dogs.

I let myself into the pen and slumped down with my back against the fence. Skaw, excited, galloped and whimpered. He thought I'd changed my mind, and was going to take him out after all. His lolling tongue cast foam and dog spit all over. I pushed him away. It was Kassie who came and laid her long skinny snout on my knee. Her nose pressed into my palm and I stroked her, feeling the skull beneath her black fur, watching her ears flatten and relax. She whined once, a long, slow, mournful noise that seemed to come right from her doggie heart. I thought she was crying for Jax, and it made me cry, too, even though I knew she really, really wanted to go home, up the East Arm, to a place I couldn't follow.

I felt mad and hurt because, heck, Jax and I were free for a while. We listened to our wild animal insides and her crazy kookum grandmother ancestors and now it was just me and the stupid fence and Mr. Anderson's dogs. That's what was left.

I missed her like crazy at first, but then the leaves turned and school started and I sort of forgot about old Jax. I went to the dog pens one day and they were empty. Kassie and Skaw were gone, maybe to Mr. Anderson, maybe with Jax. I liked to think she had snuck back and taken them but I could never be sure.

α

One morning as Ian and I are lying together, still wet and sticky after sex, someone knocks on his door. He leaps up like he's been stung and pulls on a robe, forest green with thin yellow stripes and bits of lint on it. Even I start. No one has ever knocked on the door before. There is no phone. This feels like an intrusion.

"Stay here," he hisses, and he shuts the door to the bedroom. I feel so foolish shut in the room while just outside the room I can hear him greet visitors.

"Hi. Yeah. No, not exactly sleeping. Ah, do you want to come in?"

I dress quietly then, and come out to meet the couple, who turn out to be Ian's cousin and her husband. When Ian, disheveled and sheepish in his robe in the middle of the afternoon, introduces me at last, the cousin seems pleased. Not crudely, like a dirty joke, but genuinely pleased. They don't stay long, but the man claps Ian on the back before he leaves. "*Keep in touch. We're family.*"

Later Ian asks, "Are you going to drop me like a summertime romance after school goes back in?" I don't know what makes him ask. Something in my eyes? Some worried look when I find a flyer for school supplies in the hallway? I laugh and reassure him quickly and leave the question hanging just inside my own mind.

Then, in late July, Elsie and Dad visit the *Merry-times*. That's what Dad calls it, *A Merry-times adventure*. He's like that, a little bit embarrassing, maybe, but so what?

We go to the campus together, the three of us, before they know anything about Ian. Dad walks down the courtyard to take a picture of Elsie and me in front of the old, vine-covered library. As we're standing there, squinting against the sun and smiling stupidly at the camera, she mentions a mild heart attack, suffered in the winter.

"Nothing serious. He's fine now. I've got him off eggs," she confides, as if this small detail will change everything. She tells me the whole thing quickly, as though it is a secret being kept from him and when I turn to her, puzzled and concerned, she looks directly at the camera and nudges me, muttering "*Smile, Ruthie, smile*" between clenched, flashing teeth. "We didn't want to tell you, with summer school and all."

I don't tell her summer school has been a wash, that the whole summer has gone and my courses are all incomplete. No, I barely say anything. In fact, I'd just found out my parents and another couple are touring the Maritimes, indeed, had already arrived in town, from a phone message left on my pillow. Good thing I'd gone to the co-op to get clean clothes or I could easily have missed them. They want to take me out to dinner and I ask if Ian can join us.

"Absolutely," says Dad.

"A boy?" says my mother.

He doesn't really want to meet my family and when he comes to pick me up at the co-op he's wearing a Boston Bruins hockey jersey with a shrieking black and yellow logo.

"We're going to Martha's. It's kind of fancy." I want my parents to admire him.

"Yeah, so what? Are you ashamed of me?"

"No, I just thought you might wear a jacket. Or even just a plain shirt. You look so good in the blue pullover. You know, the faded one that matches your eyes?"

"What's wrong with the way I look, Ruth? What's wrong?"

He scowls, pissed off. We are supposed to meet my folks at the restaurant at seven o'clock. It's already half past.

"Nothing, it's just that..."

"Fine." He throws the first word like a knife from afar, and it hits the mark. "I won't go."

"Please, Ian. You look fine. You look great. Please, they'll be waiting." I am begging.

At the restaurant, he talks a lot, drinks three quick cocktails, rum and Coke, while Elsie plays with the olives in her martini. He's so charming, so engaging. I desperately want this to go well.

"And what do you do, Ian?" asks my dad.

Before he can answer, I pipe up: "How's Luke? What's Claire up to? Does Jiggs ever write from Israel?" It's Elsie's cue to take over. She knows the domestic details and she perks up, prattling on about my siblings. I don't really listen. The sound I hear is the ice snapping in Ian's drink as I will my father not to ask anything personal.

"It's beautiful out in this part of the world," says Dad. "And now we have more reason to come." He pats my hand absently. "Are your people from these parts, Ian?"

"Down the coast. They've got a big spread of land on the river."

"We'll be heading down that way tomorrow. Elsie and I thought, well, we thought Ruthie, you might want to come with us. Spend a few days together. And you too, Ian, you'd be welcome to join up. It could be a convoy. What are you driving?"

"My truck's in the shop right now," says Ian, beaming goodwill at my jovial, good-hearted father. "It's a half ton, long box, good for helping out my dad on the property."

Truck? Ian doesn't have a truck. And I can't imagine him helping the Captain with anything. Ever.

Dad looks at me. He looks so hopeful. "Ruthie?"

I feel the pressure of Ian's hand on my thigh. I'd kind of like to go, to hang out with them. I'm actually so happy to see them both, so happy to have them with me for just a little while. But the pressure on my leg is increasing. "No can do, Daddy. Too much school work."

Elsie looks worried and keeps flashing me meaningful looks as Ian orders a fourth rum and Coke. I find myself studying the dessert menu intently, avoiding her green judging eyes. I answer most of the questions they address to Ian. I don't really lie. He *had* lectured in sociology, hadn't he? Even if that woman took all the credit?

While we are having coffee, Ian suddenly says we're thinking of getting married. That's how he says it, out of the blue: "We're thinking of getting married." Just like that, between spoonfuls of chocolate mousse, as though it has nothing to do with me. I almost choke on my dessert.

My mother's "Really?" is a shrill gasp.

My father is more contained: "That's big news." Pause. "But don't you kids rush into anything. It's a huge commitment. Ruth has three years left in her degree, then maybe a master's degree. Right, Ruthie?"

"Yeah. Maybe."

Afterwards, once the hugs and formal good-byes are over and my parents are back in their rental car, promising to call the next day before leaving, Ian speaks. "I don't like the way they treat you. They don't take you seriously. They kid around like you're still twelve years old, especially your old man. What a clown." When he sees how stricken I look he adds quickly, "I just didn't like the way he talks to you. Haven't you noticed how condescending they are?"

I go back to his place that night, even though I don't really feel like it. For the first time, I wonder if I'm in too deep. It's the smallest flicker, a spark igniting, and, as quickly, going out.

In the apartment, sitting in the living room, he comes to me, squats down and put his arms on my shoulders, looking straight into my eyes. He squeezes hard, a little bit too hard, and says softly, "You're mine, you know, Ruthie Callis. All mine. I don't want anything to come between us."

"Me neither," I whisper. And when he lets go, I fall forward into him, allowing tears to come. He holds me and strokes my hair.

"I won't let any of them hurt you," he murmurs. "I won't let them hurt you."

And even though I don't know what or whom he is talking about, I feel safe in his arms, against his great shoulders, safe and warm. I feel precious and small and cared for.

The fear is pushed away. I feel protected.

α

In the summer after my grade seven year, at the age of thirteen, I became the bride of Jesus. Me, a bride, at thirteen! Imagine! I was claimed, chosen from the rabble, selected for the Prince. And, not just any prince, either, I was chosen to be the bride of the Prince of Peace, the King of all Creation.

It wasn't like I had to wear a frou-frou poofy dress and a veil and all that stuff, like a real bride would have to wear. It wasn't like that at all. All I had to do was take Him into my heart. Actually, my heart had to change, which wasn't hard because everything on my big body was changing, anyhow.

It was something nobody told you when you became a teenager. I figured becoming the virgin bride of Christ sure beat the other thing I'd heard whispered about. At least I could be sure that Jesus — who was, after all, long gone — wouldn't try and stick his thing into me and feel up my two lumpy breasts now growing out of control.

Nope, there was no one trying to stick anything into your privates when you married Jesus. No bodily invasion involved, except that heart business, which wasn't too hard, considering the other. You just opened your heart. Accepted His supreme sacrifice, which, of course, I did. How could I not?

There was a big tent, and a whole bunch of kids from a couple of the churches around town, and lots who weren't from any church at all, like Lucy and me. Lucy had become my Jax substitute, not as good, for sure, but because she lived down the block and had a house almost exactly like mine, I knew she wouldn't disappear.

We were at a camp called Long Lake. There were cabins, and a swampy lake with cattails and algae. It was a skinny shallow lake — I guessed that was how it had got its name — and it had really bad mosquitoes and blackflies, but it also had canoes. There were boys, too. We were all together with a few adults who seemed more like big kids, in a way, seeing they weren't that old.

I liked the one called Brother Terry. Everyone liked him because he was handsome, but I thought he paid more attention to me than he did the other girls. He said he was worried about my soul, which I had thought was pretty okay until I got to Bible camp. Now everyone started focusing on it, saying my soul wasn't right with God, and all that. It made me feel really bad, but I had to admit having a rotten soul was good for Brother Terry's attention. I really thought he liked me, even though he was older and all. Kind of like a crush. It was possible, wasn't it?

So I slept in a cabin that smelled like mouse turds and canvas with a bunch of other girls who all seemed to know each other, but they weren't stuck up the way you'd expect. They were loving. Like angels. We called ourselves The Angels. Sister Rose — she was our counsellor — said having a name made us a team. Actually what she said was it *solidifies our oneness.* It sounded so beautiful and poetic. *Solidifies our oneness.* I'd been saying it in my head since I'd arrived.

I'd come with my friend Lucy. She hadn't wanted to come at first, being as this was a Bible camp. I'd told her that Jesus was just like any of the other guys from history, sort of like Abe Lincoln, and that we might see wolves.

Lucy used to be crazy about wolves. Up until recently we'd played wolves all the time. It was sort of like it had been that great summer with Jax, but different, more civilized. In the winter we'd made a den in Lucy's basement and always argued about who had to be the girl wolf. The girl wolf wasn't as much fun to be as the boy wolf because you never got to prowl around the furnace looking for food. The good thing, though, was the knees of your pants didn't wear out as fast. That was sometimes how we decided, by whose mom had last mentioned the knees.

I'd told her we could play wolves out at the Bible camp, or maybe even see real wolves, try to get adopted by the pack even, and that had convinced her. Or maybe it was because she'd found out Ron March would be coming. Lucy had a crush on him.

He was a grade eight boy who had a locker four down from mine. He'd asked Lucy to waltz once at the Break-Up dance last May. She did. I watched them glommed together going around and around under the disco ball, while the last record played "Nights in White Satin." Her face was pressed into the chest of his leather jacket and I wondered if she was having a hard time breathing, with all that black leather smooshed into her nose and mouth.

She told me afterwards he smelled good, like apples and tobacco. I almost said *since when is tobacco a good smell?* but I didn't because Lucy was pretty emotional these days. Elsie said it was the hormones, but they didn't seem to make *me* into a grouch. She was changing, Lucy. But she was changing in a different way than me. We hadn't played wolves yet. I wasn't sure if it was because there were too many new people or because Lucy thought it was a dumb game now.

Lucy wasn't too happy about being at this inter-denominational Evangelical One True Church of God camp, I could tell. She didn't really like being part of our group. She thought Angels was a stupid name. She thought Rose had gross teeth, which was true. I noticed teeth a lot, even though my adult teeth had finally come in and anyone would think I looked like a normal person. Rose's teeth were big and buck, horse teeth, all stained brown, but she was nice in a homely sort of way. Lucy thought the afternoon devotionals were stupid, too.

"Let's walk out to the point," said Rose. "Even Angels need some air." All the girls seemed to want to go. Lucy gave me the eye when Rose packed her bible in her cloth bag along with mosquito dope and a big jug of Kool-Aid. I shrugged and headed out the door. The point sounded more interesting than the mouse turd cabin with the cobwebs and the smell of dead leaves mixed with hormones.

Lucy came, but she didn't walk with me. She straggled behind, dragging a branch on the ground as though she had to mark the way back to the cabin. The mosquitoes seemed to get worse and worse the closer we got to the lakeshore.

Rose was humming a hymn or something, but the rest of us were scratching ourselves or slapping at the bugs that hovered and droned like miniature helicopters on the attack.

At the point it was a little better because there was a bit of a breeze off the swampy lake.

"I want you to all sit down here in a circle," said Rose. She had to be kidding. It was sort of mossy and licheny and probably wet. More than half the girls sat down, so I did too.

"Lucy, will you join us?" asked Rose.

"Nahhh, I'm just going to watch."

"That's fine, sweetheart," Rose said with her words. Her voice sure didn't have the word *sweetheart* in it. More like, *retard*. Lucy sat down and I was glad.

The devotional started out with a prayer and then a reading from the Bible and then a talk. All the girls told their stories. Me, I listened and watched and felt a bit apart from everyone until I decided that, yeah, I wanted to be like them, I wanted to be able to pray out loud like the other Angels without being embarrassed. I wanted to ask God for things. Maybe I'd ask for a dog of my own, one that I could bring home and have sleep at the foot of my bed. I'd always wanted one. But, no, that was selfish. I'd ask God to save Ron March for Lucy. Now, that was an unselfish prayer.

After our drink, we walked back towards the cabins. This time Lucy did walk with me. "I'm not into this," she whispered so none of the others could hear.

"What do you mean, this?"

"God."

"Oh."

We kept walking. The bugs were getting bad again.

"The games and the sports and swimming and canoeing and even the food is okay, but this other stuff" — she rolled her eyes — "it's bizarre."

She whispered those words a lot. *Weee-ird*. Or *biii-zarre,* emphasizing the first syllable, and making me laugh at inappropriate times.

Devotions and night prayer circle were kind of weird, I guessed, but not as strange as what happened in the evenings.

The first night, after everyone had had dinner in the big common cook shack and the plates and things were cleared away, the revival meeting started. Brother Terry began with a testimonial and a prayer and then other people started witnessing, saying out loud how good God had been. After that part was over, people started singing high-spirited songs. I didn't know the words to any of them at first, so I felt a bit stupid and just pretended to sing, mouthing the words, but I quickly picked them up. It wasn't like they were complicated songs. We sang "This Little Light of Mine," "Over Jordan" and "I Have Decided to Follow Jesus." At first I was really uncomfortable singing "I Have Decided" because, truth be told, I hadn't decided anything.

Lucy decided she wanted to go home. Ron March seemed to be spending a lot of time with a girl from cabin number three, Kathy Gilchrist, the one with the tight white T-shirts. We watched her lean back into him when he was trying to show her how to shoot a bow in archery lessons. Lucy tried to pretend she had never shot a bow either, and all she got were instructions barked at her from a fat Friar Tuck girl who was wearing a weird scarf on her head like she was from the last century.

Lucy and I were the only ones in our cabin who hadn't yet been saved. We might have been the last ones in the whole camp. If only she were able to open her heart and accept Jesus' Supreme Sacrifice. Oh, it made me cry to think of it. Jesus on the cross for me. For me, Ruthie Callis. He probably could see me coming too, when he was up there, hanging, because he knew the future and all. *This is for you, Ruth Callis*, he probably breathed as he was dying. *It's all for you*. The tears were so close to the surface when I thought about Him knowing me and still deciding I was worth the pain. Lucy would cry, too, if she only thought about it. The nails. Oh, I bet they hurt. Oh, poor Jesus.

And, just like they said, it was for me He took those nails in His hands and feet. For my sin.

It wasn't hard to open my heart. It would have been harder to keep it closed. In the big tent there were always people crying and dancing every night before campfire.

The night it happened to me, there was someone speaking in tongues, which at first really scared Lucy and me because we thought it might be Satan, who they said comes around looking for unclean souls. Tongues were actually the voice of God speaking through the counsellors, who were really more like prophets than anything else. Someone else had told me that, or I would never have figured it out. I thought you had to be dead to be a prophet and they didn't really exist anymore. Sort of like the dinosaurs.

The fact that the tongues started up that night was a true sign from God that I was going to take Him and He was going to take me. We were going to do the big "I do" with all that strange and crazy chanting in the background like a choir.

It was another language, tongues, but not a language from this world. It was really weird and beautiful in a spooky way. And because I wanted to impress him, I told Brother Terry maybe I had it too, like the gift of tongues was just something you could make up if you were sort of poetic enough, but he said no, it couldn't be, because my heart was still closed to the Supreme Sacrifice and the Holy Ghost.

The campers were all babbling away in this weird language that I couldn't make sense of and I kept hearing the word Jesus and then, like a crazy miracle, I heard my own name, *Ruth*, like they were praying for me and the angels, the real angels, were calling for me. The hallelujahs were coming thick and fast, and just when the pressure to do something was making me squirm, a large woman got up and started swaying and dancing in the aisle. Tears were streaming down her face and she started spinning around like a crazy top until she collapsed at the front. She was slain in the Spirit, was what was happening. They'd told me about that, too. My mouth was just hanging open because I'd never ever seen God strike people down before and He was doing it right here at Long Lake in the cook shack, not even a church or anything, here in the woods with a dirt floor and bugs and tinned food. It was like the stable where He was born. That was it. It all made sense. God only came when people didn't care about fancy things like stained glass and stuff.

There was a lot of yelling of commandments — "Come now, Lord!" and "Power to the Spirit!" — and Lucy looked at me like *let's get out of here,* but just when I was going to do it, turn my back on God, there were more songs, slower songs, and some of the campers put their hands in the air.

A girl further down the bench from me raised her arms and so did an older girl named Sylvia. The one girl's hands were so high it looked like she was trying to grasp something just out of reach. Like God was just past her fingertips and if she could just touch Him, she'd be okay. She had her eyes closed and her brow was gathered like a tornado in the middle of her face and it looked to me like she was going to scream or do something really embarrassing. I knew I shouldn't be looking — everyone else had their eyes closed — but it was hard not to.

Sylvia's hands were lower, bent at the elbow. She looked way more beautiful, serene and peaceful, the way I imagined an angel must look. The music was swirling around the room, and suddenly I felt all scared and trembling inside. I put my hands up in the air, low and private, like Sylvia. Lucy poked me in the ribs with her elbow, but I decided to ignore her and just keep my hands up in the air like that.

And then I started to think about the nails and about the cross and about all the bad things in the world I'd ever done. I thought about the way I sometimes tortured Luke by hiding his toys and then pretending Jiggs was the one who'd done it. I thought about the way I practised swearing out loud and the time I had taken Bonita Bennett's cinnamon stick and eaten it and then said, "Oh, my gosh, mine is gone, too," and how Bobby Whitehead had gotten blamed while I just sat there all smug and silent.

Some people in the tent were crying and singing and the hallelujahs were all around me and I knew, I just knew, that I was a sinner and the Supreme Sacrifice was all for me. I remembered they'd said in the devotionals I would be made new, like a fresh start, and I was feeling ready to be an angel and to be able to pray out loud instead of being shy and embarrassed.

Wash us in the Blood, people were calling from the altar. And they were talking to me. It must have been the Holy Ghost. *Dip her in the River of Blood*, they chanted, and even though that kind of grossed me out, I sort of wanted it, but I sort of didn't, and I half-opened my eyes to look at Lucy, who was looking at me like I was out of my mind because my hands were hovering halfway up and now I was starting to cry and the tears were coursing down my face, and the snot was coming too, and I didn't have a tissue. I was crying because of my sins, even though I wasn't sure exactly how bad they were.

I knew about Adam and Eve and the Snake, who was the Devil in disguise, and even being born, they said, was a sin, so I guessed that was me, all right. I was a sinner. I stood up and sort of staggered to the front where the altar was just half a tree trunk propped up on some birch logs.

Brother Terry called Rose over, Sister Rose who could eat an apple through a picket fence with those huge teeth, and they both laid their hands on me and prayed while I cried and cried and the Holy Ghost pried open my creaky old sin-filled heart. At least I thought He did. I couldn't really tell because I was too aware of my hot red face and all the attention. I was hoping I wouldn't get snot on Brother Terry. It was at that moment I was chosen by Jesus, washed in the Blood, new again, born again and clean as I could be. I didn't have to be me anymore. I was forgiven, but I was still crying, crying, and now Sister Rose was singing "I Have Decided to Follow Jesus," and Brother Terry was, too. They were crooning it right in my ear, like a lullaby, maybe to make me feel better about this big decision. And the whole big tent was singing, except Lucy, who had actually disappeared, forever a sinner, and I felt a bit like a traitor to her, but I didn't care. I thought the whole gospel tent was singing for me, giving thankful praise for the salvation of my soul. So I sang, too. And it was done. I had been made worthy. I was the bride of Jesus.

α

It is late August, just before classes start again. Ian is being evicted from his apartment because he hasn't got enough money for the next month's rent. My room at the co-op is paid in full, but I've got almost no money either, and won't have until my scholarship cheque arrives. So we decide to hitchhike to Toronto.

"We'll take a holiday," I say. "And we can go to Sudbury to see my family. They just moved there a year and a half ago. I know you'll like them, once you get to know them."

I miss my parents. It's as simple as that. I miss them terribly. Their last visit was so tension-filled I barely remember it, even though it was less than four weeks ago. I just want to see Elsie and Dad again. They're both getting old. I remember the shock of seeing my father small and shrunken behind the camera when they came up to the campus and he started photographing Elsie and me and all the old vine-covered buildings. I remember Elsie's poker-faced pleasure at being out and about, touring, no longer trapped in the Far North with a thousand miles of gravel road between her and civilization. When I think of her, something else is there, too, a troubling feeling I can't quite place. I remember thinking her endless prattle covered something, something I couldn't quite put my finger on, but something I'd figure out if we could just go and visit for a couple of days. I suddenly really, really want to go to Sudbury.

Ian's not keen on the idea, but we strike a deal. We'll go to Sudbury, yes, but that will be a pit stop on the way to Toronto. We'll do a loop across northern Ontario and then follow the lake down to Toronto where Ian has an old friend, D'arcy, from Quebec, from the private school he went to and was eventually expelled from. This D'arcy owns a restaurant, selling, of all things, quiche. Our visit to Toronto is all about seeing D'arcy. Elsie and Dad and whatever stray sibling might be at home I will catch up with on the way through.

How easily I discard them! I'll just pop in and see Mom and Dad, breeze through, on my way to greater things, the more sophisticated Toronto. *Hello, Mom and Dad, remember me, Ruthie? And of course you remember Ian, don't you? The second one who claimed me as his bride?*

The fact is, I've never been to Toronto. I'm not sure if I've ever eaten quiche, either, although I know it's a fancy name for egg pie. But I'm thrilled to be going on a trip, going on the road with Ian. The holiday takes on an exciting shimmer. I will, at last, meet one of Ian's friends. The fact that we are leaving because he has no place to live doesn't strike me as odd. The fact that my parents are only included on our itinerary out of necessity also seems ordinary. I am fairly out of touch with what is normal after the summer. I guess it is a little like brainwashing. I am, quite literally, at Ian's disposal.

We are going On the Road. The day we hatch the plan I sing snatches of "Me and Bobby McGee" while we move things out of Ian's apartment. The blue chair and the pink sofa traverse the crooked staircase into the basement of my co-op house. Nobody minds. People are always storing things in the basement of the communal house. One trunk containing ragged clothing and a broken badminton racket has been there since 1973. At least, that's the rumour.

The weekend before we leave, we sleep in my room. It is after all, the last place we can stay. Ian's apartment is gone, rented to some sucky student on a scholarship, much like the someone I used to be before our spring encounter at the bar.

Feeling really happy, I spend part of Saturday packing a few things in my old Trapper John knapsack, the one I got at a yard sale for five bucks.

We stay late in a different bar that night, running a tab. "We'll square up with the bartender when we get back to town," says Ian, pushing me towards the exit, hustling me out. He doesn't want to stay overnight at the co-op, I can tell, but he doesn't have a lot of choice. We're leaving early in the morning. We will follow a rising sun west.

We agree Sadie will stay on at the co-op house. I ask Shieva, the girl next door, to feed her twice a day. There will be some favour exacted later on in the year in exchange for this kindness, I know, because Shieva, despite her disdain for the material world, can't continue to live on bits of food left over from last year's food budget. She is growing thin and pale already on a diet of oatmeal, macaroni and popcorn. When my scholarship money arrives, Shieva will demand her cut. I make a mental note, pained at how quickly the money has flown. The up side is Sadie. At least she will be fed.

"Thank God this Shieva chick is a vegetarian, otherwise I'm afraid she'd tuck in herself," says Ian, as he unpacks the twelve tins of cat food I borrow money to buy at the LowFood supermarket. This is his only comment. He doesn't like Shieva. He thinks she's too ethereal, her name's too weird, she's too skinny. But he loves Sadie and he knows she'll be well cared for.

In the morning, we crawl out of my bed and Ian says good-bye to his cat. She's sleepy, still really purring.

"She'll miss you."

"Us. She'll miss us," he responds in that tender-gruff voice I love so much. I feel my throat constrict in love, uncertainty and excitement.

α

A group of young men had come to town to work on a building for the One True Church of God, because the membership of disciples was increasing and, anyway, we couldn't go much longer worshipping at the Pentecostal temple, what with its icons and idols.

The young guys were from the south, on a mission of mercy. I imagined them like Paul the apostle, trekking all over God's creation, witnessing to the truth.

We were studying Paul in the Wednesday Bible study group, so I knew a little bit about the different churches that he'd trekked to, Corinth, Galacia, and even Rome, I thought. What with their terrible habit of feeding Christians to the lions, I was surprised he'd gone there, but I guessed he'd been faith-filled enough to tell those lethal lions to lay off. I loved the story of Paul's conversion, how he used to be the world's worst Christian killer and probably kept a whole pack of lions in his backyard, until one day, he was walking along and, whomp, like a sack of hammers, he was stricken by the truth. He even changed his name from Saul to Paul.

Since I'd read that story I'd been mulling over my own change. I was wondering if I might go from boring old Ruth to Truth. I knew it was a bit of a stretch, especially when you thought of scripture like *The truth will set you free*. I wouldn't want a bunch of people thinking the Ruth would set them free. Me. Man, that would be blasphemous, like taking the place of Jesus or something. That's what Satan had done, tried to be the same as God, and look what had happened to him. The pit. Straight into the fiery pit. No, I sure didn't want anyone to worship me, especially with all this sin and stuff stuck to me like burrs to a blanket, but, truth be told, I wouldn't have minded if one of those southern mission disciples had noticed my holiness or even the fact that I existed.

They were cute. They were Elders. Sometimes I lay in bed and thought about them: Aaron, skinny with flaming carrot hair and freckles and those tiny wire-framed glasses that magnified his eyes so they looked like fish eyes; Albert, from Lac la Biche, kind of like a bulldog with heavy black eyebrows and huge hands. My face would get all hot and red when I thought about those hands. And Bruce, slightly older than the others, all dark skin and hair except for that blinding toothpaste smile. He was definitely the best-looking one, the one all the girls in the choir sang for, pretending their hearts were on fire for Jesus and not those boys, all slicked-back hair in their Sunday morning best.

Thinking about them, especially in their work jeans, made me squirm. I thought I'd better read the Bible to take away any of those evil thoughts I was having about them, particularly the thoughts of Bruce, speaking to me or maybe even doing something else. Paul the apostle said thinking something was just as bad as doing it, and if you thought about Bruce grabbing you around the waist and kissing you full on the lips with that mouth of his, it might as well have happened, and then, boom, both of you were in sin. Not that I was thinking that way. Not really.

Besides, it wasn't Bruce but Albert who had spoken to me at last Saturday's Undergrounder and he was just doing what Elders were supposed to do, teaching me to stay on the right path. He came up to me after the Undergrounder had cleared out and told me about shedding. His face was all aglow as he talked of the first disciples and I could tell that he thought of himself that way.

"We have nothing, Ruth." He held up his palms, as if to show me how empty he was. Most of the other kids like me, known in the Fellowship as Submissives, had drifted out into the street to savour the remains of a midnight sun, but Albert was set on showing me the meaning of faith. He went on, talking at me as I stood on the stairs looking at those upturned hands: "The clothes on my back, my knapsack, and a photograph of my family, these are my only possessions," he said earnestly.

"Wow." I had liked the fact that he kept a picture of his family. It seemed so sweet and sentimental. Now tonight, I couldn't sleep for thinking about it. If I ever wanted to be like them, like an Elder, I was going to have to start getting serious about the stuff around me.

I slipped out of bed quietly, making sure not to wake Jiggs, mouth breathing again in the top bunk, and I started my collection. The house was quiet. The only thing rustling was the plastic garbage bag as it received the contents of my drawers.

Elsie was furious when she found out what I'd done.

"You did what?"

"I gave them away."

"You gave your clothes away?"

"Yes."

"And to whom did you give your clothes, Ruth Dolores Callis?"

"To the poor." It was the first thing I could think of, the scriptural answer. *Unless a man gives all he has to the poor, he shall not enter the kingdom of heaven.* Elsie wouldn't know that, though. She'd told me reading the Bible at night was an affectation, whatever that meant.

She was going bright red now, and I wondered briefly if some small devil horns might erupt from the top of her tight blonde perm.

"To the poor, Ruthie? To the poor? And who the hell are the poor?'

I felt like I was going to throw up. I wished she wouldn't talk to me like that. It had seemed like a perfectly logical thing to do at the time. I had so much. Too much, really. We all did. All those clothes, the shifts, the shirts, the three pairs of leotards, two with holes, the blue jeans. How many pair had I counted? Four? Five? Summer clothes, winter clothes, coats, accessories, who needed them? If I was to become a follower, a true disciple like Aaron and Bruce and those guys, I had to give it all up, give it all away. Couldn't Elsie see? Didn't she know that her twin sets and her cardigans and her handbags and her dozens of pairs of sensible low-heeled pumps were stopping her from having a relationship with the God of all Creation?

Of course she didn't know. My mother wouldn't know discipleship and austerity, forsaking all to follow Him, if it hit her over a head with a hammer. If she were old Saul on the road to Damascus and the vision came upon her, she'd probably chalk it up to thirst, have a glass of cold water and carry on her sinful ways.

"Who are they, the poor? And where, in God's name, did you take your things, Ruthie Callis?"

She just wouldn't let it go.

"The thrift shop," I explained. "You know the one, on the second floor of the SPCA building, the one run by those old ladies, the Order of the Daughters of the Imperial Empire or whatever."

"Sweet Jesus, Ruthie. I know those women. What are they going to think? What, in heaven's name, were *you* thinking?"

She was taking the Lord's name in vain, again. She did it all the time, even though I'd pointed it out to her over and over.

"I don't need that stuff," I said again.

"You don't need clothes?"

I indicated my current state of dress: a T-shirt, a pair of blue jeans, socks, no holes, underwear, too, but of course Elsie couldn't see that. "I kept three sets."

"Three sets. Three sets." She was really mad now, I could tell. She'd gone a bit white around the mouth. It was not a good sign.

"We're going down there right now, missy, and you're going to get those clothes back. You think your father and I spend good money to buy you decent things so you can turn around and give them to the poor? What the hell has got into you?"

"I thought you'd be happy."

A look crossed her face then and it was worse than anger. Elsie looked confused, like she wasn't even sure if she knew who I was. Maybe the transformation was taking place. Maybe, like Paul, the shedding was giving me a new look, a new way of being.

Elsie put her arms on my shoulders. She held me out from her own body at arm's length. Part of me wanted to plunge right into her and hug her hard and tell her that it wasn't easy and that I did it for my own good.

"When did you do this?"

"At night."

"Every night?"

"Yes, Especially that week Jiggs was away at camp. I dropped the bags out the window, so you or Dad wouldn't find out.

"And what about her stuff? Gillian's."

"Jiggs? Oh, no. I just left it. She has to decide to be a disciple. I can't do it for her. *Many are called, few are chosen.*" Elsie wasn't going to like that, but she needed to hear.

"Who told you to do this, Ruth? Was it the people at the splinter church group? Did they tell you that you had to give all your clothes away?"

Yikes, Elsie was on to something. I had to be very careful now. She was looking worried. She could stop me from going. I knew she could. I knew that's what she wanted to do. She was looking really worried. Love and fear were beaming out of her strong green eyes and on to me, into me.

Quick, Ruth, I asked myself, what would the Elders do? What would they say? *A man must leave his father and mother to follow me. Brother against brother.* Mother against child, too, I guessed. No one had said it would be easy. I swallowed hard and thrust out my chin, like Jax used to.

"No one told me. I just wanted to."

In fact, it had been hard. Didn't Elsie realize that? All of it had been hard. Doing it, keeping it a secret. Gathering some of my favourite things, cramming them into garbage bags, tying the bags off quickly, I had felt like I was smothering someone I loved. I did it quickly so I wouldn't change my mind. I remembered feeling good about the hangers jangling, free from all my better dresses and have-to-hang-up stuff. They reminded me of bare bones dancing, some sort of weird funeral dance, like I'd seen the Mexicans do on TV. The dresser drawers weren't heavy anymore with all those things either. They felt light as a feather and I could now open them with just a pinky finger.

I was thinking about those monk guys from a long time ago, the ones who lived in castles and didn't talk to each other, as I'd pulled the spread from my bed, sending a whole bunch of stuffies to the floor. Binky and Dog and the clown woman that one of Dad's friends had brought me back from the mining conference in faraway Honduras lay there, looking up at me. I just gathered them up, rolling them quickly in the rag rug Elsie had purchased the spring before. Gone. All of my things. Gone. Given over to something, someone greater than me. I felt clean then. For a few days I'd felt really clean and now Elsie was ruining the sense of liberty my shedding had bestowed. She was making me feel guilty.

"We're going to get them back," she said, suddenly firm. "Come along."

And, with that, I was marched to the car, and we hurriedly drove through the late afternoon haze to the thrift store, in order for me to search the racks for my things.

Elsie didn't realize that I didn't want them back. I had been liberated from desire. I mumbled a prayer as I sifted through the racks of musty clothing, hoping against hope I would not stumble upon the items I had worked so hard to shed. A very cool plaid jacket, baby blue with navy and red stripes, caught my eye momentarily and I wondered how I'd look in it, but I quickly shifted away from that evil course. I felt pure and free and above reproach as I slowly shifted the hangers along the rack. I knew that I was not meant to have those things back. I wondered briefly if I would even recognize them. My belongings were well and truly gone. They had been mine and I no longer wanted them.

Elsie was talking to one of the Daughters of the Empire, a dour-faced matron whose collar seemed to pinch the joy from her face. She glared at me, shaking her head. "No, the quality stuff doesn't last. It's likely sold. Welfare cheques came out yesterday. The place was like a zoo." And she closed her mouth tightly, like she'd bitten into a lemon or was holding pins between her colourless lips.

On the way back home, Elsie was mostly quiet.

"You gave your stuff away." She said it now like a statement rather than a question.

"Yes."

"Because you wanted to help the poor."

"Yes." I would let my mother believe that if it was what made my actions plausible.

It wasn't that I wanted to help the poor at all: I didn't even really know who the poor were. I'd given away my clothes as an act of sacrifice, as irrefutable proof that I wasn't dependent on things, that my spirit would not be dragged down and defiled by material goods.

What Elsie didn't know as we drove home through the increasing gloom was that she was next. The shedding started with clothes, but according to the One True Church, the Fellowship, the next level was relationships. I had to start removing myself from those who dragged me down, even from my family; no matter how much they loved me, they were not good for me. It was the only way to purity, the only way to achieve perfect peace.

With the car humming along familiar streets and Elsie beside me, eyes on the road, two little worry lines playing tag on her crumpled forehead, I wondered if I would be able to go through with this. Would I be able to forsake all in order to follow the bidding of the Elders, the new disciples? I wasn't sure.

I wanted to tell my mother everything in that moment as the heater blew hot air onto the windshield and the town reeled past like a black and white film. I wanted to tell her about the secret meetings and how I'd been chosen to be a disciple and how I had to follow, forsake all and follow. Those who didn't... gosh, I couldn't even imagine what their lives were like.

I tried to imagine Elsie burning in hell, and I just couldn't see it. I was pretty sure she'd escape somehow, but no, not according to the scripture. The teachings at the Undergrounders said all unbelievers would perish. All of them would burn.

I closed my eyes and lay back in the passenger seat. I could feel tears behind my eyelids, threatening. I couldn't look at Elsie because I couldn't bear the thought of her damned. So I just closed my eyes and asked God to help me be strong. The next thing I knew, my mother was gently shaking me, waking me up. We were in the driveway at the side of our house.

For months afterwards, I would see my clothing on other people. I saw an Indian woman wearing my leather jacket with the tiny yellow paint stain on the pocket. I watched her head into the bar of the local hotel, a place I would never go. Two days later I saw an older woman, way bigger than I was, sitting on the bench outside the post office, head back, eyes closed, soaking up the summer sun. She wore beat-up running shoes and my Laura Ashley skirt, hiked up, showing off her big blotchy thighs and calves covered in protruding blue veins. Yuck. She didn't even seem to mind that people could see her, and for the quickest moment I wished I could order beer in a dark bar or sun myself on Main Street on a really nice day without being worried about what other people would think.

My clothing took on another, darker, life and I imagined myself left lighter and closer to God for doing without. I should have recognized that momentary feeling of doubt, the one I had when I saw other people wearing my clothes, but I talked myself out of doubt. The more I gave away, the better I'd be. The less I cared about clothes and books and things of

this material world, the more faithful to Jesus I would be.
And He was the one I was trying to be like.

I knew they wanted me to shed my family, but I knew
in my fickle little heart that I was just not ready for that. I
guessed I loved them too much and I was going to have to
work on trying to unlove them. The shedding of my clothes
had really been pretty easy. I set myself a harder task. Not as
hard as shedding the family, it was true, but hard enough. I
started wrestling with the problem of food. Sure, it was one
thing to get rid of my material possessions, but what about
my chubby body, proof that I led an undisciplined and
privileged life? None of Jesus' apostles were fat, although I
was still holding out some hope for Bartholomew, the one
who'd replaced Judas the traitor. I was thinking it was possible,
just possible, he'd been on the chunky side. I'd never seen
him in the pictures of the disciples that illustrated my brand
new Bible. He wasn't at the famous feast either, the last supper,
where all they ate was bread and wine together. He was
probably somewhere else, having crackers and water, dieting,
to be more holy than the others so he could be chosen when
they needed a new disciple to make up an even dozen.

He had a fat-sounding name, the type of disciple who
might laugh a lot, right from the centre of his big belly. I
imagined Bartholomew as an opera singer or a jolly pub owner,
even though my version of him had no scriptural basis.

The scriptures were everything, according to the
Fellowship of the One True Church of God. And even though
it didn't actually say *thou shalt not be overweight*, it was there in
the Bible.

Aaron and Terry, who now led Wednesday Bible studies
together, had pointed it out to me. *Your body is a temple of the
Holy Spirit*, they said. *You have to learn to treat it with respect.*
What I heard them say was quite different. I heard, *Ruth,
you're fat. God doesn't like fat people.* Every time the temple thing
came up, I felt disgraced and self-conscious. The Holy Spirit

had a lot of room in my temple, that was for sure. It was more like a hotel than a temple, a kind of rundown hotel at that, with no one staying in it because it had a reputation of being a bit on the fleabag side. The Holy Spirit would be wandering around in my hotel thinking *what kind of place is this? It's so huge*.

I wasn't actually even sure if the Holy Spirit lived in my body. I thought He visited from time to time, but actually lived here, no. Why would He? I was too fat. And the Evil One tempting me with chocolates had made my face break out in pimples.

I wondered if the Holy Spirit was too embarrassed to live in my fat body. I knew I wasn't created that way. I was created to be perfect and it was only my greed and gluttony that had made me so huge and unappealing to the Holy Spirit. I knew He lived in the bodies of some of the people in the Fellowship, the fit, sleek people who didn't ever smoke or drink or eat pizza or chocolate. Their bodies were like spas for the Holy Spirit. I imagined Him relaxed in there, dressed in some sort of toga and lying on one of those chaise lounge thingies, poolside. In those clean small bodies he was able to manifest Himself whenever the occasion arose.

I decided to give up food. Jesus had, hadn't He? Forty days and forty nights He spent in the wilderness, drinking only water, preparing Himself for the crucifixion. If He could do something like that for me, surely I could do something like that for Him.

I didn't tell anyone at first. It was between God and me. I wanted to prepare myself for the End Times, which were coming. I wanted to prepare my body to become a temple for the Holy Spirit so He could shine through me as a testimony to truth in the last days before the Second Coming.

"Watch and pray, people!" shouted one of the super Elders from the pulpit. "Watch and pray, oh people of Zion. The End is coming soon. Watch and pray."

"*Watch and pray and don't eat,*" I repeated to myself, sitting in the pew, wondering if the visiting Elder's head was going to explode, he was so worked up and red-faced. If Jesus was coming back to claim His own I wanted to be light enough so He could lift me up at the end of the world. I knew that all the true believers would be taken away in the Rapture, before the wrath of God rained down on the sinful world, but I was a little bit scared that I wouldn't go up with the saints, my being so big and all. Stopping eating would help that, too. Help me get taken away in the twinkling of an eye.

I knew the End Times were upon us and the Rapture was soon. I figured the Second Coming was two years away, three tops. I had to be in good spiritual shape to take what was coming, according to the Fellowship. Persecution. People would laugh at us. Maybe even revile us or hit us. *Count it all joy, my brethren. Count it all joy.* That's what they said. I was going to count it all joy, too, but first I needed some assurance that the Holy Ghost was going to take the hit for me. Otherwise, how could I count it joy?

The first day I stopped eating wasn't hard, because it was the beginning of Lent and everyone at the One True Church was giving up something. It was a small sacrifice to help us understand the Supreme Sacrifice. Brother Terry encouraged me to give up something I really, really liked as a reminder of what Jesus had given up for me. Even though he hadn't said what it was he was going to give up, I could tell Brother Terry had something tough in mind. He was very spiritual, in a good wiry way.

For the first day, I just didn't eat. I told my parents I had been invited for supper at Lucy's house, which they should have known was a lie because we hadn't hung around at all together since I'd been saved.

Instead of going there, I went to the One True Church during the supper hour, and prayed for forgiveness and strength. I prayed that I would get strength from God instead of strength from food. I prayed that He would fill me up with His holiness and I also prayed that I wouldn't get too hungry.

No one was at the Church when I was feasting on prayer. They were all at home, legs dangling under the tablecloths, bellies flush up against the tables, eating. I was sorry they couldn't see me. I was hungry enough that I thought I might have that shiny skinny glow, like the supermodels or the martyrs. I hoped so. I was praying and praying and there was no one there to see me. It was a little maddening.

I'd shut myself in one of the little rooms they used for Sunday school. There were glitter pictures on the wall with bits of cotton batten stuck to them that the Sunday school kids had made. The cotton was supposed to be sheep, I thought. I reached over and touched one of the pictures. Suddenly, the itsy-bitsy little chair I'd been sitting on gave way. The plastic legs just collapsed beneath my weight, bent outward, and snapped off on one side. I sprawled across the carpet. It was a sign. The fasting had to continue. And my prayers weren't being received, I guessed, because I had let my bad worldly thoughts about the skinny supermodels creep into my prayers. *Oh, God, I'm sorry. I'm sorry I got distracted. But thank you for this lesson, anyway, God. You're so good, speaking to me. I see the way. I broke the chair because I am a fat sinner and, not only that, I forgot that I was in Your divine presence, but You reminded me by breaking the chair and thank you, thank you for the sign. You see me all the time. You want me to keep up the fast and be holy and, please God, divine God, help me to fix the chair so no one finds out.*

But the little plastic chair was not to be fixed. I could see that quite clearly as I picked myself up. I'd have to get rid of the evidence. But where would I put it? The basement of the One True Church was just a big room with some Sunday school classrooms adjoining. There was a main bathroom and another small door beside it. I walked across the big echoing room holding the broken chair in two hands. Now I was really hoping nobody would come. *Keep them at their supper a little bit longer, Lord. Make them eat all their dessert.*

The door to the room I wanted was sticky but it opened with a sharp pull. It was exactly right, a furnace room, and as my eyes got used to the dark, I could see some janitorial supplies against the near wall. It was the perfect place to put a broken chair, especially now, when nobody would know how it got broken. As I was carefully leaning the plastic chair against the wall, and putting the leg in place so it didn't at first appear to be broken, the furnace roared to life. There was a mighty huff as the blue gas flames ignited in the roaring belly of the furnace. I could see the fire surging clear and blue, pure flames to consume evil. I thought of one of the prophets, Malachi, maybe, who went into the furnace and was not burned because he was so good in the eyes of the Almighty.

Tentatively, I reached out towards the furnace. I couldn't put my hand in the flames because there was a screen. But I could touch it and I did. The vents were warm but not hot. I could touch a furnace now because the living fire within had redeemed me. The fire in me was stronger than the fire in the church furnace. With the heat passing through my hand and up into my arm, I felt such strength and resolve, nothing would touch me. My shadow across the furnace room floor was elongated and drawn out. It was the effect of my holy fire. I'd had a glimpse of what it would be like to be slim and whole, after all the sins of my flesh fell away. God had confirmed it.

In the darkness, I smiled. God sure did manifest Himself to me in mysterious ways but, as far as I was concerned, if He was the one speaking, I was going to be the one listening. After all, it was not everyone who got direct messages like this. Only the Chosen.

The furnace duct was getting hotter now, so I drew back. But I wasn't worried. Truth had been revealed. I left the broken chair propped up by a mop handle and firmly closed the door.

As I walked home through the darkness, I was no longer Ruth Callis, but Malachi, God's chosen, touched by flames yet unconsumed. I almost hoped I'd meet a hungry dog, or better yet, a wolf, or even a pack of hungry, rabid wolves. They couldn't touch me. I was so full of power right now, they'd cringe and slink away at the sound of my master's name. *You shall have dominion over all the world, over all the wild beasts.* I was pretty sure that was a quote from the Bible, and I was hungry to try it out.

But no wild dogs came, no beasts of the tundra attacked. I walked home through the settled darkness, confident that my fast was just beginning.

The next morning, however, it was more difficult. I pretended to eat cereal, but washed it down the sink when Elsie was reading the newspaper. I knew I could throw my bag lunch away at school, but it was getting harder. My stomach was empty and groaning. The smell of toast was making my mouth water.

Supper the second day was the toughest. It was macaroni and cheese. My favourite.

"Ruthie, eat up. You've hardly touched your food."

That was the Devil, talking through my mother, actually.

"I'm not feeling well."

It was true, the food in front of me was making my mouth water again, the way it did before you threw up. I was so hungry.

Elsie's hand was quickly on my forehead and she nodded. "You're a little bit warm, Ruthie. Do you want to go lie down in your room?"

And I nodded, thinking *thank you, God*, although what I really wanted to do was plunge my head into the macaroni and cheese and inhale it as quickly as I could to fill up the hollowness inside my body. The hollowness was where the Holy Spirit was supposed to live. Why wasn't He coming? I must be clean now.

The next morning it became easy. Not easy to not eat — people always wanted you to eat — but the hunger went away on the third day and the Holy Spirit came in. I thought about it like the crucifixion. The first day was pain. The second day was emptiness when Jesus had to visit Hell. Macaroni and cheese was my hell. Today the Holy Spirit had come and I felt wonderful not needing food anymore. It was a floating kind of feeling. Everything I looked at seemed less substantial, more opaque, and everything I thought seemed invested with meaning that hadn't been there before. The scriptures took on a beauty and a wisdom I had never experienced, which I pondered and prayed upon behind the closed door of my bedroom.

It would have been fine, too, except I fainted in prayer circle just when I was starting to dream wonderful dreams and see visions of glory in my head. One of the Elders called my parents and they took me home and made me eat soup. I'd never tasted soup that delicious. Or felt that terrible eating it. I consumed three bowls of that soup, salted with tears that I couldn't stop streaming from my eyes. I imagined the Holy Spirit inside me, soggy, half drowned by my failure.

α

It is a dark Ontario night. Ian and I are in the cab of a truck. It's one of those big trucks; eighteen wheels, ten gears, all stinking of diesel and held together by the yellow highway lines and the crackle of the CB radio. Our driver's name is Marcel, but his radio handle, Longdong, is a constant amid the static and squawk that punctuates the conversation.

There are only two seats in the cab so I'm sitting on the narrow bed, hunched forward to hear, the radio between my knees. We caught this rig at Trois-Rivieres, and it's going all the way out to Calgary via the northern route, which is major good luck considering how far we have to go. The bed is behind the two bucket seats, so I am a little bit back from the conversation. The air smells of dust and body odour, and the bottom sheet is an unwashed grey. The pillowcase is stained and slightly yellowed with hair grease. It's not a great place to sit. My back is tired. In fact, my whole body is tired. I slump forward and listen.

Ian and the driver have been talking politics almost steadily since Mirabel Airport flashed past, a brightly lit oasis in a desert of darkness. The two of them scoff at the illuminated parking lot, the lit empty space, the middle-of-nowhere air about the place. Words like *patronage* and *taxpayers* rise and fall as I envision the glow of the city growing closer.

I'm pleased Ian can talk like this. He knows about government, raves about how it has failed the people. I've heard these long rambling diatribes when he's fueled by drink and full of boozy confidence. Still, I envision him and Dad sitting in the living room after supper, drinking coffee, talking about the state of the world. In this fleeting fantasy, Elsie will turn to me while we're in the kitchen loading the dishwasher. *He's such a nice young man,* she'll say, nodding towards the rumbling man voices, low and thoughtful. *So intelligent and charming.*

But of course, it isn't like that at all. When we arrive in Sudbury, Ian wants to take Marcel out for a beer.

"It's the least we can do," he says.

"It's late already," I remind him. "My parents go to bed early. We should get there and get settled or else we'll miss seeing them." My voice sounds whiny and, worse, young. Ian is pissed off as we swing onto the city bus that takes us the last few miles. He throws his pack to the floor, sits in the seats reserved for the elderly and the handicapped. I sit beside him, subdued. He stares straight ahead, feet on his duffel bag, arms folded. He doesn't look when I point out the huge nickel and the smelter near the mine site.

When I try to see it through his eyes, my parents' neighbourhood suddenly seems prissy and suburban. Bourgeois. The streets are clean cul-de-sacs. Flowering hedges or discreet low fences separate the single-family homes that line the darkened street. Instead of pride, I feel embarrassment.

That's it, of course. He's comparing this to his boyhood neighbourhood in Saint John. I remember the one time he took me there; when we left the bar and wandered the waterfront area. I remember the tenement-style housing, brick walls streaked with graffiti and, in the yard of the house he'd grown up in, a broken tricycle, without a steering column or handlebars, rusting in the damp.

"This isn't where I come from," I say, as we approach the house on foot. "My parents moved here after we all left home." He's been told this before, but for some reason it seems imperative I whisper the history again as we arrive at the door. The information divorces me from Dad, who appears, a shrunken bald man, coming to the door in a bathrobe. He draws me into his arms while bellowing up the stairs, "Elsie! Elsie! Else! It's Ruthie. She's home."

My story separates me from the silly pink flip-flop slippers pounding down the stairs, the flurry of exclamations, the quick, impulsive embraces, the pleased, quizzical re-introductions and, the mandatory snacks and questions served in the warm circle of light at the kitchen table.

As we finish the cocoa and sweep the toast crumbs from the counter, Elsie answers the question that hangs in the air, just beyond the stifled yawns.

"Ruth, what do you say we put Ian in the downstairs bedroom?"

Though it's phrased as a question, it's not. It's a statement, but I can feel Ian's eyes on me, piercing my flesh, defying me to argue.

"Yeah, that's okay," I say, quickly. "I'll make up the bed."

I leap to my feet, tongue thickened by betrayal. My parents go upstairs then, first reminding me of a picnic tomorrow in the backyard to celebrate my father's sixty-third birthday, a date I'd totally forgotten.

Ian sulks as I smooth familiar sheets over the mattress cover. "Wow, these are so white," I marvel, not looking at him.

"*We'll put Ian in the basement. The fuckin' basement will do for him.*" He's mimicking my mother, scowling and unhappy. I'm suddenly so tired. The long day of travel combined with this strange tension between people I love has left me exhausted. There is nothing left inside but empty space. I shut my eyes briefly, seeing the guest room at the top of the stairs. The narrow single bed with its white eyelet spread, and the pillows cradling a few favoured stuffed animals left over from childhood is impossibly inviting.

"I'm tired." I throw his pillow on the bed. "We'll talk in the morning."

Ian sees my impatience and changes tack. He reaches across the bed, pulls us down together. I let myself flop like some boneless jelly creature, wrung through with weariness.

He speaks first. Softly.

"Ruthie, stay with me." And then in that hurt, little-boy voice that gets me every time, "You know I'm afraid of the dark."

He is so gentle, and his hand caressing the back of my neck feels good. *Yes, I could stay here. I should stay here. I belong with my lover, not down the hall from my mother and father. I'm not part of this world. I can't be told what to do any longer.* But the chains of childhood bite into my consciousness and I squirm out of his embrace.

"I have to go up now." I kiss him quickly, somehow missing his mouth and feeling the day-old growth of his beard. I leave Ian alone in the basement, knowing there will be a price to pay in the morning. It's like Shieva and the damn cat. It's like the scholarship money and the beer.

And, of course I'm right. At breakfast Ian is distant.

"You kids come out and see the new patio," Dad offers. "I built a bird bath out of field stones." He hesitates. "Finish up here and then come out." He's got the *Globe* in hand and I can't be sure he really wants us out on the deck. Ian's lack of interest is painfully obvious. He is mashing a pat of hard butter into his pancake. He almost sneers.

Elsie raises her eyebrows and the breakfast nook, usually a place to linger, feels too intimate, too close. Outside on the porch, the only sound is the rustle of the morning paper. My father, the implacable judge, has withheld comment.

"The Torringtons are coming over at one for burgers and birthday cake, Ruth," says my mother, scrubbing a tiny spot of maple syrup off the tabletop. "Maybe you kids would like to clean up a bit or do some laundry before they get here? There are clean towels in the linen cupboard." Her voice rings with false June Cleaver efficiency. I ache for her.

"What, she thinks I'm not good enough for her friends?" asks Ian indignantly, barely out of earshot.

"No, it's because we've been on the road. She's a mother, Ian. Wasn't your mom like that? *Change your clothes, wash your face, pick up your room —*"

"I didn't live with her."

"Oh, right. I'm sorry."

It's that boarding school business again. I'm convinced something happened there. Something bad. Ian doesn't talk about it much. So many bad things had happened to Ian when he was young, maybe the stuff at boarding school is just buried beneath even worse stuff. It's too painful. Again, I feel a desire to shield him. I know the counselling isn't working. He needs me. If he would just open up.

When I've asked Ian what he and Reg talk about at their therapy session he usually tells me it's none of my business. That makes me so mad. I share everything with him and he tells me it's none of my business. I wasn't angry right away, though. It was when I was back at the co-op house picking up some clothes. The people there seemed to really know each other, really talk. And they were my age, too. I almost didn't go back, what with his *none of your business*, but then I remembered why people see counsellors in the first place and I felt sorry for him. Once, when he was drunk, he let it slip that they talked about hockey, about the Montreal Canadiens. I couldn't believe it. I thought that was pretty stupid, but I didn't say anything. Weren't counsellors supposed to help you get over your bad past? Weren't they supposed to talk about deep feelings, unrealized fears, and unconscious desires? I secretly hope that they talk about me, but I'm beginning to wonder if Reg even knows I exist in Ian's life.

"I'm going to take a shower. Join me." I give him a teasing smile but nothing comes back.

"I'm fine."

"Suit yourself. I just thought you'd feel better."

His face goes tight and he repeats each word slowly.

"I — said — I'm — fine."

I leave him and pad up the stairs to the peach-coloured bathroom, where I take a long, hot shower, but try as I might I can't wash away the bad feeling I have in my belly.

When I get out and come back downstairs, he's gone.

"Probably out for a walk," I tell my parents, feigning nonchalance, but I check downstairs to make sure his things are still there.

The bed is unmade, his clothing spilling out of the top of his duffel bag. I am relieved and I lie down for a moment, hungry for his scent. The sheets, I notice, are twisted, as though he's had a nightmare or a restless sleep. He can't sleep without me, I decide, and, pleased with the thought, I make up the bed.

He doesn't come back. The Torringtons arrive, old family friends bearing a bean salad and a homemade bottle of elderberry wine as a gift to my father. Dad barbecues the hamburgers and leaves them to stay warm on the grill while Elsie delivers potato salad, rolls and a garden salad, rich with summer produce, to the picnic table.

When it's all ready, my mother eyes me. *Where is he?*

I shrug. We start without Ian, eating, chatting as though it is perfectly normal that a guest should disappear into a strange city without a word.

"New beau, Ruthie Tooth?" quips Norm Torrington, toasting the sun and the garden and his general state of well-being with a third beer. "Good husband material, John?"

The question feels like a personal attack on my decision to bring him home, and I excuse myself from the table, afraid to hear the response.

Where is he? How could he do this?

He calls later, long after the Torringtons have left and the birthday cake has been consumed. He's at Peter's Pantry, a nearby bar.

"Why don't you come down for one, Ruthie?" He's balancing his words just so, a careful attempt to convey sobriety. "We should talk."

And I go. Against my better judgment, I go. I pull on one of my dad's old slickers before leaving the house because the late afternoon sky has closed in and the radio has forecast showers, even storms for the evening and into the next day.

α

The southern elders had left a shell of a building that summer, to be completed at a later date. But in fact, the Fellowship of the One True Church of God didn't need a building. We'd rented the church from the Pentecostals and we held our meetings in their off hours. The church was not a building, but the body of Christ. It was a human thing. It was all of us believing together and getting the blessing. When the Spirit descended, the whole body shuddered. Sometimes the Spirit was so strong, we trembled in unison. I needed to be part of the body. Without them, I wouldn't be anything, not even the toe of Jesus, not even the fingernail. Only together did we make the body.

Sometimes I imagined myself to be the flesh that took the nails in His hands. That was the most sacred, considering the Supreme Sacrifice and all. Sometimes I thought of myself as His scar, tough, twice-healed skin. When I was worshipping with the Fellowship of the One True Church, the body of believers, this felt right. It was my calling.

When I was home, with Elsie or Jiggs or Luke or even my older snooty sisters, or when Dad and I did something special together, like head out to the golf course to have a word with one of the cronies, I never thought about myself as a scar-hole.

In junior high I was trying really hard to let my light shine among men. Seeing as I didn't know any men, except my dad's cronies, I was trying to let it shine in school among the kids I knew, the heathens. I didn't actually call them that, it would have been cruel, but that was how we were supposed to think of them, the washed and the unwashed, the Christians and the nons. Most of the kids in my grade were nons. Some thought they were Christians, but if you went to the United Church, for instance, it didn't count, because you didn't take a stand. I knew. I had been United before I took a stand and was saved and became part of the Body. Some of the Catholics thought they were Christians, too. But they weren't, they were Catholic. They didn't go to my school anyway. My school was full, seething, with the non-Catholics and the non-Christians.

My job was to tell all the nons about the truth. Let my true light shine. Brother Terry had told me this was what true Christians did. They witnessed. They testified to the Truth. And the Truth — that was Jesus and the Supreme Sacrifice — would set you free.

One day in the lunchroom I decided I would witness to some bus kids. Cynthia Paul and Sherry Beauchamp were sitting at the long lunchroom table in a place we called the Boys' Basement. It was a cave of a room, hollow and painted a really ugly grey-green colour, like mould. The windows were high above,

at ground level, so it was always kind of gloomy. The Boys'
Basement was still a basement, even though during the noon
hour it doubled as the lunchroom. In fact, in between it and the
boys' cloakroom were the janitor's rooms and the furnace room.
I only went in there to eat lunch. I usually sat with the other
people in my class, other townies. I never sat with the bus kids.
Cynthia scared me a bit. She'd had two brothers expelled. She
had red hair. Some kids called her a witch. But God was stronger
than all the forces of the Evil One. I closed my eyes, prayed for
God's help, and approached.

"Mind if I sit here?"

Cynthia narrowed her eyes at me suspiciously and
squinted across the table at Sherry, who seemed so interested
in the contents of her lunch box she didn't even look up.

"Whatch'a think, Sherry? Do you think we should let
her?"

"Why don't we just tell her to fuck right off?" Sherry
responded. Cynthia hooted, and bits of her food, a few pieces
of the moist and barely chewed baloney sandwich, flew out
of her mouth and landed on my arm.

Instead of wiping the muck away, I pretended it wasn't
there. I pretended it didn't matter. *Men will revile you for My
sake.* I was being reviled for His sake.

"Well, maybe I can sit with you tomorrow," I said
quietly, looking right into Cynthia's eyes, and still loving her,
the way Jesus would. "Maybe tomorrow."

And I turned and walked away, full of what I hoped
was humility. I chose a place alone at the long table, separating
myself from all of them, and I bowed my head over the tuna
fish sandwiches packed in my own lunch, aware and glad of
the distance between me and the rest of the lunchroom kids.
I felt their eyes burning into my neck as I said my grace,
distracted from God by the thought of Cynthia's saliva drying
on my skin.

After that, the kids started to call me a Jesus freak.
Instead of being embarrassed, I was proud. I liked it. Weren't

the early disciples persecuted for their faith? People couldn't bear to look on the light. They were blinded and had to look away. That was how I was now, a blinding beam of goodness, flooding the dark places where evil dwelt. I would combat darkness and I would try not to let myself stand in the way of His light. The self, I had learned from Brother Terry and the other Elders at the Fellowship of the One True Church, was the part of each human that needed to be subdued, given over to God, snatched out of the hands of Satan.

Satan still scared me. I didn't like to admit this, because he shouldn't have been able to scare me any more, now that I had accepted Jesus into my heart as my personal Saviour. But he did. He was always there, they told me, ready to tempt. Don't be frightened, they said. But I was frightened. There was part of me that still wanted to be included with my old friends. I missed Jax. I even missed Lucy. I missed playing wolves in her basement. That was the bad part of me, the selfish part. It was the devil tempting me with my old life. I had been made new. I claimed the Blood of Jesus. *Avoid all appearances of evil. Don't play wolves. A man must forsake all others and follow Me.*

"Get thee behind me, Satan," I whispered, so no one else would hear.

I was going to the One True Church four times a week now, five if I could get away on Sunday nights for the second gospel service in the evenings.

On Wednesday nights, I had Bible study, on Friday night, Young People's group, when I got to see the other kids from my camp, on Saturday nights, we held our coffeehouse, called an Undergrounder, and Sunday, of course, was Church.

Church wasn't just church, though. It started out with Prayer and Praise, then Bible instruction for all ages, then Free Testimony Time, the Message, the Altar call and, sometimes if I hung around after service to help clean up or pray with somebody, I'd get invited somewhere for lunch. The people at the One True Church of God saw me as a bit of an orphan because I was a convert, and my family was, well, sort of looked down on. Suspect. But the more people I brought to Jesus, the more they'd like me, the more they'd recognize my holiness.

I found a boy in the schoolyard who seemed to cry out to be the receptacle of my teaching. God had pointed him out to me. He was the most needy. His name was Billy. Billy Goodyear. I knew he was the one when we lined up to come in from recess. He was in front of me. He smelled like oil, like a gas station. Sometimes I'd seen him get dropped off at school by a tow truck. He turned around to yell at a friend and sort of stopped when he saw my face. The yell never came. I thought he saw the Truth in my face. I thought he wanted my truth.

I talked to him the next recess while he smoked by the fire exit. I asked for one of his cigarettes for my demonstration. He was mildly interested. I held up my English binder in one hand and my math text in the other, books I had brought out with me expressly for this purpose.

"You're here." I indicated the binder, and laid it on the ground. "And this is God." I put the text down, too, a little way away from the binder. I laid my hand on the textbook, wishing it were the Holy Bible or at least something of religious significance. "All this space in the middle is sin. Your sin, Billy, the stuff that separates you from God." I looked up at him when I said his name. The light in my eyes must have been fierce and powerful, the Holy Spirit at work.

He squatted down, near me, drew on his smoke as though sin was just another word for adjustable wrenches. He did smell funny, like grease and wood smoke and our basement in the spring when the walls dripped with the run-off.

Now was the clincher. I held the cigarette in the air while he watched and then gently placed it between the books. "This," I said, "is Jesus Christ. He's like a bridge over sin, bringing us to God. He is the Supreme Sacrifice, Billy. The Supreme." Oh, the power of those words. I was excited, on fire with my witnessing. I smiled up at Billy just as his boot came down on the tips of my fingers.

"This is my boot," he said, "It's not a bridge between your hand and my smoke but if you don't get your Jesus Christ fucking hand off my smoke, it will become a bridge and it may have to break your fingers." He added weight. It hurt. I pulled my hand away sharply. The fingertips down to the second knuckle were bright red. Half a muddy boot print marked the cover of my English binder.

Billy scooped up his cigarette and kicked my binder and my textbook. The spine cracked and papers flapped into the wind, leapfrogging across the playing field. Billy Goodyear laughed, expertly flicked his butt to the ground, just missing my leg, and sloped off towards the door as the bell sounded.

I held my hand close to my heart. My breathing was fast. I had been persecuted for my faith. This was the first time. Oh, what a blessing. It was my lesson in loving the unlovable.

My fingers ached, but this pain was nothing compared to the cross. I thought of the apostle Paul, who insisted on being crucified upside down because he was unworthy to die in the same position as his Lord. My hurt was so small, so insignificant really, but oh, at last I was enduring something for God. The more I testified, the more I was persecuted, the more I endured for His sake, the closer I would be to knowing the sacrificial love of Jesus.

I smiled to myself. My heart was full. I went back into my classroom as Daniel to the lion's den. I couldn't wait for Testimony Time at the One True Church of God. At last I had something to tell.

α

Ian doesn't have D'arcy's phone number, but that isn't bad, it's just plain stupid. And the dirty weather has made us both miserable.

We are inside a cafe somewhere on Queen Street. It is not how I imagined Queen Street. There are no trendy boutiques, no art galleries. The restaurant doesn't have a black ceiling with the galaxies painted in Day-Glo, it doesn't have mismatched wooden chairs, sticky pots of honey on each table, and waiters with spiked hair wearing spandex and sporting phony British accents.

Rather, the restaurant we are in is a narrow, sickly salmon-coloured box overseen by a shrunken Oriental man of indeterminate age. There is a lunch counter down one side of the room and beside it, a row of red-capped stools spring like intermittent mushrooms. Ian and I sit on the other side of the room, in a booth. We are near the back of the restaurant, closest to the pay phone, just in case we actually track down D'arcy, the elusive boarding school buddy. He's not listed in the phone book and Ian doesn't have a number.

An ashtray overflows beside the Yellow Pages I've been reading for the last half hour. The list of restaurants seems to go on forever. Ian chain-smokes.

"And you don't know what area?"

"No."

"Or the actual name of the place?"

"I told you. No."

He is not being any help. D'arcy is, after all, his friend.

"The Egg On Inn. Does that ring a bell?"

He scowls. "It's not an inn."

I look again at the listings. The Oriental proprietor is tapping his pen on the counter. Ian glares at him. I try to focus on the phone book. Eglinton appears often but I'm fairly sure that's a street name or a district. Maybe looking under the Q's will produce better results. But there is no Quiche Cafe between the Quic Lunch and a long column of Quick Eats and Quick Snacks.

"Hey, look, The Quote and Quaff Poetry Café." I'm trying to cheer him up. "Maybe we could go there and catch a reading." I'm only half-joking. Part of me longs for that literary life again, for readings and papers and presentations.

Ian just grunts. "I need more cigarettes," he says, taking the last from a package of Players and lighting it.

"We should eat something." I turn the laminated menu over and over in my hands. "He's not going to let us sit here much longer unless we order something to eat."

"We'll buy smokes," says Ian, glancing at the proprietor, who has settled down to read a newspaper at the front counter, but shifts his eyes towards us every few minutes. "How much money do you have?"

I pull a few ragged bills from the pocket of my jeans, purposely leaving some behind. "Twenty, twenty-five, twenty-seven and change." Good, the extra twenty is tucked away.

"Shit," says Ian, "is that it?"

"There might be more in my account, but I need a bank."

"Shit," he says again, his voice sharp with impatience. "Let's get out of here before slant eyes over there has a fit. What's he afraid of? We're going to steal his sugar?"

"Shhh. He'll hear you." I reach for my jacket, slipping two quarters underneath my saucer, then, reconsidering, take one back.

Ian is already out the door, waiting for me under the dragon-embossed awning. His face holds the heat of anger, and I imagine the rain evaporating into little puffs of steam as it hits his skin.

I put my hand on his arm and am surprised to find it cold. "What do you want to do?"

He looks at me and I think I see his eyes soften.

"Let's go somewhere and get a drink and a bite to eat. Don't worry, there's always Plan B."

He puts his arm around me and the weight of it on my shoulders is comforting. I feel slightly less anxious, less vulnerable. We may be up against some hard times, I think, but at least we're up against them together. Just being with Ian, in this strange city, is exciting. We're like a curious couple dancing, I think, as we walk arm in arm down the street. I imagine Ian as Danger, all slick and smooth. I'm his devil-may-care chorus girl willing — no, urging — the risk. I imagine us doing our crazy tango together along the thin sharp edge of pleasure, knowing one slip could be fatal. But our dance is absolutely effortless and perfectly choreographed by a higher power. Despite seeing the razor's edge, I know I want to dance on. And Ian? I don't think he knows how to stop.

We find a pub and order cigarettes and beer, and, as an afterthought, a plate of greasy chicken wings. The pub is not crowded. It's that lull between the last of the three-martini lunch crowd and those who knock off early for an after-work quickie. I know the rhythm of a pub. Ian has taught me well.

We sit at a high table near the bar, facing away from a large television screen mounted on the wall. The picture shows two female wrestlers groping each other in a large box filled with Jell-O. The volume has been turned off. I can tell Ian wants to watch. He glances towards the screen now and then, but only briefly, pretending something has caught his eye. He's trying to be polite, focusing on me rather than the slippery women whose skimpy costumes are now pasted to their flesh.

"What do you think we should do?" I ask again, licking grease off my fingers and taking a swallow of beer. "We've got to find somewhere to stay tonight. It'll be dark soon."

"Do you want another?" He indicates my half-full glass.

"Ian, I don't think we should spend all our money on beer."

There, it's said.

"Look," he counters, bending close to my face. "Things haven't worked out exactly as I planned. I gotta think for a while about what we're going to do. Okay? I like a beer when things don't work out. It helps me think. Okay?"

"It's my money."

He leans back abruptly, like he's been slapped, and there's a look on his face I haven't seen before.

"Oh, your money, is it? It's like that, is it?" He pivots on his chair and turns directly to the television, back to me, draining his pint in one long draw.

"Hey," I touch his updrawn shoulders. "Let's not fight. We're supposed to be on a holiday. Remember?" He shrugs me off though, and calls to the waitress for more beer, ordering a jug this time.

When it comes, he pours himself a tall glass but leaves mine empty. "Help yourself." He still won't look at me.

I pour a glass for myself and drink. *Might as well get drunk*, I think, watching the dust motes float through a single ray of slanted daylight. *At least that's something we're good at.*

The afternoon, like my money, slips away as we drink more and more beer, feed the jukebox quarters and watch the patrons come and go.

I make a trip to the bank down the block and have a moment of panic when I realize the day is only a smudge on the horizon. I consider taking what's left of my money and leaving, but questions of where to go and how to get there are too huge to contemplate.

Ian, unafraid of strange city streets or the descending twilight, will surely have a plan by now. I'd left him chatting up a couple who lived in a big old Rosedale house with seven — or is it ten? — others. They seemed like an accommodating pair, as willing to share their digs as they've shared our last few frothing pitchers of beer.

But when I get back from the bank, the couple has left, and Ian, surrounded by empty beer glasses and scrunched up potato chip bags, looks lost and indecisive. He's grinning that lopsided grin again and his eyes are glassy and rcd.

"Ruthie, Ruthie." He slurs the first syllable into the second, "Little Ruthie Toothie," He's using my childhood nickname without even knowing it. The stab of memory is terrible.

"Com'on, let's get out of here."

"Did you get some more money?"

"There isn't any." It's a lie, but he's probably too drunk to notice. I'm sick of that stupid grin and the way he's so casual about the darkness outside.

He grabs me then, hands wrapped hard around my upper arms, squeezing. "What do you mean, there isn't any?"

"Ian, you're hurting me."

I try to twist away, but his hold tightens, his bar stool tilts precariously on two legs. His knees knock the table, and an empty glass falls over and rolls in slow motion to the edge. When it hits the floor, shattering, the sound seems muffled, like an underwater explosion.

"Money." I hiss at him. "There isn't any more money. None left. We spent it all. *You* spent it all. On beer. It's spent." I spit the word at him, showering his face with saliva.

"Shut up," he says. "You can't talk to me like that. No one talks to me like that. Do you understand? No one. No fucking one."

He gets up without releasing me. There is something hard in his eyes. He pushes me towards the door and we lurch together through the crowd, his grip on both my arms now brutally unrelenting.

Outside, the persistent drizzle makes him let go, but he pushes me backwards and I stumble away, striking my thigh heavily on a bicycle rack.

"Leave me alone." I'm sobbing now, drunk and crying, rain and tears distorting my vision. "What do you think you're doing? What are you doing?" I stumble behind the bike rack and crouch low for protection.

Ian's anger, like boiling liquid finally vented, seems ignited by my helplessness. He pushes the bicycle rack forward on top of me and I am barely able to scramble out of its way.

Somehow I get up. Somehow I get away. I run through the dark streets of Toronto, dodging around shoppers and late night revelers. I run for my life, to save my life.

I don't know if Ian is behind me, but fear pumps my legs, fear sucks the sight from my eyes and the voice from my throat. When I can no longer continue, I slump in a doorway, heaving and terrified. I shake and my breath comes in huge staccato gasps.

There is a sound now, and Oh God, the sound is my name.

"Ruuuuth. Ruuuuu...thieeeee." He is shouting my name. Hoarse and bellowing, Ian's voice is thick and indecipherable. Full of anger? Full of despair? Full with my name.

He must not find me. I crouch lower, forcing myself smaller into shadow. Holding my ragged breath inside my chest, I watch him lumber by, no longer large and ominous but hunched, and searching frantically.

"Ian."

It's only a whisper but it escapes my mouth without me forming the word. It is enough to make him turn and scour the darkness. When he sees me, he falls to his knees on the street and crawls towards me, curls plastered to his forehead, eyes brimming with contrition.

"Baby, oh my God, baby. I'm so sorry. My God. Ruth."

And his arms are out, pulling me towards him, pulling me out of myself, up and out onto his chest, drawing me into that safe shelter of his unspeakable sorrow.

We both weep and he strokes my face, my head, the back of my neck. The noise he makes is the whooshing of blood wrung from his heart, guttural and uncontrolled, and in his movements I feel the urging of a helpless animal rooting for comfort in the flesh of another.

I am held. I am holding. As we cling together in the dirty brick doorway of a darkened apartment building, I feel something swell inside my body, larger than pain and greater than fear.

It is pure and potent, expanding, increasing, and casting its hot white light over everything that has come before. I can absolve or condemn, pardon or punish. I now have the power to forgive. The magnanimous, Christ-like power to restore or destroy is mine. And that power renders me stronger than I have ever been before.

α

You started out being the bride of Christ, and it was all shimmer and excitement, and people just loved you because you'd made a commitment and entered into the Holy Family as a new bride, and, then, bang, next thing you knew, you'd suddenly become the housewife of Christ, and you were making coffee at the Undergrounders and people were asking you to teach Sunday school. It was a bit of a shock, really, how quickly you could lose your bride status. It wasn't that I wasn't grateful. In all things give thanks, after all. It was just that it was so much fun at first, meeting all the true believers at the One True Church and feeling part of that special club where no one else was allowed in unless they paid the price of accepting the Supreme Sacrifice and were willing to submit to the will of the Elders, which was, after all, God's will, them being so righteous and all.

I had to be really careful in the beginning about Elsie and Dad finding out. They knew I'd been redeemed of course, but I didn't think they knew how it had changed me. I could see our whole family in a new and disapprovingly flawed way.

I used to think we were okay, the Callis family, pretty regular, but now I saw the subversion and the way we had been shielded from the true face of God. My house was seething with sin, and my parents acted like it was normal. They had a responsibility to raise us to know and love God, and what had happened? Claire took the Lord's name in vain all the time, and because she was just a year younger, so did Theresa. Jiggs was so obsessed with boys, it was a wonder she wasn't already twice married and divorced. Jiggs' spiritual life consisted of her and her dumb friends using the evil Ouija board to call Elvis back from the dead.

Luke was fifteen and all he did was lie around reading Archie comics and think about the next thing he was going to eat. I couldn't stand living there anymore. The sin was everywhere and they all went on acting like it was normal and that my salvation was just like Elsie's bunion operation, or Claire getting involved with that horrible boyfriend with the Harley Davidson and the tattoos, like it was just a little blip and me finding the water of eternal life was a phase, something I'd grow out of. As if!

I tried to explain the seriousness of my commitment to my dad one day when we were working outside in the front yard. He'd planted the whole front of the house in potatoes, which was a little embarrassing when you considered that all the other people in the neighbourhood had normal things like grass and flower beds in front of *their* houses. He said it would be good for the ground, and that maybe we could have grass in a year or so.

The older girls were really in a knot about the potatoes, coming in the back door, preferably under cover of darkness, which was pretty hard to do this far north in the summer, but I didn't mind. I tried not to let the things of the world affect me much anymore. Besides, I thought of all the potatoes we'd have in the fall and how I'd be able to distribute them to the poor and just leave a little note on the sacks of potatoes saying *The Lord Provides* or something quiet and spiritual like that.

Anyway, we were working out there, weeding and picking potato bugs off the younger plants, when I brought it up.

"I'm a new person," I said to Dad.

"That's great, Toothie."

"Like, I'm really new. That name is old. It's part of my old self."

He looked up and I could see him smile.

"That's what we used to call you before your big teeth came in."

"Yeah, Dad, I remember. How could I forget? It's just that I've been born again. I'm a new person. New in Christ, you know?"

He rubbed his big paws together and seemed to be looking really closely at the little half moons of dirt under his nails. When he spoke, it was softly.

"You'll always be my Ruthie Tooth, my baby girl, but listen, Ruth, Christ and all that is a good thing. You'll never catch me saying it isn't, but remember this, my girl, a little religion can go a long way. Yes, it can. A little religion, Ruth, is a good thing but it can go a long way. A long, long way."

He ploughed his hoe deep into the ground and uprooted a small potato. "See this?" I nodded mutely. It was one of Dad's little life lessons.

"This potato will only grow and get bigger when it's underground. It needs the darkness and the soil and the rain and nutrients from the earth. It's a little bit like your understanding of God maybe, Ruth. Inside yourself, God grows. Once it comes to the surface, it isn't growing anymore. It's just there."

"You can't eat a potato when it's in the ground," I responded. *Touché, Dad,* I thought.

My father ran his hand across the scratchy Saturday whiskers on his chin.

"That's true," he said. "But these little potatoes here, they're babies. They've come to the surface too soon. You know, they aren't really formed, Ruthie. They aren't very good to eat at this size. There's not much to them and they've stopped growing. It's sort of like someone's faith. It might be best to keep your religion inside yourself until it's, well, more mature."

He didn't get it. None of them did. Only the people of the One True Church really understood the significance of being a disciple. I loved my dad, but as I watched him patiently weeding the front yard potatoes I was afraid for his soul. He didn't know the power of the Spirit. He was blind to it in his own daughter. I might be Ruthie Toothie to him, but that was my old name, my other name. By the time my adult teeth had come in, I was halfway down the path to ultimate destruction, even though I didn't know it. But I had been saved. Praise be to God.

I almost said it out loud, but I didn't want to startle Dad, who had gone back to the hoeing. There was a fine line between testifying to the eternal power of God the Father, and letting the seeds of your words fall on fallow fields. That was biblical. In this case, my testimony would be wasted. Jesus said if the people weren't prepared for the message of truth, it couldn't be heard. He said nettles would grow up and choke the Word and the people would remain in darkness. Out in the yard with Dad, my testimony would be choked by potato bugs and weeds, and even though he looked pretty happy, whistling through his teeth like that, Dad was in the darkness and the darkness was eternal.

When I was little, I used to hear them talk, Elsie and Dad. One night when Jiggs was at a sleepover, I was having a hard time falling asleep without her there and I was going to go out into the living room to tell them. But the dark kitchen and the yellow stove light trapped me, and instead of going in, I stood really still and listened to their voices. They weren't regular Dad and Elsie voices, either. They were super serious about something and so I stopped near the doorway.

"You need to come out of there, John. It's just ridiculous at your age."

"Oh, I don't know..." My dad's voice sounded sort of dreamy. "It's a different life but, you know, I kind of like it. The guys, the pit, the cage, all of it."

Elsie broke in. "The shift work, the tiptoeing around the house trying to keep the kids quiet, you sleeping all day."

"Now, Else, it's not like I'd be going back to shift work. I'd still be a shaft operator but there would be a little less paper pushing, and I'd be a little closer to the operation, the smelting, you know, the stuff I like."

His voice sounded so patient. I knew he liked going underground. He'd tell us stories about the ore, about mining ore and the veins of gold down below. Gold. I tried to imagine the gold, shining in the darkness like the brimming chests from Luke's tattered *Treasure Island*.

"How come the boys don't smuggle it up in their clothes?" I'd asked him once. "Why don't we have gold lying around the house, Dad? Gold bricks and gold taps on the sink and even beds made out of gold. I'd sure like to sleep in my own golden bed like a real princess."

He'd laughed at that. "Oh, Toothie, you crack me up, kiddo. Nope, the gold below is way, way down. It's inside the earth, Ruthie. It's part of the earth, but you've got to go down the shafts to get it. It's not pretty down there. It's dark and wet and close. And knowing there's a mile of bedrock and earth and minerals and shale and swamp above you? It gets a little scary, if you think about it too much.

"Did you know it takes tons and tons of ore to get just the tiniest chunk of gold? And there's fire, too, my girlie. It's fire that turns the gold to a liquid. Can you imagine a river of gold, Ruthie? A burning, flowing, molten river of gold? Well, that's what comes out of the cold and dark, but believe me, it all takes time. Time and money."

I crept back to my bedroom then and thought about my dad inside the earth sitting by that golden river. I used to try to imagine what the inside of the earth was like. I imagined hundreds of tunnels like the ant colony I'd seen once in a science fair where the ants built a home against some plexiglass and you could see the inside of their ant hill. I remember being freaked out by them scurrying all over with huge white eggs, like Rice Crispies, in their mouths.

I'd seen the mine from the top, the pit-head and the slag-heaps and the weird dead swamps full of grey sticks that used to be trees where they ran off the arsenic, but I'd never seen the river of gold that ran underground. I used to picture my dad, sitting there by the river, happy as a clam, while Elsie paced back and forth, back and forth, across the surface of the miserable earth, wishing he would come up.

Now all I could see was fire. The river of gold was molten lava, steaming hot and swallowing up sinners. I didn't like to think about it, but I sometimes saw that same river of fire wash over my potato-bug-picking dad to carry him down into the depths of hell.

The only place I found refuge from my heathen family was at the church where I worshipped.

There, we had a plan. There, our testimonies were having an impact and people were hearing the Word. Granted, we mostly ministered to the poor and the needy, sometimes the drunks, but didn't the lowly in spirit see God more readily? That was from the Bible, too.

Even though Elsie and Dad didn't know it, I was reading and studying the Good News every night in bed. Now I could quote scripture to almost any situation and the Elders were starting to notice.

I never looked them in the eye after bringing the Word to the group, however. I'd watched the others, and the best thing to do, especially if you were a girl, was to look down at your lap a lot. I looked down, but not too much, because I was afraid I'd have a double chin and they'd see. My holy fasting had simply not worked. It was fine when I was at the church, feasting on the word, but when I got home Jiggs had made popcorn or Puke wanted me to whip up a batch of Rice Crispie squares. I didn't want them to see that temptation ruled my life. They always talked about how a woman had to be demure and silent and I was trying to learn how to do that, but it was hard. If I was demure at home, everyone got suspicious. *What the hell is wrong with you, Ruth? Get in there, girlie. It's dog eat dog*, and that sort of thing.

Today I was working an Undergrounder, but because it was Saturday I had the whole day to kill with no homework and not much to do. Elsie said she wanted her kids around on the weekends, but after a couple of hours of us fighting and lollygagging on the sofa, she was usually happy to see us head out. It was a strategy I'd had to learn. Be present. Hang around and after a certain amount of time, a certain amount of bickering, we'd be allowed to go out. My parents seemed to think the Church was a good place to go and rarely asked questions. Tonight they told me I could stay out until midnight because it was the weekend and there was still light in the sky at midnight. Things were always more lax in the summer, so it was easier to get away.

When I entered the building, it was like entering a new but very familiar and very comforting world. The smells were candle wax and furniture polish. There was a sort of vibe, too. I thought of it as pure love mixed with sorrow. It couldn't be any other way. Instead of going up to the sanctuary where light was pouring through the stained-glass windows, making everything hushed and holy, I went downstairs. The basement was my refuge. It was my fortress. We were far from the Pentecostals with their weak and false doctrines. We were the Fellowship, the One True Church. I was so happy I could weep. These were my people. We were sanctified by the Blood, by the Supreme Sacrifice, and our job was to win souls for the only true God.

The warm, fragrant, candle-lit basement greeted me. Someone had already done set-up and seven card tables were strategically placed around the room with four chairs around each. If Elsie saw this, she'd think it was a big bridge tournament. Little did she know, miracles were going to happen in this room tonight, souls would be won and, if all went according to plan, I would have some part in the winning.

I quickly erased that thought. *I'm sorry, God. Make me an instrument. Help me to be selfless. Subjugate my ego so that your Holy Spirit may shine through me. Amen.* It was a quickie prayer, but necessary. One of the things Brother Terry, the Elder of the Elders, had told me to watch was pride and ego. I was still not sure what the word subjugate meant, but I said it anyway. God knew what it meant.

"Hey, Sister Ruth. Welcome. Praise God." It was Daryl, a big black guy who worked in the mines. He was a prophet.

"Praise God," I replied. We said that like a password, or, when we were out in the world, we used the sign of agape, the fish. It was a secret finger code that only true believers of the One True Church would recognize. When I tried it out at home on Pukie, he thought I'd Krazy-Glued my fingers together. Heathens didn't know how to respond when you gave them the sign of the fish. It was something about the guys Jesus worked with all being fishermen, I thought. They were also persecuted, so they needed a secret code for their meetings. The Undergrounder meetings were supposed to mimic the way it was in the early Church, the olden days. We made the church basement into a warm cave, a place to bring the lowly so that they could be saved. Our mission was to go out and win souls for the Lord. We were fishers of men.

Women, of course, were the best fishers. The other girls and I, we were like bait, the worms on the hook. It was kind of gross if you thought about it like that, all slimy and wormy, and Brothers Daryl and Terry and Victor and some of the other Elders said we weren't supposed to be mimicking the ways of the flesh. Still, God worked in mysterious ways and if men followed us to the Undergrounder for coffee, the overwhelming presence of the Lord in this room would carry them the rest of the way home.

"Anyone else here yet, Daryl?" I asked.

He indicated the prayer room, which was really just a Sunday school classroom off the main room, dimly lit. We kept candles and tissues in there because lots of the lost started to cry when they realized the magnitude of their sins. Gosh, so would I. So *had* I.

"Al and Vic are getting ready," he replied, waving his hand in the direction of the prayer room. I couldn't help noticing how white the palms of his hands were compared to the rest of his body. "You're supposed to make coffee tonight. The first round goes out at 9:30, the second round at 11:00. That will be the most fruitful."

"I'm only allowed to stay until midnight." I decided I might as well be up front about it.

Daryl's lips went tight together before he forced a smile. "Serve the Lord in whatever way you can, Sister Ruth. *Be unto Him as a sacrifice on the altar*. Why do you still have a curfew? Who calls the shots, anyway, your parents or the Spirit of the Almighty?"

He could tell he'd made me uncomfortable because he put his hand on my back, between my shoulder blades, as I turned and ducked into the kitchen, which was sealed off from the sacred space with its plastic folding door. Who was in charge? I thought as I filled the urn with water and carefully poured the grounds into the wide-mouth basket. Daryl must think I was a lot older than I was. Most not-quite-fifteen-year-old kids had a curfew, didn't they? I liked the fact that he thought I was so grown up, but I was afraid he was right when he asked me whom I served.

It was complicated by the fact that *honour thy father and mother* was still one of the ten commandments. How could I honour them if they were keeping me from my real work? I balanced the basket of coffee grounds on the long thin spindle and lowered the whole apparatus into the water, listening for the reassuring glug as it settled and the water bubbled up. The thrill of excitement still existed in this small chore. Would some souls be won for Jesus tonight? Would Christ manifest His spirit in this very room? It seemed that it only worked when I was here in this sacred space. Today at school had been a total disaster. I didn't even like thinking about it.

I'd just finished a social studies paper on Frobisher, one of the first English people to go out in search of the Northwest

Passage. I'd had to present it this afternoon in front of Mr. Jamison and my whole social studies class. We all had to do a presentation, not just me. It was part of our unit on Canadian history and more specifically on explorers.

Angela Thompson was at the locker next to me. "Hey, Jesus Freak, you're up today in Jamison's class," she said.

"Yeah, how did you know?" Maybe she was really looking forward to my talk. Miracles happened.

"Because I'm after you. Remember the three E's."

"Oh, yeah, enunciation, elocution... What's the other one?"

Angela snorted. "Elective information. Good thing Jamison isn't a math teacher." She started saying the words again, listing them on her fingers. "Elocution, enunciation, elective and information. That's four. Three E's and an I. He can't even spell and he sure can't count worth beans."

I liked Mr. Jamison. He was nice to me. But I also hardly ever got a chance to talk to Angela Thompson, one of the most popular girls in high school, so I said, "I think he likes Miss Bagthea. You know, Language Arts, grade nine, always wears tons of gold bangles."

"Her? She's flat as a pancake."

"Oh." I hunkered in closer to my locker, so Angela wouldn't look at my chest.

"Good luck, Ruth," said Angela, fluffing her hair in her locker mirror. "Or should I say *God luck*." She slammed the door and headed down the hall, hips swinging.

Angela must have known that I'd been praying a lot about my presentation on Frobisher, praying that I'd win some hardened hearts to Jesus. I was planning to turn it into a mini-testimonial. The story was perfect.

This Frobisher guy went to the Northwest Territories looking for gold. It was the fifteenth century, of course, so he endured a lot of hardship on this rickety boat with all these other rough cussing sailor types. There were icebergs and frostbite and scurvy and all that nasty stuff that you'd expect, but he found this inlet that he thought was the Northwest

Passage, so he went for it, and along the way he found gold, or at least what he thought was gold.

It wasn't that he was dumb or anything, but he did live a long time ago, before they knew very much about the world at all, still thinking it was flat and all that.

So, anyway, this guy Frobisher, he stopped looking for the route to China and filled up his boat with rocks and sailed back to England. Everyone there got all greedy and excited over the gold flecks in the stone and Frobisher was sort of like a hero and he got three more boats from the queen and endured a lot more hardship in the Arctic and loaded those three ships and sailed all this heavy stone across the ocean again, only to have a scientific gold guy tell him all his work was for nothing and all he'd got was a big pile of iron pyrite, fool's gold. Fool's gold for a fool, that was the Frobisher story in a nutshell.

I was mulling it over as I walked down the hall looking for a quiet place to say a prayer. My plan was to sort of turn it into a story about life without God. The kids in my class were like Frobisher, and they were trying to take fame, say, from things like cigarettes and necking and all the sins of the flesh that were happening all around me all the time. Sometimes I wondered if I was the only holy person left in the whole school, sort of like Noah, when the corruption of the world got so bad that God decided to send a flood and kill them all.

I was kind of waiting for that, but it was more likely He was going to do the Second Coming thing, the Rapture, when we were all sitting together in biology or gym, and poof, I'd disappear and everybody else would just sit there with their mouths hanging open, saying *Oh my God, help us. Ruthie was right*. And then they'd be sorry that they'd called me a Jesus freak and they'd be tearing their hair and rending their garments, like the friends of Noah did in the Old Testament. It would be raining and raining and it wouldn't matter to me a pick because I'd be totally ascended, wearing a robe of glowing white, and Jesus would meet me halfway and say *Well done, Ruth, thou good and faithful servant.*

Anyway, it wasn't like I thought the Rapture would happen during my presentation, but what I wanted Angela and all those guys to know was that the right labels on their clothes, and boyfriends, and dating and all that stuff was like Frobisher taking the fool's gold back to England. It was for fools and in the end it would all get dumped into the fiery furnace and burnt up, or, in Frobisher's case, dumped into the London harbour. I wanted them to know life wasn't worth a pinch of poop without the Supreme Sacrifice and the Blood and all that stuff.

I went into the girls' cloakroom, which always smelled like wet fur, even in the summer, and I sat on a bench between two coats. The big clock with the wire mesh over it said my presentation started in six minutes. Six minutes. There was a half-inflated balloon stuck in the clock's wire cage and as I was wondering how it had gotten there, the minute hand clicked over.

At the One True Church they said: *In all you utter, honour He who died.* I figured that with enunciation being so high on Jamison's list, I couldn't exactly utter but I needed to figure out how to honour without anyone really noticing I was talking about His Holiness at all.

Yesterday, I thought I'd try to tie the presentation into Noah — he and Frobisher both being sailors and all — but with them not living in the same century, I figured it would be too tricky, especially when one guy was stupid and greedy and the other was righteous and devout. I figured putting Noah in my explorers presentation would be too much like preaching. I also knew I had to get a good mark on the Frobisher side of things because I only had a 64% in social studies, and Elsie had said I'd have to drop Wednesday Bible study or the Undergrounders if I didn't get my marks up.

Three minutes before I was on. I sort of bowed my head, but not enough that anyone would be suspicious, and I said a quick prayer: *Help me, God. Help me, sweet bleeding blessed Jesus, in the great scheme of things. I want to do Your will. Let there be salvation for all of Mr. Jamison's class and particularly Lucy and Sherry and Angela and all those people whose hearts I know You've opened just a crack by letting me be Your humble servant, and, oh, please, by the way, let there be just enough about Frobisher in my presentation to keep me from having to quit learning and leading in Your precious Word. Amen.*

The classroom was buzzing when I finally found my way there. Robert Wong, the only Chinese kid in the school, was first. He was doing a presentation on the silks of the Orient, which to me didn't have a sweet thing to do with the explorer unit. He was even wearing this weird shiny shirt with a square collar and strange cloth doohickeys instead of regular everyday buttons. Robert was really shy and Mr. Jamison smiled at him the whole time, kind of encouraging him to speak, because he was so quiet most of the time.

When it came to my turn, I walked to the front of the class and stood as straight as I could. All the kids were looking at me. I saw one or two roll their eyes and a girl called Kathy House started to giggle behind her hand.

"I want to talk to you today about the saving grace of Frobisher. No, I mean the way Frobisher thought he was saving all this money but he was a fool." Oh, it was coming out wrong. I started over.

"Frobisher was serving the Queen and treating her like she was God and she was just a person who was greedy like all of you."

Someone else started to laugh and Pud Rankin shouted: "Hey, man, no way!"

Mr. Jamison stepped forward a bit. "Ruth," he said, his voice full of kindness. "Can you tell us a little bit about Frobisher? Where he was born? What country he came from? Maybe a little bit about his polar adventure?"

I looked at Mr. Jamison blankly. I realized I didn't know much about this Frobisher guy, after all. I had been so worried about making my presentation into a testimonial that whatever facts I'd looked up were now all blurry and run together.

I was sweating and stammering and the few things I thought I did know had flown out of my head. "He was an explorer, um, um...gold miner, sort of, um...and everything got, you know, dumped because it wasn't gold at all, so he was sort of a fool like all of you, um, chasing after the wrong things."

At first the class was laughing, but when they saw the look that passed over Mr. Jamison's face, they stopped laughing. I almost started to cry when he took me by the hand and led me into the hallway. How could it all have gone so wrong?

He was pretty nice.

"Did you do any research, Ruth?" he asked bending down a bit so he could look into my eyes.

"Yes. I just forgot because, you see, to me it's not the most important thing."

"Not doing the research?" The furrows on his forehead deepened. "Is that what you mean, Ruth? That not doing the proper preparation for your presentation is not the most important thing? Can you explain?"

And I thought I could, too, but somehow all of a sudden my Frobisher presentation and my social studies mark *did* seem important and I couldn't find the words to make it clear. Mr. Jamison eventually patted me on the head and said I would have to suffer the consequences, which meant I'd probably get a D on my presentation. He also said he was going to phone my parents on the weekend, which probably meant the end of this work that I loved so much.

I slowly put the coffee away and shook the horrible day from my memory. So far, no phone call. Tonight I had to focus on the important work to do here and now.

A blast of cool air from above and footsteps on the stairs told me some of the regulars had arrived. With three Elders and six Submissives, we should be able to do the work that needed to be done. We were called to go, two by two.

The Elders didn't like sending girls out to the streets alone anymore since Allison got mistaken for a hooker by a man she thought was opening his heart to Jesus but was really opening his fly to poor Allie. She'd cried buckets in the prayer room afterwards, said she'd had no idea what it was he *really* wanted when he offered her a crumpled twenty and put his big greasy hands on her bum. She'd felt so defiled, Victor had to take time out of his witnessing to go and pray privately with her, some sort of cleansing of the flesh, I guessed. Lucky Allison. Private time with the Elders was a rare blessing.

Tonight the Anointed were a small group. Tanya and Carol and I were Submissives. There were three teenage boys, too, Andrew and Rodney and a kid I hadn't seen much before. Andrew and Rodney were brothers. Their family had been the backbone of The One True Church since it started its work here four years ago. They were the people who organized the revival camp where I was saved. Brother Terry was their father. Rose was their aunt. There was supposed to be a mother somewhere, but I'd never seen her. Tanya told me the mother had had an affair with a truck driver two years ago and was now living in California, where she'd grown up and where the very first One True Church had started. I doubted if they would take her back, her being a sinner and an adulterer and all, a breaker of the holy bonds of matrimony.

All Brother Terry could do was wait and pray. Seven years had to pass before he could marry again. In five years and a bit I'd be twenty, old enough to be both the Bride of Christ and the bride of an Elder, although it seemed I was not the only one who was thinking along those lines.

This was the second week in a row Carol had been wearing a kerchief when she came to the Undergrounder. She was covering her head. That was usually a sign a woman had been chosen by one of the Elders. She wasn't much older than Andrew and Rodney, and only three years older than me, so I couldn't imagine Brother Terry having his eye on her, but you never knew. Our body was small and we had to keep it strong.

You weren't allowed to seek comfort from a fellow believer until they had been in the fold for at least two years. That was the rule. If you didn't obey the rules, you could get excommunicated, which was really just a fancy word for being thrown out. Brother Terry's wife had been excommunicated, but somehow this shameful thing made him more holy, not less. It was because he'd suffered.

Suffering made you holy, or at least suffering for righteousness did. It was not his fault that he'd married a woman who gratified her base physical desires instead of living in the glorious freedom of a pure and sanctified spirit.

"What's with the headgear?" I whispered to Carol as we all gathered in the prayer room for invocation and supplication. She blushed and indicated Al. "We're going into service together," she whispered. "We might be doing a mission. We're going to ask for Brother Terry's blessing."

I swallowed hard. A mission was a big step. Carol hadn't brought in her quota yet, and already they were trusting her with a mission? With Al! It didn't seem fair. I'd been in the One True Church for just under two years now, and I wasn't getting a mission any time soon.

"The mission will be around here," Carol reassured me, noting the surprise in my face. "Probably at one of the Indian villages. My parents won't let me leave home yet. They think I'm too young."

I smiled back at her. "I know what you mean. Mine neither."

Daryl dimmed the lights. Andrew lit the first candle. In the kitchen, the coffee urn gurgled and stopped. We bowed our heads as Daryl led us in prayer. Carol might be going on a mission, but our joint purpose was here and now. God was already preparing hearts to receive His Word. We were His instruments. The Undergrounder began.

α

I forgive Ian. But, unlike the old adage drilled through my head since grade school, I don't forget. I forgive him, but I vow never to let him forget. I have something on him now. And because it has been forgiven, because I have done the unthinkable thing, and forgiven him, my knowledge of his weakness is extra sweet.

The next day, outside the youth hostel we'd finally stumbled on the night before, after a sodden walk to retrieve our bags from the bar, I show him the ten bruises coming up on my arm.

"It's a perfect hand," I exclaim, forcing my short-sleeved T-shirt up and over my shoulder, revealing the purple, inflamed flesh. "Look, you can see each of your fingers where you squeezed."

"Don't," he begs. "Please, Ruth, don't show me."

"You were drunk." I take bizarre pleasure in his discomfort. "You were drunk and you didn't know what you were doing."

I repeat this like a mantra inside my head. It is the only thing that might undo what has been done. His drunkenness will somehow excuse the inexcusable.

For reasons I don't fully understand myself, I try to convince him that it does not matter. The pain brought about by Ian's unreasonable anger has purified me. I see the blood in my veins running clear and transparent. I feel as though I am not as attached to the world as I used to be. I am lighter, floating above, connected to the daily tasks of eating and walking and talking by only the thinnest cord.

Toronto is cold. I write the city off in my mind. I eliminate this trip. I've already turned it into a footnote and filed it away. This city has given us nothing. There is no D'arcy, no childhood friend to give shelter or a sense of history. There is no one to see us together and approve.

We hitchhike out that afternoon. My original intention is to go back to Sudbury, but then we get a trucker going straight through to Halifax. "We can't pass this up, Ruth," Ian tells me as

I swing up into the cab. And somehow the evidence is there, making me agree. His actions and sorrow are now written on my body, a signature, a mark that claims me.

But I know I will have to leave him soon. I know that the drinking will come between us again and the violence, once out in the air, will not willingly return to its cramped cage. I know I need to go home, back to the co-op, and the classes, the security of my known academic world. On the journey back, I feel disconnected. I sleep a lot, lulled by kilometre after kilometre of spruce and asphalt. Ian is there, but not there. He is someone who talks to the driver, the person who lets me be alone. We stop every few hours for coffee at gas stations and trucker joints and, once, to pee on the side of the road. *They are pissing on the Plains of Abraham*, I think as I watch Ian and the driver through the tiny window. Beyond them, I see the wide flat fields before they drop off into the grey-green swiftness of the St. Lawrence River.

I do not eat or drink. I pretend to ignore Ian's concern, his attempts to draw me out of myself. I struggle with thoughts that roll around randomly in my brain.

He didn't know what he was doing. He didn't mean to hurt me. He was drunk. I was drunk too. But he did it, drunk or not.

I replay the bar scene over and over in my head, the parts I remember. I hear myself saying, *Where will we sleep? What will we do? Where will we go? It's raining, it's cold, I'm tired, I'm scared.* I don't feel scared any longer.

It's clear here, in the back of this rig. I'm in a new space where the air is rarified and purer somehow. This is what happens after pain. This is how it feels to know betrayal. Oh, but I glory in it. I feel big and powerful, and somehow above humanity. Christ must have felt like this, I think briefly. Pain brings you closer to God. It's a feeling I like. It gives me so much power.

Not the power of Ian, the pathetic power of physical force. No, mine is a clean, sweet power. The body's pain sears and sharpens the mind.

As our truck rattles Ian and me back to our small town on the side of a different river, I feel for the first time I know his sorrows, for, at last, I have my own.

α

You weren't really supposed to go upstairs. That was sort of an unwritten rule. We just rented the basement. The Pentecostals were pretty particular. I'd heard they considered us a splinter group, a sect. Some even called the One True Church a cult, but that wasn't true.

Because there was something weird about the light, I paused on the landing. One flight of stairs went up to the Pentecostals' meeting place, the other went down to where our Undergrounder was in full swing. I could hear a murmur of voices from below, but there was something strange about the sanctuary, some movement and some voices. I went up to see.

There was someone in there, all right, a couple of people, but I couldn't tell what they were doing. I slipped into a back pew where it was dark. When my eyes got used to the light, I saw two Elders, Simon and Vic, at the front of the church. They were with a woman. She was not very tall and she was dark. There was something familiar about her.

She was probably a working girl. They sometimes came to the Undergrounders to get coffee and warm up. I didn't talk to them. Because of their work, we Submissives were supposed to leave them for the Elders to deal with. Even Jesus talked to the prostitutes, so we were not supposed to condemn them but, to be honest, they gave me the heebie-jeebies. A lot of the working girls were native. That was what we were supposed to call Indians now, so that it didn't feel like we were superior to them or something. They wore really red lipstick and short skirts even in the winter or, if they were younger, jeans and jean jackets with skimpy undershirts cut to show off their boobs. I didn't like to admit it, but I tried not to get too close to them, knowing where they'd been.

Most of the women hung out near the bunkhouses at the mine, but sometimes they came right into town and started work as the bars let out. That was when we got to minister to them.

I squinted to see more clearly, but for some reason I didn't move. Something was wrong at the front of the church. The girl was shaking terribly and there was a raspy moan, almost a growl, coming from inside her chest. She was standing before Vic and he was laying his hand on her where the moan was coming from, right near her heart. He had his eyes closed, so I guessed he was praying, but I wished he wouldn't touch her there. It didn't seem right, even though the girl wasn't pushing his hand away.

Now Simon was laying his flat palm on her head. He was praying out loud. I couldn't hear everything, because they were speaking in low voices, but I heard them call out something about Satan. The girl's rattling anxiety was swelling over the sounds of their words. They were calling out against the forces of the Evil One.

"Daughter of Satan. Daughter of Shaman. Daughter of Darkness, we commend thee to the Light," chanted Simon.

Suddenly I knew. They were trying to cast a demon out of this poor girl. They were trying to exorcise an evil spirit. But the way they were touching her was wrong. She was overwhelmed now, crying, and she fell to her knees. I couldn't see what was going on because she had sunk below the front pew but when Vic and Simon helped her back up I realized immediately who she was. It was Jax. They were trying to cast a demon out of Jax.

Simon was standing in front of both Jax and Vic, but he was backlit from the light on the piano. Even with the light around his head and his face in shadow, I could tell he was calling down the Holy Spirit. His arms were raised in the air and he was speaking in tongues, evoking the power of God against all the evil energy flowing out of Jax. Or was he?

Vic had his arms around her waist and she was standing rigid like a cardboard doll. It was definitely her. She looked way older. Maybe she was drunk or something. She was swaying back and forth and her eyes were rolling around and around in her head. The sharp little chin all of a sudden fell to her chest and she started to howl, like a wolf or a dog. I thought of our pups and that summer and all that we did together and I wanted to push the Elders away. *Leave her alone. Just leave her alone.* But I didn't. I just sat there, staring, unable to budge.

What was happening? Jax wasn't evil. Why did they think she was evil? Bad people had hurt her in the hostel, she was from the East Arm, she loved her kookum, she was my old friend, the only one who didn't care about the ugly retainer and the hideous fake teeth back before I was made new.

I moved to stand, to go to her and tell them they'd made a mistake when I saw Simon, with his eyes closed. He was trembling too and he ran his hands down the front of her body. Like Vic, he lingered at Jax's little breasts, cupping them in a quick massage before he dipped lower. I watched his palms spread across the tight expanse of her jeans. Kneeling, he continued to run his hands down each of her legs. His face was at her crotch, pressed into the space where you're not supposed to go until you're married. Jax's upper body was arched backwards, away from him and I could see the expression on her face. It was fear. I was frozen and horrified. This wasn't how Jesus did it.

The expulsion, the exorcism was complete, because all at once, Jax fell forward again, sobbing and Vic caught her and held her in a different way, like a brother would hold a sister. Simon came up and joined the tangle of arms and legs intertwined and all three of them hugged. I stood up and they turned to me. Vic's mouth dropped, Simon shook his head quickly and then I saw that it was not Jax at all. It was some other Indian girl. And she couldn't take her eyes off the floor.

Vic smoothed his face out fast, and started to walk towards me with his hands out, ready to explain. But I had already seen too much and I turned quickly and bolted down the stairs to the landing. Grabbing my parka from the coat rack, I pulled the door open a crack and slipped out of the One True Church of God into the winter night. Ahead of me, somewhere in the darkness, was home, and I knew that's where I had to head.

α

How strange the human mind, how wonderfully complex we are created. Oh, after that awful thing in Toronto I know my relationship with Ian has to end. I know, but part of me likes it. Not the pain part, but the grown-up part, that weird power I have over Ian. I glory in it. I feel so wise and compassionate. I have the ability to forgive. Or not. Imagine.

I know it has to be over, but extracting myself proves far more difficult than I anticipate. I think with the new term beginning, the buzz of excitement on campus, it will be simple to ease out of my relationship with Ian.

I think, naively, he will want it that way too. The incident in Toronto, the entire trip, is surely something we both want to forget. It's something I file away in my mind. I pull forward the symbolism in D.H. Lawrence, the dusty old files on George Herbert, Thomas Hobbes, seventeenth-century poets and philosophers. I reshuffle and reassemble. A dark compartment closes, best forgotten. Our bond has weakened, the glow of mutual desire faded.

September brings cool winds off the river, and while the elms paint their leaves the mad, clinging colours of fall, the air is sharp with starting again.

Ian is not interested in new beginnings. Nor is he interested in seeing anything end. He wants to see me. He *needs* to see me.

"I can't come, Ian. I have timetable troubles. I have to set up some space. I have to rearrange some classes. I can't come over yet. Maybe later in the week. Maybe later. I have to get back in the groove of school. You know, essays, assignments, workshops and presentations." But, of course, he doesn't know.

What I realize is simple. I'm no longer in love. Love doesn't care for timetables and schedules. Love wants to be with someone, no matter what.

The summer, I tell myself, has been an anomaly, a blip in my usually conscientious routine of study and work. Back in classes, I am shocked to see titles on the reading list I haven't heard of, let alone read. Usually I am miles ahead.

Ian phones the co-op house often. He is staying in a motel south of town. It's a roadside motel. I have seen the place before. It's called the Riverview Arms, although it offers no glimpse of the river from its perch above the highway. It's a long, narrow building, a series of vinyl-sided mobile homes strung together in a clumsy V. The Riverview Arms is run-down. Doors sag on their hinges, and even in the summer when tourists flood the Maritimes, the Riverside is often the last to turn on its no-vacancy neon. Ian has rented one of the motel rooms by the month. It's cheaper than renting an apartment, he tells me, and besides, when he's in town he can always stay at the the chicken coop, the co-op.

"I don't know," I say, twisting the telephone cord into a snarled knot, my belly fluttering and sick feeling. "They're cracking down."

"Who? What do you mean cracking down?"

"On overnight guests. You know, people who sleep here but don't contribute. It's more strict in the fall when school's back in."

"You're telling me those assholes are dictating who you can and cannot sleep with?"

"No, of course not. It's just that they don't want people taking advantage of the house. You know, using it like a flophouse."

He snorts. "Fuck them and their flophouse. We can do whatever we like in your room."

We. Ian still thinks of us as we. A couple. I've been trying to sidestep the issue. The message is getting jumbled. He's not reading me because I'm not telling the truth. The way it really is. I'm trying to make it easy and less painful. I try again.

"Umm, Ian, I want to see you, but I just need some time to myself right now. Maybe we could get together on the weekend?"

There is silence on the other end of the line, then a click and the sound of the dial tone, buzzing flat and loud in my ear.

He comes that night, while I'm out. The roommates tell me. He sits on one of the old sofas on the porch, silently smoking, stroking Sadie and waiting for me to come home. He waits two, two and a half hours, and leaves just minutes before I arrive from the library. I am relieved that I've missed him.

That night, I have a dream. I dream I am in my room, the new attic room I have chosen for the school year. While I am in the room, the walls begin to close in. At first it is subtle, barely noticeable. The minuscule blue flowers on the maroon wallpaper come a tiny bit closer, become a little bit larger as the walls slope inward.

In the dream, I am lying on my back on a narrow bed draped in a white gauzy material that resembles mosquito netting or a transparent white gown. Maybe a hospital gown, maybe a bridal dress. I can't move, but there is no physical object holding me down. I am restrained by the weight of my own limbs, arms and hands, feet and legs, even my head is pulled back so I am forced to look straight at the slowly descending ceiling.

It is the feeling of helplessness that lends the dream its nightmarish quality. The walls press in, threatening to enclose me in a tight floral box, the type in which fancy candies or costume jewelry comes in.

Just before I am totally encased, Jesus comes to me. In the dream I know it's Him even though I can't see His face. He lies on top of me whispering, *Let me take everything.* That's all. *Let me take everything.*

I jerk awake. Sitting up too fast causes a rush of blood to my head. I almost expect to hit my head on the closed-in walls, the dream is so vivid, but they stand away at their proper distance and the flowers, indistinguishable again, blink benign innocence from the shadows. Jesus has gone.

α

I arrived home almost breathless, feeling like the Elders know what I've seen, what I've thought. I am afraid they will track me and I will suffer some sort of penalty for witnessing the exorcism. I wasn't expecting Elsie when I got in. Immediately I knew she was tired. Elsie was always tired. That was Elsie's way.

She cornered me as I was slipping into the bright kitchen, looking for leftovers.

"Where have you been, Ruth?"

I knew that tone. It was an accusation. No matter what I answered, I would get in trouble.

"Church."

She said it back, like a question. "Church? On Saturday night?"

"Remember, the Underground...er, I mean, coffeehouse, the one in the basement?" I knew I'd told her about this, probably when she was in the middle of some dispute with Jiggs or Luke. The older girls had left the nest, and Elsie was more vigilant than she used to be.

"What did you do tonight?" It was the third degree.

I watched the spirit of Satan fly out of an Indian girl. I saw some men who were supposed to be righteous touch her the wrong way. I remembered playing with Jax and what it was like before the Supreme Sacrifice. I failed to win any souls and I'm not allowed go on a mission or wear a headscarf or even think about having an Elder as a boyfriend. I spent my evening secretly hoping Jesus wouldn't come back. I worried about frying in hell.

"Nothing."

I turned my back to Elsie and opened the fridge. "Is there anything to eat?"

"Nothing. You did nothing. You go to that church all the time, spend hours there, and you did nothing? Is that right, Ruthie? Because I can think of a hell of a lot of things you could be doing around here for all those hours of religious nothing."

It was the word *hell* that made me close the fridge and really look at my mother. She was sitting upright in a straight-backed chair. She had a cup of tea in front of her, but I could tell by the rings on the newspaper it was already cold. There was no steam. No nothing. She'd been sitting there for a while. Waiting. She was tired, she was waiting up for my older brother and sister, and she was in interrogation mode. I just happened to come in at the wrong time.

But suddenly I saw her through the eyes of Jesus. She really was tired. She was mad at my siblings who were disobeying her. She was alone. My father was sleeping. Elsie was tired and angry and alone. She was in the perfect space to receive the love of God.

I walked towards her and put my hand out, touching her lightly on the shoulder. "Mom?"

I felt her shoulder sink under my touch and the stiffness went out of her body. I looked into her eyes, deep sea green, the colour of growing things. "Are you okay?"

She smiled up at me wanly and pulled me down onto her lap. I let myself go weak and curled myself up small against her. I hadn't sat on Elsie's lap for years.

"Are *you* okay, Ruth?" she asked gently, and then, remembering my question, she sighed. "Yes, I'm fine. It's just that sometimes I wonder about that organization that calls itself a church. I worry, Ruthie. I do."

It was so weirdly warm. I felt so safe that even though I was supposed to be winning her over to the light, I didn't want anything to change. Even though I knew I should defend the faith by leaping up and telling her the Good News, I said nothing. I chose to say nothing. I was worried, too.

Elsie continued: "Your father and I have been talking about it. We want you to spend more time at home, or maybe join Junior Rangers, take swimming lessons, something..."

"I want to go on a mission." Oops, I'd let the cat out of the bag. I struggled to sit up.

Elsie turned my face towards her, but gently with the palm of her hand tucked under my chin. "A what?"

"A mission."

She looked puzzled. Of course she didn't know what a mission was. How could she? Elsie thought digging the garden was a mission, grocery shopping, getting her kids signed up for summer camp. Elsie thought getting her daughters through their teenage years without any of them getting pregnant was her mission. How could she understand a real mission?

"What kind of a mission?"

"To save."

"You're saving for a mission?"

"No, I want to save others. Sinners. I want to go on a mission to save others."

Elsie made an elephant sound deep in her chest. "It's that church again, isn't it?"

"What do you mean?"

"Have they planted this notion in your head? That you have to save sinners? Good God, Ruthie, you can start right here if you want to do your mission work. Start with Gillian." She glanced at the kitchen wall clock. "Where the hell is that kid?"

"*A prophet is never recognized in his own country*."

Elsie looked at me sharply. Scripture still had the power. "And what is that supposed to mean?"

I faltered. "The Elders are all from away because their power isn't recognized in their hometowns. Remember Jesus shook the dust off his feet when he left Nazareth? That's because in his hometown, his mom and dad and all the shopkeepers and everybody didn't recognize his power. That's why it's important to do a mission. The Elders are all on missions. They're here. I could go away with one of them if I get my quota. Then I could maybe wear a headscarf."

Elsie looked at me like I was speaking Japanese. The furrow between her eyes had become a crevice. Her eyes were dark green now, the same way the Red Sea must have looked after it flowed back in and drowned all the unchosen.

"Ruthie, it's late. You need to go to bed." She put her hands on my shoulders and drew me into her, looking straight into my eyes. "Go to bed and we will talk about this in the morning. We *will* talk about this, Ruth. I'll speak to your father first thing. Now go." She pointed me down the darkened hall to the room I shared with my sister. I went.

Their solution was simple. No more Fellowship, no church or church-related activities. And it came almost as a relief. I didn't know what to do with myself at first. No prayer circle. No Bible study. No Undergrounders. No services. No healing touch. No nothing, just my room and my family and school. There weren't any disciples of the One True Church in my high school. There were a whole bunch of kids I had testified to, but no converts, if you didn't count the school counsellor who'd called me into her office for a "little talk."

"Ruthie, do you know what it means to be a Christian?"

I'd looked up at her, met her earnest gaze with one of my own. "Yes."

"What does it mean to you, dear?"

"Living the Word." I'd said it really fast so she might not hear.

She'd leaned forward. I could smell old tuna fish on her breath. It was gross, but I hadn't flinched.

"What's that?"

"Christians live the word of the Lord."

She'd seemed satisfied.

"That's right, Ruthie. We live our faith. It's here." She'd laid her hands on the flat tight spot between her breasts where a mini crucifix dangled on a gold chain. "People see our faith by the way we live. It's not something one broadcasts. Do you know what I'm saying, dear?"

And I'd nodded and backed out of her office, stammering thanks.

In the yearbook I drew horns on her head. She was in cahoots with the Evil One. Most of the Catholics were, but they were too dumb to know.

Most of the One True Church converts came from the street, from the people who were already out on their own. At the rate I was going, I would never have worn the headscarf, I would never have won my quota of souls and been ripe for a mission with one of the Elders. It was a lost cause.

But the Elders didn't think so. Three weeks after I left the Fellowship, as grade eleven wound down into exam week, I got a phone call from Brother Daryl. He was not as high profile as Pastor Terry, but still pretty high in the ranks.

"Ruth, we haven't seen you for a while and we were wondering if you're in Paul's predicament." That was code for being imprisoned by your parents, not allowed to attend the services.

"Ummmm, not exactly." I felt the colour flush in my cheeks.

"Do you need our prayers?"

"No. I'm just taking a break."

"You can't take a break from your faith, sister. He who is called is chosen and he who is chosen is predestined. You have been chosen, Ruth. Your path is clear."

"Not to me, it isn't. Not right now."

There was silence on the other end of the phone. "The way of the cross is clear. There are no breaks. We'll send someone over to pray with you if you'd like, but you know it would be better for the Fellowship if you came here."

"I can't. I just can't. I want to, but I'm not allowed…" Oh dear.

"You *are* being persecuted for your faith, sister? Praise God."

"Well, no, it's more like I can't because I don't want to. Yet. I don't want to come back yet."

A longer silence.

"Daryl? You still there?"

"The angels are weeping, Sister Ruth. Remember, your stubborn resistance is making the angels weep. Not to mention Satan. *Anyone not for me is against me!* You remember who said that, don't you, Sister Ruth? The Supreme Sacrifice, that's who. And now you're making a mockery of that sacrifice. The demons are cackling, the End Times are near, and you must decide…"

I felt a chill run through the phone cord and down my arm and I pulled the receiver from my ear and replaced it quietly on its cradle. Daryl sounded crazy. He sounded mad, Not only mad, but angry, too. They didn't want me to leave.

I didn't have any friends, so I whiled away the summer alone, reading and thinking. I didn't read the Bible. Instead, I read novels, and when school went back in that autumn I poured myself into my final year, getting the best marks, achieving the highest scores. And it worked. Upon graduation

I received a four-year scholarship to any Canadian university. Elsie was happy, my dad beaming

"I knew you would do it, Toothie, just a little elbow grease, some head-down can-do hard work, and Bob's your uncle." He grinned ear to ear.

I was pleased, but I couldn't seem to get the other stuff out of my head. The One True Church had wormed its doctrine into my brain and although I had physically left, mentally leaving was much, much harder. All I really wanted to do was get away, start over, go where no one knew my name.

α

Ian comes to the co-op house the next evening. I know he will, so I'm ready. He's been drinking. I can smell alcohol on his breath as he leans forward to kiss me on the mouth. He tastes like a stain, nicotine mixed with rancid oil. I feel shame, entertaining this drunk man in my house. My roommate Lisa walks in, sees us and quickly looks past as he sprawls on the living room sofa. She says a shallow, tentative *hi* before heading into the kitchen where most of the others are. I hear shrieks of laughter and pots and pans clanking out of their cupboards. It's not my night to cook, thank God.

"Let's go for a walk." I don't want him here. I don't want him in the new room I've chosen upstairs, either. He's too large, too male, and too angry for the small sloping room with its low, single bed.

Since our trip to Toronto, I see Ian differently. He is no longer my tender, intelligent lover. He is not the sensitive poet struggling for truth and justice in his own life. The violence has transformed him into someone altogether different, someone with whom I would rather not spend time.

We cut through the grounds of the old folks' home and cross the tracks towards the rail yards. There is a moon, but it is only a sliver, hanging in the sky like a fingernail chewed off, or a sickle, a strange instrument used in a magic show. Everything in the sky has disappeared except that thin blade on the black velvet backdrop. That is tonight's moon.

In the air there is the skunky odour of decay — dead leaves and stagnant water — and on the ground, just below the surface, I can feel the winter the same way I knew I could feel the spring five short months ago. Winter is just beneath this unyielding field muck. The first frost is not far off.

Ian speaks.

"What's wrong, Ruth? You're mad at me."

"I'm not mad. Dogs are mad. Foxes are mad." I try to stop the way this is coming out, take a breath. "People get angry." I sound like Elsie.

"Yeah? So why are you angry, Ruthie?"

"I'm not angry."

"Oh, like I'm not mad."

"Something's changed, Ian. I can't explain. I just don't feel like I want to..."

"To what?"

"To be with you anymore."

"To be with me?" he echoes. "What the fuck is that supposed to mean? You don't want to sleep together any more? You don't want to see me anymore? You want to see other guys? You want to fuck other guys? Is that it? You want me to just disappear so you can fuck other guys?"

"There are no other guys."

"So you want me to disappear so you can be by yourself. Is that it?"

His voice is getting louder. There is a desperate quality, a dangerous edge to it. I must be careful.

I try to sound casual, try to swallow my fear. "I want some time to think about where our relationship is going. We can't just drift along like we did this summer. I've got to get serious. I'm trying to get a degree. You should get serious too. Try to find a job."

I've said too much. I can tell. The ground suddenly feels very unstable.

Ian leans close to me, his hand large and heavy on the back of my head.

"I am serious, Ruthie. I'm serious about you."

There it is again in his voice, something absolute, as though some secret knowledge of me has been attained without my permission. It is like our second date, or the announcement of our engagement. How can he know things about me that I don't know myself? Engaged. Did my heart really flutter when he told my parents that? No. I remember confusion, feeling stunned. The baffled feeling smothered the anger. Not this time.

"I know you are, but..."

"But what?"

"I'm not so sure we're right."

"Because of what happened?"

It's the first time he's mentioned the violence of Toronto and I can see by his face that speaking it is hard.

"In part, yeah. I don't want to live like that. You know, drinking all the time, not knowing what to expect from you. I was scared of you, Ian."

I pause and frown and repeat it. "You scare me sometimes."

"What about now?" he asks, backing me up against a wall of the old rail yard warehouse. "Are you scared of me now?"

He seems to enjoy my discomfort, so I shove him away, trying to make it a joke. "No, you big galoot. Of course not."

It is the wrong thing to do. His hand is at my throat in a flash, and I am pinned against the siding.

"Don't push me away, Ruthie. You know I don't like being pushed away."

Then the hand drops and he smiles. It's more frightening somehow than his hand pressure at my neck. That serpentine smile is now infused with threat and his blue eyes, like crystal marbles, are not smiling. They are clear and hard and cold and I remember seeing those same eyes somewhere else but I cannot remember where.

I duck away and start walking across the field, tense with the possibility that I might be struck from behind.

"I'm going home," I call over my shoulder, and when I get far enough away and the lights of the house shimmer in safety, I start to run.

"You can't get away, Ruthie. I've already decided."

His words ring as loud as my ragged breathing. What has he decided?

The house is warm as I enter. Paulette, a dark-haired new girl from the North Shore, sits with Brian, playing cribbage at the kitchen table. She has fried doughnuts. Every counter surface is covered with them, some just cut-out dough, uncooked, some ready to be eaten, still sizzling and sugar-dipped, and others cooling, dripping with creamy icing. The air is sweet with oil and yeast and sugar.

"Ahh, Root," Paulette says, looking up from her game. "You okay?"

"What happened?" says Brian, narrowing his eyes, frowning.

"It's nothing. I just..." What? Just what? "I just saw someone I didn't want to see." Yes.

"You look like you have — how you say? — seen the holy ghost?"

"Holy ghost." Brian laughs and I am grateful for this distraction. "Have you just seen a holy ghost, Ruthie?"

"I'm fine," I say, not feeling fine at all. "I'm going up to my room. If anyone calls or comes around, I'm not home, okay?"

They nod absently, already reabsorbed in their card game.

I close the door of my room and walk quickly across to the window. A streetlight casts long shadows on the parking lot of the old folks' home. Beyond the darkened field are the tracks and the buildings. He's out there, I think, and then revise it. Ian would not hang around a deserted rail yard on a chilly September evening. He's in a bar, the Chestnut or the piano bar at the Holiday Inn. He's probably drinking draught and watching a pool game. He's brooding. I've seen him, silent and withdrawn, wrestling with some private demon he refuses to reveal.

But now I don't care anymore. I don't give a shit. I'd tried to help him. Lord knows, I wanted to help heal the pain he refuses to surrender, but he wouldn't let me, he wouldn't give me anything, and now fuck him and his messed-up childhood and his secret traumas. He can carry a hate-on for his mother and the Captain for the rest of his stupid life if he wants to. He can carry around the same feeling for me. I pull the curtain closed and look around my new room.

He can't touch me in here. This is my safe place. My home. I am among other students here, people my own age with common interests, common objectives and common goals. Ian is a freak. He couldn't cut it at university but hung around anyway. He's a pseudo-intellectual snob. He'll always be on the outside looking in. It's too bad, but there's nothing I can do about it. I'm better off without him. I just need to forget about him. Move on. I gather my bath things and go down the hall to the bathroom.

There are blond hairs in the tub, residue from someone else. Despite how much simpler it would be to shower, I clean the old claw foot. I want a soak, a steaming long, muscle-relaxing soak. A meditation. A treat.

I run the water hot, almost scalding. Quickly the room fills with steam and I strip to my panties and bra and look at myself in the rapidly fogging mirror on the back of the bathroom door. I suck in my stomach and run my hand over my rib cage, made prominent by the concave hollow of my belly. The beer drinking all summer shows.

I'll join a gym or at least make an attempt to swim at the university pool every second morning. The summer of lounging and drinking has accumulated on my hips and waist. Like Ian, who has invaded my body, this fleshiness must be gotten rid of. I know it will be painful at first, but there is a certain purity in ritual cleansing. I remember the shedding of years ago and smile to myself. The image in the mirror is softened by the steam and I suddenly feel quite hopeful. I've never been afraid of hard work. Elsie always told me hard work would get me places prayer never would. It's funny to think, all these years later, Elsie is right.

α

My escape from the pull of the One True Church came in the oddest way. In the spring of my last year of high school I bought a coat at a consignment store, a spring jacket, an in-between coat for the days that weren't quite warm enough to be without. It was unusual, this coat, vaguely Indian in design, but with small pastel sheep hand-stitched to the robin egg blue cotton background. It was reversible too. The design could be worn inside with just the blue colour showing, a hint of sheep at the cuff and collar. I liked the idea that I had the option of being either way in this new-to-me coat. I could be playful and bright by displaying the animal pattern or I could be more conservative with the design inside. I smiled, thinking of the sheep next to my body. I could be a conservative with a secret. The coat was only fourteen dollars. I paid and left, clutching the bulky bag next to my parka as though I had captured spring in a sack.

As soon as I got home, I modeled my new coat for Elsie.

"Won't lose you in a shopping centre, Tooth," was her distracted comment.

It was true, the coat was somewhat garish, but I didn't care. I liked the carefree spirit of the little mauve and pink and yellow sheep running across the hills and valleys of my body. "Look, it can be worn this way, too."

"That's better," said Elsie, nodding.

Inside out, I noticed the jacket had pockets on both sides. I stuck my hand in and found a folded piece of paper. It had one word written on it in ballpoint pen.

Nimbin.

"Mom, what's a Nimbin?" I called after her, but Elsie didn't hear me; she'd already gone downstairs.

Nimbin? Was it a thing? A person's last name? Was it a place?

I put the paper back and repeated the word over and over. Nimbin. Nimbin. I loved the sound of the word. It sounded whimsical, free, like the frolicking sheep. Nimbin. I dragged out the heavy Oxford and looked it up. Nimbin was not a word in the dictionary. Because it had a capital letter at the beginning, I decided it must be a place. I went to the world atlas and flipped to the index. It was there.

Nimbin, Aust...Pg 97

I flipped through the atlas with growing excitement. Surely, this was a sign. Someone was telling me something. Nimbin was a tiny dot on a continent on the other side of the world. It wasn't a city, not even a town, according to the map. But it was there.

Nimbin, I discovered after a trip to the library to get all the books I could on Northeastern Australia, was a mountain village, a spiritual energy field, the home of a holy sage. Nimbin, I decided, was where I wanted to go. It was my mission, my personal pilgrimage. It was also a way to escape the One True Church and the apostasy that marked me as strayed, the one fallen from Grace.

I felt like God was in charge again. He had given me a sign and a mission that was all mine. I would find the holy sage. I would be a seeker again.

The timing was perfect. Dad had been offered a job in Sudbury and the plan had been that I'd help my parents move and then go to university somewhere in Ontario. While they packed I scribbled out applications. Trent. Waterloo. Windsor. York. I was entirely unenthusiastic, ill-prepared for post-secondary education. But what else was there? The others were ensconced in various institutions and careers. Claire and Theresa were sharing an apartment in Kitsilano, both going to nursing school in Vancouver. Jiggs was at art college in Toronto, hoping to go to New York City. Luke had decided to work in the mines for a while to make some money. They were all living away from home. All but me.

I proposed something before university, a little jaunt across the ocean, a little overseas trip, this mission of my own making. They were at first dubious about my destination.

"Australia, Tooth? Are you trying to break the old man's wallet?" It was evening. and Dad was out back, reading a book in the fading daylight.

"I need to go, Dad. I just need to."

"What about finding a friend to hook up with? You know, Toothie, a friend to share the big adventure?"

"I don't have any friends."

"Now, now."

"It's true, Dad. Ask Elsie. The only friends I've ever had in this town are, you know, part of the cult."

Ever since I'd decided I couldn't go back, we'd referred to the One True Church as the cult. That made me feel less like an traitor, less like Judas, and more like someone who'd been rescued and deprogrammed.

"What about that kid you used to hang around with when you were little?"

"You mean Lucy?'

"No, a little native kid. You two played outside for hours on end. What about that friend?"

I was shocked. I'd had no idea they even knew that Jax and I had been friends that one great summer so long ago. I'd looked for her for a couple of months now, on and off, ever since I'd left the church, ever since I'd discovered that it wasn't her they'd touched. I was glad it wasn't Jax that Vic had felt up, telling her it was good for her, and how the devil lived in her. Jax would have punched him right in the holy gut. I smiled.

I was glad it wasn't Jax, all right. She'd had enough shit in her life to deal with — the disappeared mom, that weird thing with Mr. Anderson. But it didn't really matter who that girl was. She was just some poor down-on-her-luck Indian girl. She was Jax. She was me. She was all of us.

"She's long gone," I said. "She got to get out of this stinking small place."

My dad pulled me down beside him on the swing Elsie had set up in the backyard. "Would it make you happy, Ruth, to go away for a while?"

I bit my lip. He just wanted me to be happy. *A little religion goes a long way*. "Yeah, Dad, I do. I want to go away and figure things out for myself."

"I'll help out, Ruthie. Count on me."

And I laid my head on his shoulder and curled my legs underneath me as he began to swing us, back and forth, back and forth, while the day faded into darkness.

We made a deal. Dad agreed to pay an open return ticket to Australia in return for me helping with the move. Maybe they wanted me to discover myself. Maybe they wanted me to discover something to replace the gaping hole the Fellowship of the One True Church had left in my heart. Maybe they wanted me to learn something about life. Or maybe they just wanted me gone.

My father's new job was at a nickel mine in Northern Ontario. Elsie was ecstatic. He'd been offered a managerial position. My dad could at last climb out of the earth to work on the surface, and Elsie could leave the north forever.

Two months after my parents sold our family home and moved to Ontario, I flew from Ottawa to Australia. It felt like I finally had some forward momentum in my own life after months of sorting and sifting and packing and preparing a house to sell. My only distraction from my parents' move had been books. Books were food, but faith was fire. And I was burning to find a guru, any guru, who would help me discover my purpose.

α

I'm nervous, preoccupied, the next day, on the lookout for Ian. But he doesn't come. He doesn't come the next day either. He waits until I feel safe. I'm reading when he comes, lying on my bed, catching up on some Shakespeare. I'm reading *Othello*, the story of the Moor with his immeasurable grief, the guilt he suffers when he realizes how wrong he was. I am absorbed in the book, thinking about guilt and grief in an abstract way, never once drawing a parallel between the text and my own situation. The 1600s and today are worlds apart. People back then were more anguished, weren't they? Weren't they always wringing their hands and rending their clothes? Me, I lie on my bed and read.

Suddenly Ian appears at my door, in my room.

"Oh, it's you."

He closes the door softly behind him, waiting for the deadbolt to engage, a smothered click.

"Yup," he answers, grinning, "It's me. Expecting someone else?"

"No, it's just that I didn't hear you on the stairs and I thought..."

"What? That I'd call first?"

"You could have," I say, easing off the bed, standing, trying to look purposeful and in control. "You could have called, but you didn't have to. I mean, I guess you want to talk."

Ian exhales sharply. "No, I want to fuck."

He says it like that, with all pretense stripped away. He says it like it will hurt and hurting me is the best part. *Fuck.* The brutal, unyielding word hovers, caught on a tense tightrope strung between us.

"There are people home downstairs," I say quickly. "I'm going down."

I take a step towards the door, knowing it will be futile. He grabs my hand and wrenches my arm behind my back, slowly pulling upward. Now his mouth is in my hair and my back is pressed against his chest. I can smell him. The smoke and alcohol of a recent barroom linger on his body.

"What's wrong, Ruthie?" he croons. "You don't like old Ian anymore? You used to like me. I know you used to."

He is slowly backing up and all I can do is stumble backwards with him. Any thought of resistance is banished by the pain in my arm. It will break or surely be wrenched from my shoulder socket. I hear small whimpering sounds coming from my mouth. He pushes me backwards onto the bed where Sadie sleeps in a nest of blankets and discarded clothing. She leaps up and launches herself off the bed with a yowl, but she is caught mid-flight in Ian's great hand.

"Stole my fucking cat, too," he growls, and, placing his free hand over Sadie's head, he yanks down, snapping her neck so her head lolls back, mouth open, tongue slack. I watch, transfixed in horror, unable to make a sound, and he grabs a handful of fur on the cat's underbelly and thrusts the limp body into my face.

"She fucking loved me once, too," he says in a hoarse whisper. "But you can't stop, Ruthie. You can't stop loving someone. Or look, you see what happens? Look..." His voice goes softer still, and takes on a sing-song quality, "...look what happened to Sadie. Look at poor little Sadie. Poor kitty got hurt, didn't you, little puss? Poor Sadie. Poor little old Sadie cat. She loved me, but she tried to get away, didn't you, puss? Tried to get away from loving old Ian, eh? Poor little Sadie."

The cat's fur is now matted with blood that comes from her mouth and ears, and her head swings crazily back and forth as Ian dangles the body over my face. I can feel warm blood dripping on my cheeks and then my eyes. Bile rises in my throat and I turn my head to vomit at the same time Ian drops Sadie's warm body against my neck. The fur, the vomit and the blood are now all in my mouth, suffocating the scream that has finally risen. And when I fight my way to open air, Ian towers above me, undoing his belt.

I raise my head and he smacks my face with the back of his hand, sending me spinning, bouncing across the bed like some crazy out-of-control top. The back of my head hits the headboard of the bed and I crumple there, willing myself to cry for help.

But I don't scream. Not once, as he hauls me to him, forces my buttocks into the air and wrenches down my jeans and my panties. His forearm is on the back of my neck and my face is mashed into the slimy sick-smelling fur of the dead cat. I can't fight back, can't move, and there is so little room to breathe.

He's on me now, ripping his way into me. He penetrates me from behind, pumping his angry, stiff member again and again into the unprotected place between my legs. His thrusting is wild and blind. He is intent only on hurting me, and the pain courses up my back, splits me in two.

I'm there, but no longer there. I hover somewhere near the ceiling. Everything, everything except the pain is surreal.

"You like it. You like it. Say it. You like it."

With each phrase, he stabs, twists and withdraws, his stomach slapping against my lower back until he comes in one final spasm. He emits something between a growl and a moan, and he falls forward on top of me.

There is only room for pain, shooting behind my eyes in red and black and yellow. Vaguely, I feel something lift and he is gone, but this knowledge is too far away and still too small to find a place in the throbbing colours of my mind. My body does not belong to me. I am detached, floating somewhere on a turbulent, churning sea of pain. And, as the pain stops screaming in my ears, as it recedes slightly, there is another sound. This one different, overriding the piercing sound of hurt. It is a voice.

As I lie on a tangled bed, jeans around my ankles, blood and semen and the contents of my stomach spewed on the sheets, a voice whispers *It's not his fault*. I realize it's my own voice.

In my room there is little sign of violence. How much time has passed? A few minutes? Half an hour? Has everything been erased by the stillness? Sadie's body is gone and there is so little blood on the bed I wonder if it was real. The lines are blurring badly between what is real and what isn't. My book is still at the side of the bed, open to the text I was reading.

I stand up carefully, gingerly, not sure if my legs will support me. I sway for a moment, dizzy and confused. I smell my own vomit first and almost instinctively I strip the bedding without looking at the mess, and roll it up in a bundle, dropping it outside my door. This act is too much effort. I collapse on the bare mattress.

Outside the window there are birds twittering. I wonder if this noise is possible and decide, yes, birds are chirping. The sun is low in the sky.

Sadie is dead, or maybe not. Is she stalking those birds, causing the shrill outrage just past my window? I think of going to look, going to chase the cat from the nest, but I can't get up. I continue to lie on the bed. It is the only thing I know how to do and the only reason I know I'm doing it is because I can feel the buttons of the cheap mattress underneath me. I am naked. I know that, too.

My hand passes over my body, feeling for anything. I want some sensation. I start between my legs at the clump of hair, the part he stole, and I hold the tender, coarse part of myself. Yes, warmth. Faint, but through my cupped palms, I can feel heat.

My hand moves up to my shallow hipbones and down to the hollow of my stomach, over the rise of my belly. Higher still I feel my breasts. The first one, the left, is a horizontal line that falls off to the soft weight where the ribs come up from my back. I slide my hand over to the other, cradle it and feel the steady thump of my heart. It is still there.

My heart still beating, my body still intact, birds singing amid the gathering dusk, these simple things are what anchor me to the world.

I cannot think of the other thing. I cannot name it. I can only think of what is here, now. My body is still here. I can feel it, but there is something intruding. It's a certain smell. It's a bad smell and it's inside me.

I rise from my bare bed, this time not so dizzy, and go to the bathroom. In the bathroom mirror I can see no marks. My neck hurts when I turn it a certain way. That's all. I vomit into the toilet, quickly, with no mess, and turn on the hot water.

I let the water pour down on my neck and shoulders until someone yells, telling me I'm taking all the hot water. There is a phone call for me somewhere during this time, but I am in the shower when it comes. I hear the ringing and my name being called. I don't answer. I am wrapped in a towel, unable to bear clothes, curled up on my bed, when someone comes to the door and taps.

"Hey, Ruthie, are you coming down for supper?"

It is my roommate Brian. I can't see him yet. I don't want to see anyone.

"No," I answer.

"Are you sick?" he asks.

"Yeah, I'm sick." It is enough to keep them away, and I'm briefly thankful he thought of it.

I know I should call someone, tell someone what has happened. But who to call in the late afternoon on a Saturday?

And what to say? *Remember that guy I told you about?* But the problem is, I haven't really told anyone about Ian.

Lisa, one of the roommates, knows something has been going on between us, but she has said little, just flashed me a knowing smile when I've left the house or when the phone rings. Besides, Lisa's gone home for the weekend to visit her grandmother in Halifax and isn't expected back until tomorrow. I think of the police, but going downstairs to the phone is too impossible to contemplate, let alone what I would tell them. It's not like Ian and I had never done it before. It's not like he jumped out from behind a bush on the shortcut to the campus. He isn't a stranger. He was my lover not so long ago. He is a friend. He was a friend.

Suddenly it's Jiggs I want. I want my big sister with a longing that I have never felt before. I want us to be small again, in the shared bedroom in the house on the rocks. When one or the other was hurt or scared at night we would crawl in together. Usually it was Jiggs who came into my bed to comfort me, but sometimes it was the other way around. If I peed my own bed, or if I heard a strange noise or just wanted company, I would go to Jiggs and stand near her head, willing her awake until the covers were drawn aside and I could climb up the ladder and snuggle into the warmth of my older sister.

But Jiggs is somewhere else. I'm not even sure where she is. I can't believe I've lost track of my own sister. Gillian. Gillian Callis, also know as Jiggs. It seems incredible that somehow we have grown so far apart when not so long ago we shared the same sweet sleep.

I can't seem to get warm. I go to my closet where I have stashed extra blankets. Elsie has sent three extra blankets over the course of the last year. She would send a blanket, then, forgetting, and feeling a chill in her own Sudbury home, she'd send another. It was her way of keeping me warm.

Now, pulling one of her blankets down from the shelf, I am so grateful for my mother. I wrap it around myself, and lie again on the bed. But it is impossible to block out all the pictures in my head. I move to the floor below the window and, still curled in the blanket, close my eyes. I cannot get warm. The space around me is too big.

I go to my closet then and, pushing away the accumulated clutter of shoes and boots, I make a space on the floor to lie down. It smells strongly of feet, and faintly of perfume still clinging to my better dresses, but at least it does not smell of him. My mother's blanket is prickly new wool and I am beginning to feel it against my naked, scoured body. I am still cold, but in this small dark space, little by little, I begin to feel warmer. I pull the door of my closet closed, shutting myself inside. I think I am safe and, somehow, despite everything, I fall asleep in my wet warm wool cocoon.

α

Australia was lonely at first. Until I met the girls, the ones that seemed so nice, with their flashing eyes and brightly coloured sarongs. Thin Mira with her bleached blonde surfer hair, and the other bigger, darker one, Anna.

I was so honoured when they singled me out to be their new friend, to come away with them, off to that distant mountaintop where a holy swami lived with a bunch of other blokes who, according to them, would *really, really like to meet a Canadian*. I should have been suspicious at how quickly their duet dissolved and reformed itself into a trio, but I thought myself an essential third side of the triangle, the completed trinity.

Nimbin turned out to be an old forest ranger post turned into an organic spiritual community. It was back in the hills, away from the beaches, an area the Australians called "the green behind the gold." It was rain forest up there, and certainly off the beaten track. We were going to catch a ride with Anna and Mira's friend Lloyd.

I was thrilled to be going inland with locals. I was heading off to a place I had only imagined a few short months ago. Now it was happening as it was meant to be. God had put me together with these new friends, and set us all on a path of enlightenment and adventure.

True, Mira and Anna said they were skint, which I understood meant broke, but neither sounded too worried. Maybe the blokes had some cash, or the swami. I still had some traveller's cheques left, but not a lot. The community would be a way for me to live cheaply, in the moment. I imagined peace and harmony, a spiritual energy field. I was a disciple of an unknown guru and I was willing to go anywhere.

When Lloyd arrived in his Jeep, the face that appeared from the swirl of dust was appraising and suspicious.

"Hi. I'm Ruth." The old reflex to put my hand over my mouth was still there. Instead I smiled.

"She coming with us?" His accent was so thick, I could hardly understand him.

Ever the leader, Mira stepped forward. I couldn't see her face but I could hear her. "Yes. She's cool. Ruthie has *everything we need*. Very cool. You'll see."

It was an endorsement. Anna smiled her beguiling smile and the three of us crowded into the back of the Jeep, tucking some supplies I'd purchased under the front seat. Mira perched beside Lloyd, who casually slumped at the wheel, elbow cocked on the driver door. He flicked the cigarette burning in his hand into a small banana plantation, where it smoked briefly before going out. From the back seat I couldn't see much of him, just the back of his head and his lank grey hair hanging down past his collar.

We roared off, took three corners too fast and started climbing a twisting mountain road. Anna, beside me, put on sunglasses. With the wind in her hair she looked like a movie star. I started to relax. This was fun. I wondered briefly about the swami. What kind of religion had a swami? Hindus? Buddhists? I wasn't sure, but I needed to know if any of my faith was real. I needed to see if this holy man would recognize any holiness in me. I wasn't sure if it even existed anymore. Or if it had ever existed.

Half an hour later Lloyd stopped the Jeep at a roadside pull-out and, gathering supplies in a pack, we started along a trail that became increasingly narrow as we climbed. Soon we were spread out single file; first Lloyd, then Mira and, a few yards back, Anna and I, both jostling for third place on the trail. The strain of the climb was beginning to show on Anna's face. Her cheeks were bright red, the veins in her neck pulsing. I slowed a little so she could catch her breath. The slope, although steadily winding upward, wasn't the mountain goat scramble I had expected. I talked so Anna could focus on something other than the rising trail.

"Have you been up here before?" I asked. As I waited for a reply, I realized she hadn't the wind to answer. "It's really beautiful. Imagine, getting off the beaten track like this. It's not something a lot of tourists do, I'll bet. I sure was lucky running into you two. Imagine, all of us heading for the same place. What a coincidence. It seems like it was meant to be. I love Australian people. They're so friendly and down to earth. How much farther is it to the camp? And who will be up there? Do you know?"

Anna didn't answer any of my questions, she just picked up her pace in order to catch up to Lloyd and Mira. I couldn't figure out if her silence was rude or if she just deferred to Mira all the time. Perhaps she didn't know the answers to my questions.

We walked on and on, ever upwards.

As the sun became lower in the sky, the surrounding jungle began to look strangely foreboding. Who were these people I was with? What had brought me to this place? I tried to recall the sense of adventure I had felt when I met the girls in the youth hostel earlier but it would not come to me. Instead, the dark beasts of the jungle stepped forward in my imagination. The jaguar awakened, stretched, and felt the hunger clapping in his belly; the snake, fanged and hissing, stuck out his forked tongue and slithered towards the trail, his red markings brilliant in my mind.

Lloyd and Mira paused beyond us, waiting for Anna and me to catch up. By the time I reached them, Lloyd was passing around a water bottle and all three drank deeply. The inside of my mouth felt furry and dry at the same time. All my saliva had dried up. I felt if I didn't get some water, I would die.

I spoke, hoping to draw some attention to myself. "Will we get there before it's dark?" The three of them looked at me. No one answered. Lloyd grunted. Mira narrowed her eyes. Even Anna looked vaguely contemptuous. They spun around as though on cue, and continued walking up the mountain.

The sun behind us cast long shadows that wove and twisted on the trail. I couldn't distinguish my own shadow from the shadows of the gum trees, the arbutus, the spice trees, the sago palms and the palmettos. All the vegetation danced in dappled light, bowing and breaking up the trail in front of me. I could do nothing but follow.

We arrived at the camp at dusk. Three men were already there. From what I could see in the rapidly gathering darkness, there was a small hut with a watchtower built beside it. A fire burned outside, a smoking mess, and the night creatures, the cicadas and other creeping things, pierced the night with their shrill continuous peeping.

The men were glad to see us, or at least glad to see Mira and Anna. There was much celebration, a jug of wine was uncorked, there was dancing and the thick potent smell of hashish. Bodies pressed together in the darkness of the hut. I couldn't tell who was who and there seemed to be no discernible sleeping quarters.

I went outside to the fire where a skinny mongrel dog nosed about looking for bits of food. She was shorthaired, brindle in colour and ugly. I could tell she'd just had puppies because in the firelight I could see her underbelly, flaccid and pale. The stretched milkless sacs flopped about, dark nipples sagging as she sat on her rump in the dust and scratched at fleas in her neck and around her ears. I wondered how long ago she had given birth and where the pups were now. I thought of the dogs of my childhood.

A man with bare feet and a long shaggy beard came up to me and spoke. I had no idea what he was saying. His eyes appeared wild, not mellow and placid, the way Mira's had looked last time I'd seen her, bedded down with Lloyd in a corner. I had no idea what had happened to Anna. I was here alone. I had no bedroll to speak of and the cold, sudden and very real, rolled in like moist fog almost immediately after the sun dipped below the horizon.

I poked at the fire, trying to coax some warmth from the spent coals. I thought about going foraging for wood, but that would have meant a trip into the darkened jungle and I was not prepared for that. My vision of dangerous creatures still lurked at the shadowed periphery of my imagination.

I was tired and cold and scared. Strange moaning sounds were coming from the top of the watchtower and at first I thought it was the mysterious swami chanting. The moaning became louder and suddenly I recognized the voice. It was Anna. She was up there with one of the forest dwellers. I hoped, for her sake, it was not the unkempt bearded one with dirt between his toes and the crazed look of the addict upon his face.

I briefly imagined them entwined, but the vision made me feel disgusted, guilty and lonely. A well of self-pity flooded my belly as I sought a small place to rest. All I wanted was to lay my head down and sleep until morning restored the bright tropical colours and my sense of well-being. I wanted tea with honey, and bright batik sarongs and birdsong, but mostly I wanted a bed, a place to sleep.

In the hut, the strangers were still talking and drinking, passing a bottle from hand to hand. There was no glass in the windows, no door in the doorframe, but at least inside was a sense of shelter. I found some empty burlap sacks near the wall and pushed them together into a makeshift nest. I was shivering with cold and yet it made more sense to have them under me than on top. The floor was hard and I could smell animal droppings. Rodents might come in the night, but I had no other place to lie down.

I took out my contact lenses, stashed them in my money belt and closed my eyes against the ugliness of the situation.

Sometime in the night, the brindle dog came and sniffed at my face, waking me up from an uncertain slumber. I tried to get her to lie beside me, patting a place on the floor, making a cave of my body. I wanted desperately to steal some warmth from her ripe dog body, but she ambled away, oblivious to human need. She scratched again, leaving a trail of hair and fleas and the strong scent of canine dander.

Somehow I slept again and was awakened, at first dawn, by the sound of shouting from outside. There was Anna's voice — *Fuck off* — and a male voice growling some groggy response. I heard a scuffle and then silence. I knew I should get up, go see, but I was so weary, still so tired from my terrible sleep and my circumstances. Big Anna was on her own.

I must have slept again with the warming edge of the sun, because when I woke the third time it was broad daylight. I quickly learned my new friends, and my money belt, were gone. So were my contact lenses. Everything was blurry. I couldn't distinguish faces unless I got up close. I recognized Lloyd and approached him.

"Have you seen the other girls?"

He just pointed into the bush. "They must have split."

"Is that the way down?"

His eyes glazed over like he couldn't figure out what I was saying.

"Down?"

"Yeah, down. Out. Back to the town."

"Down town?" He wasn't getting it.

I walked to the trailhead. How could I get back when I couldn't see? And what would I do without money? My jaw was aching. I must have been grinding my teeth during the awful sleepless night. Surely, they'd be back.

But, of course, Anna and Mira were gone for good. I looked around the compound, hoping somehow they would materialize, that I was mistaken and they would appear, cheerful and bright and laughing, from behind a palmetto. All I could see was the burned-out fire pit, the forest hut and the watchtower looming at the edge of the clearing. Trails seemed to snake away from the area where the jungle had been cleared, but without my contact lenses I couldn't see where they went.

I walked slowly back to the building I'd slept in, hoping to find someone who could tell me what was going on. There were three men inside sitting cross-legged on the burlap sacks I had used as my mattress last night. They were all facing the same direction and not one of them moved a muscle as I stepped across the threshold of the open doorway. They seemed to be waiting for someone and so I sat, too.

As the silence settled on the room I noticed different sounds. A low hollow plunking came from a bamboo wind chime hung in the door frame. There was the sound of water running somewhere and far away a bird called and another one, with a deeper voice, seemed to answer. Without my sight, everything sounded closer and more potent.

A movement, a flash of orange and brown, and a small stooped man with wire-rimmed glasses came into the room. None of the others moved. He carried a magenta cushion that seemed to wink and shimmer in the morning light as though it were covered with jewels. It was the swami. The holy swami.

I barely dared to breathe. Was I in the presence of God, at last? Was this skinny little man in saffron robes some sort of divine conduit? Would he have a message for me?

Suddenly I became aware of my clothes, slept-in and wrinkled. There were splotches of ash on my T-shirt and my jeans were filthy. Would the swami notice?

He sat down at the front of the room, facing us, and pulled his legs together like a pretzel. I realized all the men were sitting that way and so I tried to force my own legs into the position, but they refused to bend. The best I could do was sit semi-cross legged. I pulled my shoulders back, straightened by spine and tried to look spiritual.

No one spoke. We just sat and sat. Minutes ticked by, more minutes. My shoulders were starting to hurt and I still didn't know what to expect. The meditation reminded me of silent prayer at the One True Church. What would I pray for? That Mira and Anna would come back? That they hadn't stolen my money, after all and it was just an elaborate hoax to test my faith?

All of a sudden the man closest to me bent at the waist and touched his forehead to the floor. He was bowing, but from a seated position. It seemed impossible. I wondered if Nimbin wasn't a retreat for contortionists, a religious circus troupe, and someone had neglected to tell me.

The next man dropped too and the one farthest away. *What? What?* I tried to bend over, but my head and neck hovered halfway to the floor. Outside, someone started pounding a drum and the sound made me sit up again. The swami or whoever he was appeared to be asleep at the front of the room. The drumming was getting louder.

I suddenly had a powerful urge to get out, to stand up and run back outside. I felt like they could all see what a fraud I was, sitting there bent double in a room full of strangers, bowing to a blurry guru without the faintest inkling why.

I stood quickly, too quickly. My moment of dizziness receded in time to see a drummer enter the room, followed by a parade of dancing, gyrating people dressed in rags and throwing flowers over their shoulders. They all looked skinny and unkempt. Two of the women, neither whom I recognized, were topless and their breasts swayed back and forth in time with the drum. There were some raggedy kids in the chain of swaying worshippers. One girl, maybe five, with a garland of flowers in her hair, was picking her nose and flicking boogers at the back of a smaller boy, who looked bored with the ritual, as if he'd done it hundreds of times before.

"Ommmm, ommmm," they chanted. I watched. More and more people came in. If I was ever going to get out, it would have to be while the room was full of activity. As quietly as I could, I slipped through the door.

As soon as I was outside, relieved to be away, I saw a man stride purposefully over to me. It was Lloyd.

"What did you leave?" he asked.

"Leave?"

"At the blessing ceremony. You have to leave something. What was it?"

"I don't know. I don't have anything." I had no idea what he was talking about. Did he mean money? Mira and Anna had already taken my cash. I didn't have anything left of value. How could I leave something?

"This ain't a free ride, baby," Lloyd snarled. "Nobody here takes without giving. We don't like takers." His voice suddenly dropped and I could hear lewdness creep into his growl. "His Holiness might like someone like you, though. He might find something worth taking.'

"The old man with the glasses?" I couldn't believe what he was suggesting.

"No, that was today's messenger. I'm talking about His Holiness." Lloyd nodded towards the jungle. "He's coming back tonight and he might like a virgin to keep him warm. It gets cold up here. You are a virgin, aren't you?"

I was shocked. It was none of his business. Why would Lloyd presume I'd be interested in sleeping with some counterfeit god, a man I'd never met? The thought disgusted me. In fact, Lloyd disgusted me, too. They all did.

He stood there, leering, "You are, aren't you? Aren't you?"

"I'm leaving," I said, glaring into his squinty rodent eyes. "I may not have anything to give, but neither do you. You're a bunch of hypocrites, Lloyd. Hypocrites. You've already taken my money. Okay? And that's it. There isn't anything else."

Lloyd looked me up and down quickly. "He probably wouldn't want you, anyway." With that, he turned on his heel and walked into the shack, where the chanting was growing louder and more insistent.

I stood there, my mind reeling. I had put my faith in friendship and it had failed utterly. Mira and Anna had brought me to this purportedly holy place only to leave me penniless, sightless and bereft. And now the experience was further tainted by Lloyd's suggestion that my virginity would be an appropriate sacrifice to this absentee god. I'd crossed an ocean and climbed a mountain to see a spiritual man whose only desire, according to his disciple, was a warm body in bed. Did he already have a chorus of virgins at his disposal?

It felt like I was reliving my experience of the One True Church all over again. I'd travelled down that sanctimonious road only to find that the pathway of the Fellowship was about self-gratification after all. Now this.

"Ommmmm...ommmm." The chanting droned on. "Ommmmm...ommmmm."

Or was it Home...home? Either way I knew I would leave, and the sooner, the better.

A contingent of hippies was going down the mountain midday to see if they could find work. Apparently the holy swami needed more money. I didn't even want to find a guru any more. I just wanted to get out. I tagged along behind the group that was descending, keeping their blurred silhouettes in sight. Their backs blended in and out of the greenery and although I knew there were times the trail fell away in a dangerous precipice, I couldn't see enough to know when or where that happened.

Down, down, downcast, downhearted, down the mountain I went, barely able to formulate a thought beyond getting to the bottom. My head hurt from squinting, my teeth and jaw ached from clenching and my body was weary beyond belief. More than that, something had filled the space where trust used to live.

In the town, I went to the bank. A woman put a trace on the traveller's cheques and sent me to the Saint Vincent de Paul society. A man there gave me grocery vouchers and reassurance.

"We'll help you out, darling," he said. "Sad to see this sort of thing happening on home soil. What's wrong with the kids of today?" And he doled out the chits, redeemable at the same grocery store I'd shopped at the day before. I didn't understand his generosity, his charity to me, a stranger. "You'll have a chance to help someone down the road. Remember this gift and pass it along when you're able," the man told me after giving me coupons for two free nights at the youth hostel. *Pass on the goodness.*

It was new mandate I mulled over as I pulled the musty hostel blanket around my shoulders. I wondered if I had any goodness left to pass on, and, even if I did, I was not sure there was anyone left in the world who deserved it.

I stayed in Australia until my money ran out. I bought the cheapest glasses I could find in Sydney, big thick rims with Coke-bottle lenses, and saw all the sights through them. I stayed in hostels, thought a lot, read a lot and occasionally met other traveling people. After a few weeks on the coast, I headed inland by train to the outback. It was cheaper, hotter and less populated. I walked everywhere in that scorching wilderness. I walked until I was lean and suntanned and calm. My clothes became ragged from washing them too many times and I refused to buy new ones. When my sandals finally broke and I had no money to repair them I decided it was time to go back to Canada.

The only thing left for me to do was go to Sudbury. It was a desolate city on the edge of the Precambrian Shield. My parents welcomed me, but it was easy to see they had become used to the empty nest. I slept in the guest room Elsie had done up in white muslin and eyelet pillow shams. The room felt purposely sterile. It was not the type of place one settled in.

My dad brought home stacks of university and college brochures. They lay on the kitchen table like a gentle reminder that I must move on. And I did. Although I was accepted at four universities in Ontario, I chose a St. Thomas college in the Maritimes. Saint Thomas, named after the doubter. Thomas was the only disciple who saw the risen Christ and asked for evidence, hard facts. *Show me your hands*, he said. *I want to see if you're the same one they crucified.* Good old Thomas, I thought, the only one who needed proof, living proof, of the existence of God.

α

The day after Ian rapes me, I abandon my attic room. I need to get away from the space where he hurt me. I can't be in that room at the top of the stairs anymore. It has been defiled. Even though I loved it last week, I don't love it anymore. I need to be somewhere Ian has never been before.

I know he will come back for me and I must be gone. I move to the neighbouring co-op house that has one room left open. Students who have applied to live there are trickling in as their timetables demand an end to summer. Because I stayed through from last year, I have some seniority in this shared student housing.

I choose the last available room in the house. It is a large room in the basement. I don't see it as a basement room, dim with only one small, ground-level window. I choose it because it is alone, removed from the two stories above full of strangers. I choose it because I see this room as a haven, not unlike the basement coffeehouse of the Fellowship. This new room in a new house is a safe place. I want a cave, a den, a warm place to lick my wounds. I want time to heal. The healing will be in books and study and classes and papers. I think briefly of my Bible and the healing grace of God, but that was before this. I know too much now to go back to God and, besides, I'm not so sure He would want me anymore.

I am in my den only two days before Ian finds me. It's a Monday evening and the washer and dryer have been running all day, as everyone carts down their clothes after the weekend. I like the sound of the washer and dryer. They are across the basement from my room in the junky part of the cellar where all the discarded stuff is stored.

The sound of the churning washer and the snaps and buttons clanking on the dryer drum is distant, lulling. It's becoming a familiar background hum in this new room I've claimed and lined with books. I've made the room strictly functional, positioning a good reading light over my large desk and a smaller one near the bed, which is different from the bed in the other house. This room is for study and sleep. My only concession to comfort is an easy chair near the door, a place to throw books and dirty clothes.

I don't hear him come down the stairs. When he knocks, I go and open the door, completely unsuspecting, completely unprepared. It's him in the doorway, my boyfriend, the person who is not a boy and is no longer a friend. My rapist. He carries a bottle of fury wrapped in the bright guise of apology.

I know I should slam and bolt the door right then, but something in the wrapped bottle, floral paper clumsily taped around the neck, makes me pause and look at him. It is the split second he needs and he is inside my room.

"1 brought you a present."

"I'm studying."

"Well, maybe I'll have a little drink then. You don't mind, do you?"

"Ian —"

Ignoring me, he looks around my new room.

"Nice place. Different. Got any glasses?"

"I'll go up and get some."

But he sees right away what I'm thinking.

"No, that's okay. I will."

He leaves then and I think of running upstairs too. But where will I go? What will I say? There's a small basement window, but I can't really imagine breaking the glass. With what? Will I fit through?

"Hey, buddy, Ruthie and I are having a little celebration downstairs. Got any fresh glasses?" He's talking to Donny in the kitchen at the top of the stairs. They are laughing. I imagine Ian in the kitchen, bear-like but charming, seemingly without menace. They won't be able to see him like I do now. But what can I do? Hide? He's coming back down the stairs, clinking glasses like we're really going to have a party. It's too late to hide. I go to my desk, open a book, pretend to read. Maybe, oh God, maybe, if I ignore him, even have a friendly drink with him, he'll go away. I sit down at my desk. I can get through this.

He's holding his blue binder in his hand when he comes back with the glasses. I wonder where he got it. Inside are his poems, the lyrics to songs that run inside his head, the ones that he insists will one day make him famous.

"What did you say to Donny?"

"I told him a little joke, that's all. He won't come down here, Ruth, if that's what you're thinking. I'd have to kill the skinny little fag if he did."

The way he says it, I'm sure he would do it. I don't speak. I just shake my head, mute. Ian seems intent on getting something done. He sits on the arm of the easy chair.

"I thought I'd work too, seeing as you're so busy. I thought we could both just work down here together and, you know, have a little drink, pass a little time. Like we used to." Pause. "Last time I saw you wasn't so good, was it?"

I swing around in my desk chair, angry. "No. No. No. It wasn't so good. It was goddamn awful."

My voice is trembling and high pitched. I'm livid, raging, but he widens his eyes at me, a veiled threat, and says, "Hey, hey, calm down. Have a drink."

He rips the paper off the bottle and pours two large tumblers of a thick brown liqueur into glasses. It's called O'Darby's, a cheap version of Bailey's Irish Cream. Ian hands me one of the glasses. "Cheers," he says. "I wouldn't want that to ever happen again, Ruthie."

"No." I'm so scared my mouth is dry and I can't swallow. I take the tiniest sip of the liqueur. It is sickeningly sweet and creamy like cheap chocolate milk straight from the carton, but it burns on the way down.

Ian pushes the clothes off the easy chair and opens his binder on its arm. He has a yellow legal pad and a pen. He seems to just want to be with me, to work in my presence, so I pretend to go back to my book.

"I want to see your face."

"I have to work, Ian." I'm begging him. My voice quivers.

"Maybe we could just move your desk around so I don't have to look at your back. I'd much rather look at your face, Ruthie."

I swivel again in the chair and face him, trying to make my voice casual.

"I can take a break for a while. We can have a drink and then we can go back to work. How's that? You can have the desk for writing. I just have to do some reading for my American lit class, so I don't really need the desk."

He smiles then, and pats the armchair. "Why don't you take a break here, near me? Or would you rather lie on the bed?"

He is filling up his glass again. I want to scream. The moments are an underwater film. I am trapped. He pours again and reads me a poem. It is something about a man losing his woman to the racetrack. Is that possible? The racetrack.

I bet on you, despite the odds,
but my bourbon mare ran away, ran away.
Now I'm in despair
and you're in another man's care.
"Do you like it?" It sounds like one word. *Dooyalikit?*

Ian has been drinking before he got here, likely a lot, and now he's drunk. I edge towards the door. If I pretend to go get something — a pen or a book or something — I might get out.

But he is not so absorbed in his writing that he doesn't notice me inching toward the door.

"What's wrong?"

"I have to pee."

"Pee here." Crudely he thrusts out the bottle of O'Darbys. "I'll just finish up this little bit and you can pee in this little bitty hole. Think you can pee in this little hole, Ruthie? Can you hang your precious little pussy over this little tiny hole?"

I lunge towards the door while he's pouring but I knock his arm and the bottle flies to the floor, smashing. Enraged, Ian jumps to his feet and I feel him on top of me throwing me face first to the floor with the glass and the sticky liqueur.

"You don't think it's good enough, do you, smarty-pants? You don't think my poetry is good enough, Miss English major. Miss fucking know-it-all."

He has grabbed my hair and is smashing my face into the floor and the glass is cutting into my head and there is no way to get up, to get away, and I think it is the end because he twists me upright and hits my face over and over with his fists. Then his hands have gone around my neck and he is squeezing, squeezing, and there is no air and my blood is all over the front of his shirt, and everything, the blood, his face, the air, is bright red, blurring and blending into crimson and, oh my God, no, no, not like this.

I can't breathe and I slip away as unconsciousness steals the red, and only darkness is there, and I am somewhere that is not a place. I am everywhere in the room except in the rag doll body. When he lets me go, I fall limply and don't respond when he shakes me. *Oh my God*, I hear him whisper.

The room is hot and somehow I know in my bones that he believes he has killed me. When the darkness recedes I feel the anger that surged through him dissipate. There is a brief lightening. I see two papers, one under my desk, dark with blood, the other wet with drink, a different shade of red. There is the blue binder. Spattered with dark drops. And then I am gone again.

He leaves through the small window, pushes it out into the night and snakes his body through onto the lawn, pulling his papers and his fear after him. Too terrified for sorrow, he worms out onto the grass as my lungs fill with air. I sputter and stand, fall again, oblivious to the glass in my head, the blood all over my face and dripping down onto my sweater. A shriek that will not stop rises to my throat and I stumble out of the room and up the stairs, blinking and crying and dripping blood. I stagger into the kitchen, where five of my roommates are sitting at the kitchen table.

"What the heck?" calls someone. Another voice. "Oh my God!" Is it them screaming or is it me?

I have my hands over my face, but I can feel blood flowing down between my fingers, rivers of blood, pooling in my eyes, sluicing over my cheeks and my chin and falling like heavy rain to the linoleum.

"Call the police!"

"Call an ambulance! Who has a quarter?" And while they scramble for the pay phone in the dining room I go jellyfish weak and collapse where I stand. One of the roommates gets her legs under my head and cradles me, pressing an orange tablecloth to my head. "What happened? What happened?" And, of course, I have no voice to tell them.

"He'll kill Donny," is the one thing I manage to croak out. "He'll kill you. He wanted to," I cry, finding Donny's pale face in the kitchen and knowing now that it is out in the open he can't kill any of them. Now that he has tried to kill me, the rest of them are safe.

Suddenly there are big bodies in the room, two men in white, two in blue, police. Too many people. The orange tablecloth is removed and the blood on the floor — my blood, I realize — is like a thick lake. A policewoman stoops down. Her face blurs then comes into focus.

"Move aside."

Her voice helps. She is both calming and authoritative. I am helped to my feet by strong arms that don't seem attached to bodies and a blanket is draped around my shoulder. I'll get blood on it.

"She just came up out of the basement. We were just going to call everyone for supper and I heard this scream," says one of the girls. I notice she still has an oven mitt on. Her face is ghostly white, her eyes wild.

When I manage to choke out parts of the story, the policewoman radios for someone to bring tracking dogs. She addresses the roommates standing slack-mouthed in the kitchen. "Do any of you want to accompany her to the hospital? We also have to take her to the station to make a statement. Anyone?"

There is a terrible silence. Many of the roommates are new. Some of them I haven't even met. I see their awkward shuffling, the quick glances, one to the other.

"I'd rather go alone."

I want to go. I want to disappear. I don't want to move. I don't know what I want.

The policewoman escorts me to a car and I get in. From the back of the police car, I see broken glass near the ground window of my room. I wonder, briefly, if Ian cut himself on the way out. I hope not. I do not know that I am still bleeding and that it will take twelve stitches to close the three holes in my face. I am in shock. I listen to the police radio as I sit alone in the back seat. They are calling an APB, an All Points Bulletin. He is armed, they say. With what?

The dogs arrive and I watch them sniffing and yelping excitedly outside the car. Do they smell blood, I wonder? And then the policewoman is back. She opens the door.

"We have to go to the hospital, because you need some medical attention."

I nod dumbly. We pull away from the house to go up the hill towards the bright lights of Emergency. I am grateful that they do not turn on the siren, and relief tinged with shame takes up the slow dance with sorrow.

Emergency is all bright lights and professionals. They show no surprise that a badly beaten and bleeding patient comes to the hospital in the early evening accompanied by a policewoman. The people in the waiting room look, of course, but there are forms to sign and I focus on my blocky, wobbling writing.

Almost immediately, a nurse comes and leads me into a small room. "Please remove all your clothes and put this gown on. It ties at the back." Once I've changed into the paper gown, the nurse reclaims me, and we walk past some curtained beds to an examination room.

"Wait here," she tells me. "A doctor will be with you shortly."

The room is blue and white and chrome. Every surface gleams. There is a mirror on one wall above a sink but I do not look into it. I am afraid I will have no reflection.

Although I have tied the gown as instructed, I am acutely aware of my bum hanging out. I sit on the plastic chair in the icy examination room waiting for someone to come and tell me everything will be all right.

But they don't say that. Everything is not all right. The doctor comes. He is young, mid-thirties and though I see him struggle not to, he winces when he sees me. It is barely noticeable but what I read is distaste. Not pity, not sorrow. Mild distaste.

He tells me to lie on the table and he begins to touch my face lightly.

"Was she raped?" he asks the nurse. *What? Does he think she has more information than me?*

"There's an awful lot of genital bruising and some vaginal lacerations," she says, shaking her head, absently stroking my face. "Did he rape you, dear? Can you tell me?"

Yes, Yes, I shout inside my head. *I was raped. Three days ago. I was. I was. I just didn't know who to tell.*

"Could be just rough sex."

Did the nurse actually say that or am I hearing things?

"Let's stitch her up now."

I'm not sure who the doctor is speaking to, or what he's talking about. Are they going to sew me up down there? The nurse has disappeared. To get a needle and thread? To get more information from the policewoman? But wait, he's coming around to my head.

He touches my chest. I wince.

"Three of your ribs are broken. You really took a beating, didn't you?"

He seems to be addressing me, but I have no words to respond to what he has stated. What can I say?

The nurse comes around again and gives me a shot of something for the pain while the doctor swears under his breath and begins to bind my ribs. There is such pain in my back where the bruising has already flamed to the surface in an angry purple red that I start to cry, and he stops to let me collect myself before continuing.

The stitching of my face doesn't hurt as much as the binding of my ribs. They are sewing me back together.

The pain in my flesh is dull. A topical anesthesia has been applied to the parts of my face that have been opened and exposed by the glass. It reminds me of the freezing that Dr. Gartenberg, my old dentist, used to use. That numbness, combined with the swelling, makes it impossible to speak. The nurse says the cuts on the top of my face and in my scalp, the ones made by the glass, are clean, easily closed. The lower cut is jagged. It's where his fist connected the hardest, where my teeth went through my lip before they broke off. This takes the most time.

"I'm sorry, but this will scar," he says. *A reminder* is what he doesn't say.

My neck is badly bruised and twisted but, according to the doctor, not permanently damaged.

Signs of asphyxiation accompany the words *severe genital trauma* on the medical record the police take away. I only see it by chance as I am bundled back into the police car to be taken to the station for photographs. The phrases mix into my head along with the radio that is calling backup cars to Glengarry Heights. My policewoman speaks code into the radio while I shiver in the back seat.

The police station is worse than the hospital. The photographer asks me to pull up my top so he can see the area around my back where my ribs have been broken. They are photographing me for evidence.

Even with the pain, I try to smile when he takes the headshots. I forget that the two front lower teeth are gone, sheared off at the gum by the force of Ian's fist.

My policewoman goes off duty. She stops into the waiting room where I sit to say goodbye. She doesn't actually say anything. She just nods to the photographer and squeezes my shoulder on the way by. After the photographs, I am taken to a room where two plainclothesmen are waiting for me. One is tall and thin, greying, with a grave, hollow look about him. The other is blond. He's got a crewcut, and he's younger. He looks like he should be a lifeguard or a ski instructor. The older one asks me to sit down.

"This man who assaulted you, do you know him?"

He asks as though he already knows the answer, but there is urgency in this question, different from the doctor.

"Yes. He was..." I don't know what to call Ian anymore.

"Your boyfriend?" Good, he's said it for me.

"Yes."

"Well, Mr. Bowen, this boyfriend of yours, is now in Glengarry Heights. He is holding a woman and two small children hostage in their own home. He is armed and dangerous. We are trying to establish phone contact, but he refuses to speak to anyone except a man named Reg Straker. Do you know that name?""

"That's his counsellor, his therapist. He works at the university, I think."

The young one nods to the other, and quickly leaves the room. The older man continues. "Now, Mr. Bowen apparently believes you are dead. What we need, Miss Callis, is for you to speak to him. Tell him to turn himself over to police and release the hostages. Can you do that for us?"

I'm stunned. Hostages? Two children? A woman? What is Ian doing? None of it makes sense. It's like something in a movie except it's very, very real.

"Miss Callis? Ruth?" The older man prompts me.

"Yes. I can try."

"You'll have to be careful. He's very volatile. Please don't say anything to make him react negatively. We can't stress how important it is to keep him calm. Talk him down. Do you think you can do this?"

"Yes."

The young man, who has slipped back into the room, pulls a telephone out from below the table.

The older man speaks briefly to his radio. On a signal I don't see, the younger one dials a number and hands the phone to me. It rings once, twice, three, four times. It rings and rings. I don't know whether to hang up or not. The ringing is in the room. I am on a speakerphone. The ringing is in my ear, in my brain. The police are listening.

Finally, "Yeah?" It's him.

"Ian?"

There is a long pause. The seconds count off.

"Who is this?" I can hear the doubt and hope in his voice.

"It's me, Ruth."

"Ruthie?" Then, his voice turns suspicious. "Who is this?"

"It is me, Ian. It's Ruthie."

"You're not dead?"

"No."

"Where are you, Ruthie? I thought..."

I look at the police officers. The younger one nods.

"I'm at the police station. Ian?"

"What?"

"They say you have some hos... some people there. Some kids."

"The kids are upstairs. They're asleep now."

"Oh, good. Will you let them go now, Ian?"

No answer. Then, "Ruthie, you're not dead."

"No."

"I thought..."

"I know."

"It wasn't you I wanted to hurt..."

"No."

"Ruthie?"

"Yes?"

"Can you still love me?"

The words are all over the room. The two men are looking at me. They seem to be holding their breath.

"I guess so. I don't know."

And then, because I see the fear in the policemen's eyes, I speak louder, with conviction.

"Yes, Ian, I can. I still can."

I know it's a lie, yet I tell it anyway, and while it may save the children and their hysterical mother, it will not save me. Nothing can save me now.

There are things to be seen to. The most pressing are my teeth. The two teeth Ian knocked out punctured my lip before snapping and falling into my mouth. I don't remember any pain associated with this at the time, but now the problem is huge. The hole in my mouth has been temporarily filled with a cast, a porcelain bridge that spans the gaping hole. A dental surgeon does the work for me at the hospital the day after the police arrest Ian and take him away.

The dentist has to clean out the roots and he freezes the whole bottom half of my face, from my eyes down, to work his equipment into the ragged swollen gums and extract the live nerves rooted in the bone of my jaw.

The numbness feels almost normal. The dentist works bent over my face and I feel nothing as the long roots are pried out of my mouth. I imagine them like two carrots growing in the dark soil of my jaw and it is only when I open my eyes, see the flecks of blood on the surgeon's mask and the red pulpy hole that is my mouth reflected in his glasses that I feel panic.

I remember Dr. Gartenberg and Zelda. I remember a recurring dream I used to have of Donald bringing me my Jell-O, but instead of Jell-O that weird fancy parfait glass was filled with baby teeth and Zelda would laugh like some kind of maniac and her smile got bigger and bigger until it took up almost the whole dream. Dr. Gartenberg would fade her out and he would smile his tight smile from the background and say *Open up, Ruth*, in that mocking, gentle way he had, and I would open up. Thankfully, it was always at that moment I'd wake, my mouth gaping, prepared for invasion.

I remember how much I wanted those teeth. How I wanted to be normal. Now, even that has been taken from me.

I go back to the co-op, but I cannot face my classes. My professors are understanding. Days move into weeks. I keep track of nothing, not even day or night, until the first phone call. The first time I see him is after the phone call from Paul, a guard who has befriended Ian. He must be off-duty when he calls, because there is the sound of a child wailing in the background. He's hesitant on the phone and I'm pretty sure he's broken the rules.

"Yes, hello, umm..." Long pause. "Can I speak to Ruthie, um, Ruthie..." His voice trails off. He doesn't know my surname.

"This is Ruth."

"Oh, well, I'm calling about Ian."

My heart lurches.

"Yeah?"

"He wants to see you."

"Is he okay?"

"There's been an incident." Pause. "I know he'd feel better if he could talk to you."

"An incident?"

"It's not something I can talk about on the phone. Can I tell him you'll come?"

"I'm not sure."

"He says he needs to see you, needs to explain"

"Oh."

Silence.

"He's in solitary. We had to protect him, from himself, if you know what I mean."

I hear some impatience in this man, but he is straining to keep his voice under control. Cajoling, he lowers his tone into gruff confidentiality. "Look, old Ian and I have been talking a lot, you know? He's a good guy, but it's eating him up, you know? What happened? Between you two? He doesn't want to go on, thinks it's hopeless. So he tries to check out, if ya catch my drift. I tell him, *Ian, call her*, but he can't now. He's in the hole. Anyways, he wants you to come on Thursday. I won't say any more. Come or don't come, but now at least you know." This is relayed in a rapid monologue, the two-pack-a day voice low and gravelly.

"Tell him I'll come," I whisper into the receiver. "Thursday. Tell him I'll come on Thursday."

There, I've done it. I'm committed. Paul hangs up quickly, erasing his interference.

I have to go. I have to see him. He'd told me he couldn't go on without me, now he's proving it. Checking out? It sounds so pedestrian, like leaving a roadside motel or taking books out of a library. But Ian has tried to check out of life. He's tried to kill himself.

Greater love hath no man than this, that he lay down his life for his friends.

This Sunday school scripture burns a hole in my head. Greater love. But who is he laying his life down for? Not for me, surely. Not some redemptive gesture. He tried to check me out, too, and now he's so sorry he sees no reason for living. What am I supposed to do?

He is in a holding cell, in custody, they call it, at the local remand centre behind the police station. I learn this by making a phone call, pretending to be someone else. He is awaiting trial. The trial has to do with what happened. I am not pressing charges, but the Crown is representing me. Who is the Crown? It must be a representative of the Queen. I imagine a man in a long cloak, a funny curly wig, maybe draped in an ermine stole. This has quickly gone out of my hands and taken on its own life. Nothing is explained.

I go to the remand centre at the appointed time. There is the door and I go in, as if to pay a parking fine or to complain about a dog defecating on my lawn. I see a long counter stretching across the entire entranceway. Behind the counter are people busily processing papers.

Two swinging doors, one to the left and one to the right, flank the counter, which is high and slightly intimidating. I look to see if I should take a number, but there are no clues on how to proceed. This is a foreign world.

At the counter no one pays attention to me.

"Excuse me." I focus on one woman — a policewoman? — and try to catch her eye. The woman goes from the filing cabinets to the desk, speaks briefly with a small, bald man, goes back to the files. Do any of them work the counter?

"Excuse me."

My voice is almost inaudible. Can't they see me? Ian must be waiting by now. Maybe he thinks I'm not going to come.

I try again. "Excuse me."

This time someone looks up. It's the bald man. He comes to the counter. He's very short. Only his head and shoulders are visible and his eyes look directly into mine across the officious plane of countertop.

"What can I do for you?"

"I've come to see someone."

"You a visitor?"

"Yes, I want to visit Ian Bowen. He's here."

"He works here?"

"No, actually, he's a prisoner here."

It sounds so silly. A prisoner. Images of the Tower of London, the rack, rats, balls and chains float through my mind.

The short man doesn't blink. He just looks at me and repeats the name. "Bowen."

"I'm supposed to see him at two o'clock."

The man indicates the swinging door to my right. A policewoman is called and she has me spread my legs and arms. She pats me down quickly and after they record my name in a ledger, the bald man leads me down a narrow corridor and opens the door to a smaller room. It is almost completely taken up by a large table. Ian is there, wearing blue coveralls.

My mouth is dry, my heart thumping wildly. Can they hear it? He looks up as I slide in on the other side of the table and I notice his eyes are filled with tears. I see the bandages on his wrists, white against the blue, cuffing his hands, and I feel a flood of sorrow.

"Ten minutes," says the man. He closes the door and is gone.

"I had to tell..."

"Why did you...?"

We both speak at once, our words overlapping.

He looks much smaller than I remember. He shrugs his shoulders back all the time trying to shuck off the coveralls. When he speaks again, it's as though he hasn't spoken for a long time.

His voice constricts. "I did that to you."

At first I don't know what he's talking about. Then I remember my face.

Yesterday I'd bought some concealer at the drugstore, gooey beige paste designed to cover pimples and blackheads, but it hasn't worked well on the area where the stitches have been recently removed. The lines are obvious. They run in three seams across my face. One on the bridge of my nose, one in the fleshy part of my forehead running from above the eyebrow to my hairline, and the worst, although by no means the longest, below my lip, where the teeth have gone through. There the proud flesh is rugged and uneven. I think most of the bruising is covered, with just some purple-green around the eyes. I pull at the cloth around my throat, the purposely chosen turtleneck.

"Oh." I don't know how to respond.

"I'm sorry." He looks down at the tabletop, ashamed.

"Me too," I whisper, unable to stop tears springing to my eyes. "Me too."

Then we are both crying. Tears roll down Ian's cheeks and he doesn't try to stop them. He just looks at me straight on. I wish he wouldn't. Or at least I wish he wouldn't do it so openly. I don't look that bad.

Out of nowhere, I feel hysteria rising in my belly. It's like the time Daisy, one of the Submissives, got baptized and, sitting in the pew at the back of the Fellowship, I just couldn't stop laughing. It was something about the size of Daisy's large awkward body and the faint memory of other infant baptisms. I laughed so much I had to leave, but at least I'd been able to disguise the convulsing shoulders and hunched back as some more appropriate emotion. That was at the height of my zeal for the One True Church when I still believed I was shedding white light all over my world.

But this is ridiculous. Here we both are, crying away our time together in a small room. We've survived, haven't we? I've survived despite the fact I can hardly begin to understand how things got so violent. He's survived despite this suicide attempt. The cousin that he took hostage and the kids all survived. There's no time for tears. I want words.

I crack a small smile and Ian picks up on it right away. He wipes his face with the back of his hand and offers me a sheepish grin.

The feeling in the room shifts; the air seems easier to breathe.

"You're okay, then?" he asks.

"I guess so."

"Things just got crazy for me, just blew up."

"Yeah."

"I never meant to hurt you. You're the last person I wanted to hurt. I just..." His hands hover for a moment, then fall.

"Oh."

"I love you, Ruthie. I know it's hard to believe." His eyes are misting again.

"You wouldn't let me go."

"I know. I couldn't stand to see you leave me, too." He's crying again. He's probably thinking of his dad, his mom, maybe even that woman before me.

Elsie and my own father flash through my mind. I haven't called. I haven't told them. I am a thousand kilometres away. They must never know.

"Yeah." I don't know what else to say.

"It's too late now, isn't it?"

He is so desperate. I can hear that thickening of his words with that tiny flicker of hope at the end. *Isn't it?* That weird power floods through me, again. This is the moment I've been dreading.

"I don't know." *God, Ruth, what are you doing? He tried to kill you. He'll do it again. What are you saying? Don't lead him on.*

"What?"

"I don't know whether it's too late or not."

But by then there is light in his eyes again. Before he can say anything, I speak again. "I don't know what to do."

"Nothing. You don't have to do anything." He speaks quickly.

"You won't kill yourself?"

He just casts his eyes down, not replying.

"What about the trial?"

"It doesn't have anything to do with us."

I can't believe he can say that. It has everything to do with us.

He must register my disbelief because he adds quickly, "I mean, we can't let what happened destroy us. They're going to try and rip us apart, but we won't let that happen, will we, Ruth?"

"I don't know."

It's true. I don't know what's expected of me. What does he expect? What does the court expect? Apparently there will be a trial after Halloween. I will be called to the stand.

"I have to testify." I might as well tell him.

He slumps back in his chair, deflated for a moment, then leans forward, reaching his hand across the table. The bandages on his wrist look fresh and clean, as though they have been changed for this special occasion. Underneath the white, I imagine a ragged cut, badly stitched like a Frankenstein mask. He wants me to hold his hand.

I look to the door. Is there movement behind the little square window at the top? Is there a policeman there with a gun, ready to shoot us if we touch?

Ian's eyes watch me intently. This is some sort of test. I tentatively reach out and then drop my hand back into my lap.

"I can't."

Ian's large hands curl into fists and I imagine blood oozing out into the bandages. He pulls back and is silent for a moment. His face has gone from white to bright pink.

I speak quickly because I can't bear the silence. "Look. I don't know what happened. I'm not mad at you. I just need some time. Please understand. I don't want you to hurt yourself. I'm okay. I'm fine. Really."

I smile the smile that says I'm fine and he searches my eyes, wanting to believe me.

"You need time?"

"Yeah. I do. I don't know what to do."

It's the fourth time I've said that. I'm beginning to sound like a broken record.

"It's two weeks until the trial. Will you see me again?"

"I can't." It's a lie but maybe he won't know. "They said there should be no contact until after the sentencing."

"Oh. What about then?"

"When?"

"After."

"I don't know. I'm not sure."

"But you'll think about it."

Is he talking about the trial, me thinking about the trial or the possibility of seeing him again? I'm not sure what he's talking about, and there is a buzzing in my head that won't go away. I'm afraid to ask him what he means. I don't really want to know.

"I'll see you at the trial, I guess."

"Ruthie, I might be sent away for a long time. My lawyer is going to try and get two years less a day, but it could be more. If it's more, Ruthie, it means the big house. Maximum. Do you know what that means? They'll kill me in there, Ruthie."

Maximum security is a place where murderers go, people who kill children for the thrill of it and bash little old ladies over the head with hammers so they can steal their pension cheques. It seems impossible that Ian should go there. He doesn't belong there. I've seen him gentle and caring. He bought me the purple moon woman. He taught me about fiddleheads. He writes poetry. He just doesn't know how to deal with his emotions. He's afraid of people leaving him. Didn't he just say that? My head pounds. He's still talking.

He's afraid. For a brief moment, I'm glad he's afraid. Now he knows what it feels like, I think, but that fades and I see him frightened.

"You'll be all right." And then I say it again, with more force. "Everything will be all right."

I know it's true. The buzzing in my brain has quieted. It's out of my control now and whatever comes next is no longer up to me. It's out of my hands. I deliver it all to God, whether real or not.

"We'll have to see what happens." As I speak, the door opens and the small man is there again. Ian looks at the man. He looks at me and then he rises, waiting for me to get up.

"Time's up. Let's go."

At that moment I see his feet are shackled together. He can't walk properly because there are metal bands around each of his ankles and chains between the bands. He didn't want me to know. The man is behind him, herding. The chains drag on the floor. Ian doesn't look at me as he leaves through a small door I hadn't noticed before.

Now, the man and I are together in the room. The door I first came through is open and he indicates I should go by nodding his head towards it. I feel dismissed. "His feet...? Is that normal?"

The man looks at me blankly. "He's up on forcible confinement, assault causing grievous bodily harm and weapons charges. Is that normal? Ask the people he hurt, lady, not me."

I am shocked into silence. I gather my purse and walk out of the room, shaken. I am the person he hurt. It's my memory that will be hanging, a dead weight, around his neck forever. I hold the key to those awful leg manacles and now, more than anything else, I want him released. He is chained to me. If he kills himself it will be because of me. I need him to be released or I am afraid I will have no freedom.

In the Maritimes there are no legal abortion clinics. I am afraid of the alternative, a backstreet, illegal variety. I think I will die. I have a futile meeting with the panel of the local hospital to determine whether or not I could stay in town, go discreetly to the local hospital, and emerge fixed, the following day.

The meeting is confusing. Somehow I say all the wrong things.

It is a meeting in a hospital, in a boardroom.

They, all in suits, sit on one side of an oak table. I, awed by the table, the boardroom, the strange suited men, sit on the other side. I look at the walls hung with certificates and framed black and white photographs. I try not to look at them.

They refer to the lump in my middle, which is indistinguishable from the fear in my gut, as my *situation*; the same way I think of it, if I think of it at all.

A situation doesn't have the makings of a human face, semi-formed arms and the buds where fingers and toes will grow. They are trying to appraise, through a series of questions, whether I meet the financial, physical and emotional criteria for a hospital termination.

The word termination comforts me. It doesn't sound as deliberate as abortion. A termination is something you might do for someone's own good, or just because it's necessary, involving no choice: *we are terminating his medication,* or, even better, *the train terminates at Crestwood station.*

The men — one is a physician for sure, one is a psychologist and another is introduced as a member of the board and may or may not be a doctor — seem quite casual about the meeting. They drink coffee out of Styrofoam cups and laugh about some mix-up on one of the wards, a nursing error, but not life-threatening. I can't help but feel it has something to do with sex. It's in the way they were laughing and the way the laughter stops when I arrive, early and a little out of breath.

The questions are quite simple: I am a twenty-year-old second-year arts student at the university?

"Yes."

On a scholarship?

Again, "Yes."

I am physically fit?

"Yes, except for a bout of scarlet fever as a child."

Any psychiatric history?

"No."

The father is informed?

"No." A few raised eyebrows. The men shift in their chairs, suddenly uncomfortable. The one with the mustache, the psychologist, continues, gently: "But you do know who the father is, Miss Callis?"

"Yes."

They seem relieved by this answer and nod, one making a note in a spiral-bound book. I know this information has pleased them. I smile tentatively. Then, like a child, I remember the fake teeth and I pinch my lips together. Did they see? It reminds me so much of being a kid, being self-conscious about my funny little baby teeth that refused to fall out and of the retainer I had to wear for so long. What will Elsie say when she finds out all that dental work was for nothing?

I should tell them, of course, that the father is in prison, that he raped me, but for some reason, I assume they already know about the assault. It was all over the newspapers. Everyone knows, don't they?

I am perfectly calm as I answer these questions. I am an automaton. My answers are sensible and delivered in a measured, even tone. I think about each one, deliberate for a moment, and then respond as honestly as I know how. It is the well-tailored suits that make me calm. That, and the shining table smelling faintly of lemon furniture polish. It somehow assures me these solid, kind men will see my predicament and help me.

I put my faith in a table. Somehow polished wood equates understanding. What an idiot I am. What a dupe.

There is one final question before I am dismissed like a truant teen making up a missed examination. Could I, with the help of my family, support a child?

I pause, answer truthfully. "I guess so."

As soon as I say it, I realize I should have lied. I should have wept and railed and flung myself on their mercy. I should have told the whole sordid story, the awful fear, the coercion, the ensuing violence, the guilt, all of it. I should have told them about the blood, the dead cat and the rape, especially the rape part. But the words, fully formed, sit inside my mouth like my fake front teeth and the plastic moulding that suctions to the roof of my mouth, impossible to spit out without making a big mess on the table.

They don't help. A letter, marked confidential and private, comes to the co-op house the following week. In terse, formal language, the letter explains that I do not meet the criteria required for a first trimester dilation and curettage procedure. The local hospital will not offer treatment. The letter is brief and to the point. It does not say how very sorry they are, nor does it suggest other options or offer alternatives. The letter closes with the word *Sincerely*. Underneath is an illegible scrawl, as if the author wished to remain anonymous.

I take it down to my room to reread. I am having difficulty breathing now, and I lie on my bed. This thing inside me is growing, getting bigger every day. I slip my hand down the front of my pants and probe the unyielding flesh above my pubic bone. With increasing clarity I know I must face the fact that this changing mass of tissue, this lump rapidly becoming flesh and bone, is not going to go away. It demands action. And yet all I can do is lie there, hand in my pants, paralyzed with indecision.

It's not hard to do the math. We met in the spring. It was in the lovey-dovey spring that we met and made out like rabbits. Toronto was in August, so was Sadie's death. I was putting things in plastic bags that weekend. I remember looking for her body but I couldn't find it. He must have taken it with him when he left. That was moving day, early September. And after that, all hell broke loose.

The calendar feels clammy in my hands. I don't want to count backwards but I already know the truth. This lump in my stomach wasn't conceived in that violent ugliness, no, this baby was from when I still wanted Ian. This child was conceived in those fleeting weeks when I couldn't get enough of him, when I imagined us together forever. It makes me shudder now.

One thing is sure: I will get rid of the baby. I know this with an unwavering certainty. If I allow it to live, I will be eternally, irrevocably, connected to Ian. The thought frightens me and brings my body's betrayal into sharp focus. I will have an abortion. Soon. But how? And where?

The answer comes three days later with a telephone call.

"Dad?"

"Hi, Toothie. How are you?" He sounds so close, so familiar and loving and close. I swallow hard, choking back the desire to tell him everything.

"I'm fine, I guess."

"You don't sound so good, Ruthie. Are exams getting you down?"

Yes, exams and assaults. Court appearances, impending abortion. Yes, a few troubling things.

"No, yeah, well, sort of. I haven't had a great term, dad. I've got a lot on my plate."

"I know, baby, but if anyone can do it, you can, right? You've got what it takes, the right material up top."

I can almost see him tapping his bald, freckled head as he speaks. He has such faith, blind faith, I think, in my abilities. The thought brings tears to my eyes but I blink them back quickly, biting my lower lip and focusing on a series of dust motes escaping under the radiator. I'm not going to give it away now.

Concentrating again, I hear him talking about plans for Christmas. They are contemplating going south to Florida — Elsie's always wanted to — and what do I think of meeting Jiggs in Montreal?

"You two could spend Christmas together in a posh hotel, see some sights, do some shopping. I'll send train fare and book the hotel if you like the idea, Ruth. Of course, you're welcome to come to Florida, too," he adds, afraid of hurting my feelings. "It's just that the condo is part of a seniors' complex. Wouldn't be much *action* for young people."

His heart condition, I think. Winters are hard on old men with bad hearts.

"Yeah, Dad, sure. That sounds great." I babble on about how good a change of pace would be, how nice it would be to get together with Jiggs again, what a great city Montreal is and all the while the words *train ticket* and *hotel* are making me weak with foreboding and relief.

I am probably sixteen weeks pregnant when I arrive in Montreal, a city that feels like a foreign country. On the phone I have told Jiggs I will come right after Christmas exams. We are booked into a hotel in downtown Montreal for a week. I arrive two days early, planning to have the abortion before Jiggs comes in from Toronto. She's at the University of Toronto in women's studies, or philosophy. Or is it film studies? I realize I don't actually know what it is she studies.

Snow falling from the sky and gathering on the ground causes me to blink and readjust my vision as I trudge up the stairs from the cavernous underground Central station.

Lounging on the stairs near the entrance to the Métro, a boy is silhouetted against the sky. At first I think he is begging, but there's a taut urgency in his voice that betrays my first impressions. He is spare, sunken-eyed, dressed in a black leather jacket and tattered jeans tucked into high lace-up boots. He seems anchored to the stairs by the heavy soles of these boots, rocking back and forth, heel to toe. He's speaking French. As I get closer, I see his head is shaven and the snow melts as it touches the boy's scalp, the imperfect circle of his skull painfully exposed beneath a faint stubble of growth. He speaks rapidly to the crowds of people that swarm past, ignoring him, drawn instead to the relative warmth of the underground trains.

The boy pauses in his monologue long enough to watch me ascend, struggling towards the wan, overcast skies with my suitcase dragging behind, banging on each stair. "Tête carrée," he hisses as our eyes meet briefly. I don't know what he's said but I feel as though he's guessed my secret. He knows what I am going to do. He is warning me away from my mission of death, but I hurry upward, past the boy, into the daylight, and as I emerge I feel the arms of the city, hostile around me.

The abortion clinic is in East Montreal. I have found it through a women's resource centre, Place des Femmes, advertised at the YWCA, where I stay the first night. The resource centre is located near the Y in a two-storey walk-up on the verge of either being remodeled or demolished, I can't say for sure.

I deposit my bag at the Y and hurry through the winter dusk, anxious to make contact with someone who can help. When I get there, I find that the woman who speaks English is gone for the day. A young woman with a pierced nose leads me inside the office to a shabby sofa in the corner. She puts a kettle on for tea and as the steam fogs up the windows to the street, sealing us off in a secret sisterhood, she explains, in a mix of French and halting English, the options.

This is what I understand: The clinic they usually refer women to has been closed. Another clinic has been recently bombed, perhaps as recently as yesterday. The staff is scattered and someone is awaiting trial, either the bomber or the abortion doctor, I'm not sure. Rallies and demonstrations are being planned but, until the clinic re-opens, choices are limited.

The woman shows me a Xeroxed pamphlet with a photograph of the remains of a building. The photograph shows police tape surrounding the site and what looks like smoke still curling from the rubble. Over the photograph and surrounded by question marks is printed the word *Choix*.

The young woman scribbles two addresses on the back of the pamphlet but shakes her head as she writes, implying that neither establishment is recommended. It would be better to wait. Can I wait? And as I nod my head, I think she asks if I would like someone from the Place des Femmes to come with me.

In long buried high-school French, I agree it is best to *attende*. Yes, I will wait. Inside, I know I will *not* wait, I may have already waited too long, but the woman smiles now, relieved that she has been understood. She moves to close the office.

We part, me clutching my pamphlet and promising to come soon to talk with the English-speaking counsellor. Before I leave, however, the woman lays her hand on my sleeve, detaining me. "Bonne chance, ma soeur," she says.

Outside, the Salvation Army bells of a skinny Santa ring out a message that reminds me of birth not death, and I begin to weep in the darkened, slushy streets as my feet find their way back to the narrow bed I will share for the last time with my unwanted child.

In bed, I think of Mary and Joseph and their run from a crazed baby-killer king. The only thing I know for sure is I want to kill the life within me. And when at last I sleep, it is a poor, troubled sleep.

In the morning I take the Métro first, then a city bus. I watch the numbers on the buildings closely as they expand block by block. It is shortly after ten in the morning and the bus is almost empty. Another passenger, a young woman with bleached blonde hair, fiddles aimlessly with a packet of cigarettes while her toddler tries to put a penny up his nose.

There are two older women on the bus, their profiles remarkably similar as they stare out the window at the passing landscape. They look beaten, I think. Not physically beaten by some pugnacious bulldog husband with a short fuse, but more emotionally beaten, as if a large machine came along and sucked all prospects of joy, present and future, cleanly out of their lives. The bus lurches down the boulevard, past pawn shops, used car dealerships and down-at-the-heel restaurants selling dubious food.

The clinic is on the main street, but I continue a full bus stop beyond to disguise my destination. From whom, I don't know. By the time I walk back, my feet are wet and cold. The bottom floor of the building is for lease and at first I think I have the wrong address. Walking around the building, I discover a side door with a sign. *N.A. Nashist, M.D.*

The stairwell leads to a second-floor office. The reception area is pleasant and I feel relieved. It is spacious and clean, not my nightmare vision of blinds drawn on a dark room, a table strewn with sharp, unwashed instruments, bloodied sheets.

There is a skinny man sitting alone, looking at the floor, and another person with their back to me. Behind the desk, a tiny dark-skinned woman with hooded eyes motions me over and begins to speak in French.

"Je ne parle pas français," I say quickly.

"Ahh, English, yes?"

"Yes."

"And you have the money?"

"Yes." I hold up an envelope.

"When did you last bleed?" The woman sighs as though she has seen too much of this and it makes her sad. Or angry.

"October." That's not true. I can't really remember when my period stopped. It was probably mid-July or early August, although I cannot even be sure of that. Too much has happened. Too much has gone wrong.

"October, yes, and what day in October?" asks the woman, her eyes narrowing as she continues to fill out the form.

I have worked this part out in my mind. Abortions up to twelve weeks are legal in Quebec. Anything after that is illegal. And more expensive. I have only five hundred dollars. I know they will demand more if they find I am farther along. Or maybe they will refuse me altogether and call the police. I do not think about the foetus, its size or shape. I think only of myself. I must save myself.

"October fifth," I say, praying it will not make a difference, praying by the time they discover my false calculation, it will be done.

The woman refers to a chart, hidden behind a calendar advertising painkillers. She frowns and looks closely at me.

"You're on the border," she says tersely, and reaches across the counter for the envelope of money. After flipping through the bouquet of red and orange bills, she seems satisfied and tells me to sit.

"You will be called when your time comes."

The expression sounds strangely grotesque, a prophetic reminder of my own mortality. *What if my time comes here? What if I die here?* I suddenly think, as my forearms turn into uncooked turkey flesh. *Who would know how to find me?*

The room goes fuzzy and I sit quickly, putting my head down between my knees.

A voice comes from behind. "It's not that bad."

I look up to find the blonde woman from the bus. Her eyes, pale blue, are heavily ringed with black eyeliner, one stroke below the eye, one above. The eyeliner matches the colour of her hair where it has grown out at the roots. The platinum against black is shocking.

"I'm Rhonda," she says, sticking out her hand, fingernails ragged, bitten to the quick. "This is my third."

"Third? Third what?"

"Third time here. Do you want a smoke?" She holds out a package of Players. Ian's brand before my money ran out and he had to start rolling his own.

"The little boy? The one on the bus?"

"Oh, him," says Rhonda, pleased I've remembered. "He's at my mom's. She lives down this way."

"What if they call us while we're out smoking?"

"We're not going out," Rhonda snorts. "Anyways, it'll be a while. There's only the two of them and they just took some girl in bawling. Half an hour, forty-five minutes, depending on whether they vacuum or not."

Vacuum? Glancing at the desk, I see the woman is gone. The reception area is empty except for Rhonda and me. She lights a cigarette after dragging a huge, silver canister ashtray across the carpet. It is full of butts, most marked by heavy lipstick.

She nods towards a door on my left. "They lock the doors between sessions so no one can come in. I think they're afraid of a raid, eh?"

I nod dumbly, wishing to be somewhere else. What the hell does she mean, vacuum? Rhonda is enjoying her cigarette. She holds it away from her mouth and looks at it. She pulls on her cigarette suggestively.

Before I can speak, Rhonda does.

"Give me a cigarette over a john, any day. It's when some fuckin' jerk begs for something else I get in trouble. I've never been on the pill, you know? I'm afraid I'll gain weight. So I end up here. My boyfriend is paying this time though, 'cause he thinks it's his. "

Rhonda seems to want to talk, so I ask the question that's been bothering me.

"Does it hurt?"

She laughs again, stubs her cigarette against the blunt dish and buries it in the yellow-white sand.

"Nah, not really. It's like going to the dentist to get a rotten tooth out. It hurts for a while afterwards, but then you forget about it 'cause it feels so much better when it's gone. Like after a toothache, y'know. "

I do know. I know all too well.

"How come you have — kept — the boy?"

Rhonda scowls. "His daddy said it would be different. He talked about a house, a kid, a life different than this shit. But, you know what? He didn't deliver. Who the fuck does? He was history before I even popped the baby. Never even saw his own kid. Can you believe it? Fuckin' men, eh? Fuckin' assholes."

Rhonda slouches and is silent. She folds her arms across her chest and closes her eyes, deflated by our exchange. I notice a green tattoo across her upper arm. *Roger Forever* it says. I wonder if Roger is the delinquent father, the man who could spin fantasy into belief, tantalize Rhonda with a picture of a small family on a beach picnic or before a fireplace, toasting marshmallows. I think of his sugar-coated words catching fire, burning into charcoal, the bitter carbon crumbling to ash.

But his lies saved that baby.

The door opens briefly and the tiny dark-skinned receptionist walks back into the room. I think she must be East Indian and I try to imagine what she would look like in a sari or a Punjabi suit.

She takes something from her desk and without even glancing at us, leaves again.

"What about you?"

I jump. *What about me?*

"Why are you here?"

"I'm not married." I realize how ridiculous this sounds. "I mean I'm not ready to have a baby. I'm still in school. Besides, my fiancé had to go away for a while, up north, and I — we — decided I couldn't deal with a baby by myself. Right now, that is. We want kids later on, you know, when we're married and all." The lies dribble out into the empty, unbelieving space.

"Oh yeah? That's nice."

She doesn't say anything else and I am grateful. I imagine Rhonda recognizes the subtlety of half truths and knows the importance of self-deception. She lights another cigarette and leafs through a fashion magazine. The woman returns, calls her name and I am left alone with the skinny man in the waiting room.

The air feels stale and I long to be outside. Suddenly I wish I were a kid again, on the rocks, near the lake, the muskeg and the wind, the yapping of dogs, the freedom of such a long time ago. A stirring in my belly brings me back and I wonder vaguely if it could be hunger. In my pocket I have taxi fare back to the YWCA, and my room, a single, has been reserved until tomorrow morning. I feel the few remaining bills in my pocket, their substance reassuring me this will soon be over.

A young woman emerges from the back room and the skinny man across the room rushes over to her, speaks softly to her in French and supports her with his arm around her shoulders. The girl's face is hidden by greasy shoulder-length hair, and she slumps towards the exit without looking up.

I want to see her face, but she doesn't raise her eyes from the floor. The couple creeps across the room in a huddle, guarding some fragile thing at their centre. I am forced to turn away.

There is a bitter taste in my mouth now and I realize bile has risen up my throat. I am literally scared sick. Again. I am scared and alone and powerless to do anything but rise and walk with the receptionist through the swinging doors when my name is called. My time has come.

We go together down a short corridor. Someone is lying on a gurney, curled inward, fetal, doubled up and facing the wall. A blanket covers the person, but as we pass, I see the distinctive crown, black on blonde. I am led into another room that smells strongly of antiseptic.

"Please take off all your clothes, put on this gown and lie on the table," says the receptionist, thrusting a thin paper wrap towards me. "The doctor will come soon."

Her voice, authority overcome by intense and overwhelming boredom, is easy to obey, and I strip down, shedding my emotions with my clothing. I stand naked, ready.

The paper gown feels like the skin of a snake on my cold flesh. I sit on the table, mindful of the steel stirrups protruding from the end.

The doctor enters. He is a tiny man, also dark. He glances at me, and then turns to wash at a basin and draw on plastic gloves, snapping each of them like a judgment.

"You must do as I say. There will be some pain, but not too much. You must trust me. If you must cry out, please take this towel to cover your mouth. The other patients must not be alarmed. Do you understand?"

I nod and shift down on the table and spread my legs, feeling the cold instruments before they actually touch me.

Then there is pain, hot, sharp pain, a different sort of pain, deep within, shooting upwards, scalding my innards, sweeping up my back, searing my belly and my breasts. It is like nothing I have felt before, and as I stifle a shriek, sweat leaps out on my brow.

The doctor, intent, pokes and prods. At one point he mutters, curses under his breath, and calls for forceps. The foetus, like a spirit unwilling to be exorcised, is dragged from my body in small bloodied pieces, and I feel its life drain away in a hot wash of fluid.

I lie rigid with horror as the last instrument is withdrawn, as my legs, like numb phantom limbs, fall back together, as the blood is stemmed with industrial padding.

"It was too late for this. Too late. Very bad business. Very bad." He shakes his head angrily and turns away. "Get her out," he says to his assistant.

The woman is kinder. She helps me dress, pulls my pants on over thighs still faintly smeared with blood. She leads me to a gurney; the same one Rhonda occupied, and tells me to rest until I am ready to go.

"I didn't think it would be like that," I choke. "I didn't know. Please help me. Please. I'm sorry." The Indian woman stands beside me and pats my shoulder.

"Be quiet," she urges in a hoarse whisper. "It is over now. It is finished."

It is finished. Have I killed something sacred? Have I rid myself of the hope of God? I lie alone in the dim hallway, feeling wave after wave of nausea washing over me. I cannot stand, nor do I trust my legs to carry me, so I remain inert, wretched, curled on the thin mattress.

A door opens nearby and I hear the sound of liquid being poured from a great height. Without looking, I know what it is, and the sound of the toilet flushing, soon afterwards, confirms my suspicions. Like sewage, unwanted kitchen grease, table scraps, human waste, the thing is flushed away. I imagine severed arms and a limbless torso, mutilated genitals and a shattered sightless skull floating momentarily in a swirling red sea. And then, magically, mercifully, it is gone.

I rise from my pallet and find the floor, a miracle beneath my feet. Tentatively, I stand, sway slightly, and walk through the waiting room, open the heavy door and descend the stairwell to the empty wind-blown winter street.

I step forward, steadying myself against the side of the building. A bus flies by, churning up dirty snow and I feel the moisture against my burning cheeks. I walk toward the bus stop slowly, weak and slightly light-headed, afraid to move too quickly in case the world spins out of control or my guts slide down my legs to splatter on the sidewalk.

The smell of strong coffee and spices emanates from a storefront with a sign in both Arabic and French. Without hesitation, I enter, anxious to sit among people who do not know me or where I've been or what I've done.

Inside, the restaurant is dirty crimson and tarnished gold: a gypsy caravan abandoned on a street in east Montreal. The people in the room appear darkly exotic. I feel an underlying excitement here. It smells of cashews and coffee and steamed milk. A waitress in an emerald skirt flies by enveloped in a babble of language and I see it all, hear it all, the richness, the very joy and wonder of life.

A man approaches, almost dancing. He swoops low, close to my face and I smell mangoes and cigarettes on his breath.

"Une café. Forte." I don't care if my language is correct. "S'il vous plait," I add, knowing it does not matter what he brings, just that I am here and still connected to the world.

When the coffee comes in a tiny demitasse it is so perfectly bitter and potent and rich, I swallow it in two short, scalding mouthfuls. It is healing my ragged innards, cauterizing the recent wounds, and almost immediately I ask for another.

Outside the wind has dropped and snow has begun to fall in fat lazy flakes. The proprietor of the restaurant has turned on Christmas lights and tomorrow Gillian arrives from Toronto. She will bring news of the city, gifts from our overindulgent maiden aunts, who, I know, anxiously await the birth of a child to grant them a greater immortality.

Immortality. Eternal life. It is too much for me to think of now. I will go back to the YWCA. I will rest my body and purge my mind of the last few hours. I will not tell Jiggs. I will make this awful experience disappear, but now, just for these next few moments, I will gaze out the window and watch the snow fall between the coloured lights. I will sip my coffee, savour its sharp goodness, and rest in the knowledge that soon I can sleep.

The hotel Dad has booked isn't really a hotel at all. It's more of a guesthouse, one of those stately old Montreal row houses converted into a pension. It's called l'Hôtel Blanc. The White Hotel. Hotel of Purity. A Hostel for Unaccompanied Females. When I found the place earlier in the afternoon I visualized a sign in the window: Rooms for Rent. Virgins Only. Apply Within.

The landlady, or more properly the concierge, is a Madame Dupont, a friend of a friend of our father. Madame Dupont is a thin, angular woman, all starched, button-down collars, hand-knitted cardigans and grey hair wound into a tight bun and held in place by steel bobby pins. Like the people in the Arab café, she seems like a caricature of herself, wholly exaggerated.

She greets me gravely in the grey afternoon light, offering just the tips of her sticklike fingers before leading me up one flight of stairs to our assigned room. She hovers at the doorway, waiting for approval, while I enter and place my bags near the bay window.

"It's lovely," I breathe, causing Madame Dupont to nod and acquiesce, smile tightly at my obvious good taste and superior judgment.

And the room is lovely. It is filled with old furniture, pieces that could have been antiques, but lack the spindly inadequacy of antiques. Two poster beds in dark wood are covered in quilts and flanked by side tables holding squat brass and green hooded desk lamps. Striped towels are folded on cedar chests at the foot of each bed and an oval pine table occupies the space in front of a large window, facing the street but concealed by lace curtains that filter and soften the winter light.

There are flowers on the table, silk blues and purples, and a variety of writing equipment, as though any guest of l'Hôtel Blanc would have an intimate relationship with the post. Beyond the table, a wooden wardrobe separates a sitting area where two overstuffed wingbacks with worn upholstery huddle around an electric fireplace that casts feeble warmth around the high-ceilinged room. Like gigantic flightless birds, the chairs perch on the edge of a faded oriental carpet. A floor lamp stands by, ready to chase away the creeping shadows of twilight. It is a cozy Christmas retreat, and I bless my father for finding it. I am almost certain Jiggs will approve.

The first thing I notice as Gillian trips off the train is that she's wearing a man's overcoat. She looks spacey and disheveled, smiling a Cheshire cat grin as big as the boughs of plastic pine hung in the station. I'm smiling, too. I'm so glad to see her.

She carries an enormous amount of luggage, and not just one or two easily transportable bags. She has five small packages slung over various parts of her body and, strapped to her back, knapsack style, an easel, and a huge, ungainly roll of paper held together by a multitude of ribbons.

"You look like a peddler," I say after hugging her and dislodging a paunchy carpetbag. "What is all this stuff?"

"I'm going to work while I'm here. These are some of my supplies." Her smile is disarming. It's so great to see someone who's known me forever."

"I thought we were supposed to be on a holiday," I tease, starting to shoulder some of the mismatched baggage. I crouch, the stab in my womb a reminder.

She halts, mid-step, doesn't seem to notice my cringing. "I'm an artist, Ruthie. I don't holiday from my own creativity. It's fundamental to who I am and how I express my inner voice."

"Oh." I raise an eyebrow "Is that right?"

The tension walks with us as we make our way through the labyrinth of shops that spin off the central station in an underground maze. My relief at seeing my older sister has evaporated. *She might as well be French*, I think bitterly as Jiggs steams through the crowds, elbowing her way past last-minute shoppers.

She turns back to me, her easel barely missing a woman in a fur coat, who mutters some curse in French. "So where is this place?"

"Off de la Montagne." I take the lead as we make our way up the stairs into the city, "It's nice, really old-fashioned, but nice."

Now, heading back to the hotel, I'm not quite so confident that Gillian will like it. My sister is dressed oddly, artistically, I assume. She may balk at the faded, floral gentility of the room. But Jiggs does like the room and she settles in right away, setting up her easel by the window, bouncing on both massive beds and even turning on the taps in the tiny en suite bathroom.

"We have a bidet!" she shouts, laughing and drawing a bottle of wine from the depths of one of her packs. She flushes the bidet and mimics putting the wine in the low basin.

"Ah, Jiggs, I don't know if that's the best place..."

"Just kidding, Ruth. It's so gauche. Don't you think?"

So unsanitary. I bite my tongue so as not to spoil my sister's pleasure.

"Colin gave me this before I left. It's a Christmas present. For us." Smiling, she fills the sink and partially submerges the bottle. "He told me to drink it on the train. Share it with some handsome stranger, he said, but, you know, I don't think he meant it. The handsome stranger part. I think he really wanted me to drink it with you."

"Who is this guy?"

Jiggs shrugs. "Colin? He's a friend, sometimes a lover. We hook up once in a while."

"You what?"

"Sleep together. You know, have sex. Com'on, Toothie, stop looking so shocked. You remind me of Elsie."

I try to readjust my face.

"You're careful, aren't you?"

"Oh God, Ruthie, of course we're careful. We take precautions." She draws out the long-sounding *aw* sound, twangs the second syllable in a mock Texan accent.

"Why, it would take a mindless bimbo some doing to get knocked up these days, what with our little white pills. Or, maybe down your way, in the back of beyond, they haven't discovered birth control yet and they're still using the quick draw method." She mimes a gun being drawn from a holster and falls laughing on the bed. "Gotcha."

"I just didn't know you were involved with anyone."

"I'm not really," says Jiggs, suddenly serious. "I can't afford to lose my focus right now. A relationship would just suck the energy out of my art. Colin's just a friend."

"A friend you have sex with?"

"Yeah. Any objections?"

Don't get pregnant, I think, but I keep my mouth closed.

"What about you?" Jiggs asks innocently, taking a crumpled blouse out of her pack and trying to smooth it with her hands. "Any new men in your life?"

"No," I say, "nobody special."

We decide to go out then to eat and find some entertainment for the evening. I suggest a movie. The thought of settling into a dark theatre and watching something impossibly sentimental to get rid of this obstructed grief is enormously appealing, but I'm overruled by Jiggs.

So we go out into the unfamiliar streets of downtown Montreal, Jiggs full of a restless, churning energy and me trailing behind, beleaguered by my red weeping womb and a false sense of cheer.

I want a dim, calm, candles-on-the-table restaurant and Jiggs wants somewhere upbeat, with slick, sexy waiters and jazz playing in the background. We finally settle on a busy restaurant off the main street called Le Palais d'Or. It's got both candles and live music but at least the server is not pretending he wants to be our new best friend.

"Allo, beautiful woman," he greets us. "You like, ah, cocktails?"

Jiggs orders something called a Greyhound and I choose a virgin Caesar because I can't think of anything more exotic. The drinks come, elaborately adorned, and Jiggs snaps hers back quickly.

"Hair of the dog," she grins. "I've been wanting that all day. A bunch of us went out last night and really tied one on. I've been suffering since I woke up this morning."

"Feeling better now?"

"I'll feel great in a sec." She dips into her bag, removing a tiny enamel box. She extracts two small black pills, and rolls them in her palm. "I use these beans as a pick-me-up when my energy is down. They help me paint."

That's it, of course. The pills explain the huge dilated pupils, the vacant look in her eyes, the way she's lost so much weight and the fierce, wiry energy that seems to push her along.

"What are they?"

"Beauties. Black Beauties. They're just a cheap upper."

"You don't need them."

Jiggs laughs as if I've made some outrageously funny faux pas.

"Of course I don't. You're so right, I don't need them." She leans across the table, rolling her eyes around in her head and sticking out her lower jaw so her teeth protrude horribly. "What do you think I am, Ruthie? A drug addict? There's a difference between what you need and what you want, silly."

"These," she says, throwing the pills back with a great gulp of the second Greyhound, "I want. They're a harmless little boost, that's all."

Maurice the waiter materializes, and we order, suddenly civilized and proper in the presence of a stranger, and the meal, when it comes, is consumed with little conversation. Jiggs picks at her food, moving it around on her plate in a charade of eating, her head turned towards the band that is playing an old Miles Davis tune.

The sax solo is slow and I feel a great gulf separating me from my sister. I am also finding it difficult to eat. Everything tastes flat and bland. In part it's the teeth, which Jiggs hasn't even noticed or at least commented on, but I feel as though my taste buds have been scraped from my mouth and replaced with cardboard. There is also a lump in my throat I cannot dissolve no matter what I swallow.

We don't linger. When Maurice comes to take away our plates, we pay the bill and leave quickly, neither of us sorry the supper is over.

Back on the street, there is a moment of indecision.

"Why don't we just walk?"

And so we do. Trudging side by side, we navigate the icy streets of Montreal, each absorbed in our own thoughts. My body aches. My belly feels like it's been hollowed out, like the seeds have been scooped out of a not quite ripe melon.

Somewhere in the distance, there is the sound of a choir singing and, without acknowledging it, we walk towards the voices, drawn to the faintly familiar strands of Christmas music.

The sound — hundreds of voices singing Handel's *Messiah* — is coming from a huge stone church and both of us pause on the sidewalk outside the arched stone doorway, caught in the majesty of the song.

"Let's go in. It's just started. Come on." Jiggs pulls me towards the broad frost-worn steps. I hesitate — *Hallelujah. Hallelujah* — then follow.

Inside the church, it is warm and close, smelling of wet wool and bodies pressed tightly together, many swaying to the swell of the music, which swirls and dips and soars again, enveloping and transporting the congregation. The dappled light of hundreds of candles adds to the magic of the room. Beside me, Jiggs has closed her eyes and stands with her face upturned towards the music.

She suddenly looks very young to me, beautiful in the candlelight. As the *Gloria*s sound again and the trumpets take up the triumphant refrain, I know we are forgiven everything. Everything, that is, except the silence, the lies of omission, which keep us separate and very much apart.

I go to see Ian for the final time in the spring, one year after our first fateful meeting. Something is driving me. Something unexplained, unfinished, is compelling me to go. I've been picked up by a van driven by an Elizabeth Fry volunteer, who looks suspiciously like a nun out of habit. *A nun out of the habit. Ha.* I smile to myself. Most nuns must be out of the habit.

I've prepared an answer for anyone who asks me why I'm going on this prison visit. It's not the answer that's ringing inside my skull, the answer that lives where the baby used to live. I whisper it to myself as if to test its validity as the van speeds towards Dorchester, Canada's oldest and bleakest maximum security prison. Even when I whisper my reasons out loud, my stomach lurches and I feel sick and lightheaded. My body, since the trip to Montreal and the fake Christmas cheer with Jiggs, is not behaving the way it used to.

The hollow sick feeling persists as the miles fall away. The other women in the van sit silently engrossed in their own private thoughts. I have one night ahead of me. I don't have to go to the prison until tomorrow. I feel like I'm coming down with the flu and I need a good sleep before I face Ian.

I plan to be perfectly composed when I sit before him, but I don't feel composed now. I feel carsick, heartsick. I know that if he finds out about the baby, and what I did to it, he will kill me. He cannot know. I need time to become composed, to recompose, to create a believable fiction. The night with the nuns is my reprieve.

One of them is on the porch of the old house when the van pulls up. The other women seem to have other places to go, and I am the only one who gets out. The nun and the driver speak to each other, quietly. I can't hear their words, although I assume they are discussing what time I should be picked up tomorrow. I'm glad other people have arranged things. The less detail I have to think about, the better. This is my garden of Gethsemane, I think. This is the time I need to get myself prepared.

The nun approaches, holding out a hand. "I'm Sister Marie-Claire," she says. "You are welcome here."

"Thanks. I'm Ruth Callis." I look around at the grounds, trying to think of something else to say. "I just have to visit somebody."

"Yes, of course. We often have prison visitors as our guests. Have you been there before?"

I shake my head and cast my eyes down to the crumbling cement walkway. The nun points north as she leads me up the steps.

"Dorchester is that way. It's less than two miles from here. Sometimes we walk."

I say nothing, but look in the direction she has indicated. All I see is a lilac bush, stripped bare of blooms, and beyond that, a few other older houses facing the sea. I can't see the prison.

"It's pretty here."

"Yes, we find it very peaceful. It's quiet, especially now before the summer, but our work keeps us busy."

For the first time, I look at the nun, who has paused in the wide foyer and stretched out her hand for my coat. I'm surprised to find the face of a woman not much older than me, with lively hazel eyes and a smattering of freckles across the bridge of her nose. As she smiles, the white headdress, the scapular and the flowing black skirts fade. "Marie-Claire. Are you French?"

"Acadian. My parents are from the North Shore. Do you know Bathurst?"

"No. I'm not really from around here."

God, I sound so vague and noncommittal.

"I used to go to university in the city, and my parents live in Ontario, but I'm actually from the north. Or, at least, I used to be." I don't even know where I'm from anymore.

"Ahh, a citizen of the world." She smiles, releasing me from more explanations.

"Yeah, I guess."

The nun leads me up a staircase to a different, broader landing. The wide, dark hallway is carpeted in a moss green short shag that absorbs the fall of our feet. She opens one of many doors, which leads to a second, narrower staircase.

"We gave you the room at the top of the house so you can see the ocean." The sister pauses as I take in the stark, small room with its single bed, solitary reading lamp, and straight-backed chair by the front window. It's bright compared to the gloom below.

"There's a widow's walk off this room," said the nun, indicating the four windows. "The view is quite magnificent. This used to be the home of a sea captain. Apparently, his only son wanted to become a priest, but he was killed in the first war. Years ago, the old man left the house to the Church in his memory."

"This is great."

She suddenly becomes businesslike.

"It's warm up here," she says, pushing up a side window.. "Have you had supper?"

I nod.

"Well, we breakfast at 5:30 and have morning prayer at seven o'clock. You can join us for either or both, as you choose. We will go to the prison at 9:30 tomorrow morning after matins and morning devotion. Sister Monica is the chaplain. She'll show you where to go and what to do. Between now and then, you're free to do as you wish."

"Thanks." I drop my shoulder bag to the floor. "I'll wash up and maybe go for a walk."

"Very well."

Together we descend the stairs. The nun opens a door on the second-floor landing and shows me the bathroom. Nodding her head slightly and smiling, she turns and seems to float down the second set of stairs into the main part of the house, leaving me alone. The heavy wooden doors, all closed except for the one in front of me, march backwards down the dim hallway. They remind me of something, some other place, but I can't remember what or where.

There is an old house smell in this place too, of wood rot and damp, and something else. In the bathroom with the door closed I identify the faint, musky odour. It's the fuggy smell of women living together, so synchronized they all bleed at the same time. A big box of sanitary napkins is stashed under the sink, along with spare rolls of toilet paper and cleaning supplies, and there are suspicious-looking uniform bundles in the trash, each wrapped in white toilet paper.

They don't have babies, yet they bleed. Here is the evidence of the baby-less brides of Christ. I am shocked. It is too human thinking of these virgin brides of Christ bleeding, their soiled pads wrapped in paper, clean and white on the outside, red and bloodied within.

The only one to ever have a baby was the Madonna, the Mother of them all.

I sit on the toilet and notice a crucifix hanging on the wall directly across from me. It's Christ hanging on the cross, dead. It's the perfect sacrifice, the perfect denial of self.

Without thought, but with a fury that rises out of nowhere, I grab the crucifix and tear it off the wall. It comes off easily, too easily. Drywall breaks and powders on my shoes. There is a gaping hole in the wall, black and yawning. Behind are studs and condensation and mildew and rot, but the thing in my hand is still perfect. I madly wrap the crucifix in toilet paper and heave it into the garbage with the other neat bundles of discarded and disguised menstrual pads. They'll have to open them all, everyone single one, to find the bloodless body on the cross.

My body is trembling now and an impossible rage is upon me in that small bathroom in the nuns' house.

I am muttering out loud. "I hate you. I hate you." I hiss the words to Ian, and to God, and to the bloodied baby I could not love, could never save. My anger is growing, leaping like a fire suddenly alight. It fills the room and my body begins to vibrate, out of control. This time I am in it, present in my own body, feeling my own feelings, occupying myself completely. *It hurts. It hurts. It still hurts. I will not forgive. I am not a sacrifice, I am not a fucking martyr, I am not, will never be, selfless.*

The bathroom is small and close and moving. It's vibrating with all the anger coming out of my mouth, oozing out of my pores, boiling up out of my subconscious like a living thing that can no longer be contained. It feels so good, so liberating, to at last let out my unvoiced rage, and pain and grief. It feels so good, I begin to moan, louder and louder still, until the moaning becomes a language of its own, and I'm shouting and I hear the sound of footsteps hastening up the stairs.

When the nuns approach, I fall silent for a moment. I can feel myself swallowing the emotion. It's exactly what I don't want to do. They knock on the door of the bathroom calling, "Are you all right?" "Is everything okay?" I hold my breath, and when the doorknob turns and they pour into the small room, I grab the wrapped pads and hurl them into the air.

They fly up and begin to unravel, streamers of toilet paper, flapping and sinking and coming undone in great swirls of white and red.

"We're human," I shout. "Human. We bleed. We bleed." I scrabble through the trash bin, grabbing more and more of the bundles, whipping them into the air, flailing and throwing the sanitary napkins into the faces of the startled nuns.

"It hurts," I cry, frantically looking for the mummified icon. "It hurts. Don't you know? He hurt me. He did. It hurt. Why did He say it wouldn't hurt?"

I find the crucifix and quickly twist it out of its sterile paper cocoon. I hold the crucified Jesus up in front of their faces, moving it up and down back and forth in the sign of some clumsy cross.

"Liar," I cry, laughing hysterically now. "It's not my fault. It was a lie. We all bleed. Look. Look. Look at these." I kick at one of the fully opened pads, its menstrual blood exposed.

I see flashes of Dr. Gartenberg and Zelda and Ian and someone who is either Frobisher or the Captain. I see all the co-op roommates, Brian and Lisa and Donny and Kevin, sitting in tiny desks while Mr. Jamison and Miss Gordon ask

Miriam Cohen to spit her teeth into a golden bowl. Angela Thompson is laughing even though Kassie and Skaw are biting her ankles and Billy Goodyear is dancing around in her ankle blood while Mrs. Bagthea speaks in tongues to the Elders, Brother Terry and Brother Vic.

"It hurts. It hurts," I howl to this shifting of faces and voices that have lived inside of me for so long. "It's not my fault."

"No, no, it's not your fault." This is the only voice that penetrates, the only one that reaches me through my momentary madness, as the anger and crazy need to shout dissipates as quickly as it came. I am left weak and panting, slouched against the cool tiled walls of the bathroom. Toilet paper and menstrual pads are strewn about the room. The crucifix lies face down on the floor.

"Help her upstairs," says an older nun, one I haven't seen before. Her face goes in and out of focus as I try to stand. Someone helps me up, brushes off the bits of toilet paper that have landed and tangled in my hair.

"I'm okay now."

I feel suddenly clear and focused, confined only by all these women in this one small room. They crowd around me.

"I need some air." And they nod and murmur and slowly leave the bathroom and regroup like fluttering crows on the landing, excited by this unbridled display of emotion.

Sister Marie-Claire comes forward. There is a scratch down one side of her cheek and a swatch of red hair has come loose from her hairpiece and curls on the calm plane of her forehead. "Let's go upstairs," she says gently. "Let's go upstairs, Ruth, and we'll get you settled."

Amazingly, the room is as I left it. My bag still sits where I dropped it on the floor, and the bed still stands, blankets smooth and untouched. But everything seems altered. It has all changed. I go to the open window and stand looking out, letting the sea breeze cool my face. I see the sun still anchored in the sky. Shifting my vision across the backyards and alleys,

I can see the rolled barbed-wire walls of Dorchester Penitentiary in the distance.

I look briefly at those insurmountable walls and turn away. The door is closed. The nun has gone. I go slowly to the straight-backed chair and pull it across the room and sit at the window facing the sea. I see it all, the four panes of glass, an empty cross, and, beyond, only ocean. I feel something move inside me, filling me where the emptiness has been for so long. Like the swell of the sea, barely visible from this height, I feel peace descend. I have told the truth and the truth has set me free.

Men and women are allowed to kiss and embrace but not for more than half a minute. Each chair is to be occupied by one and only one person with the exception of babies and toddlers. Fathers can hold their small children for the duration, but each child will be subject to a body search both before and after the visit. No loud voices, no sudden movement, no body rubbing, necking or sexual touching. Nothing can pass between the prisoner and the visitor.

After each statement, we nod. I am one of a group, all women and children. A female guard has frisked every one of us. Two women are on conjugal visits. They'll go to one of two trailers set up for a night of pretend normal life, sex and smoking and more sex. They are asked to stand aside while the rest of us are led to a large steel door with a small window.

The visitor room is a small space with very high ceilings. This windowless area has eight orange tables and thirty-two blue plastic chairs bolted to the floor. On a metal catwalk suspended above, two armed guards pace, back and forth, back and forth, their eyes trained on the reunions below.

I pause just inside the door, uncertain, edgy, unwittingly moving my weight from foot to foot, trying to act like everything is normal. He's not there. People near me are embracing. Children cling to their fathers. One woman is sobbing. I feel my shoulder blades high inside my coat and hear the thunk, thunk, thunk of my ridiculous heart. I look towards a door on the other side of the room, expecting him to come through, so when he walks into the visitation area through the same door as I did, I am half turned away.

He comes up from behind and lays his hand on my shoulder. I start and whirl around. It's him. Ian, older, sadder, but it's him.

He steps back, also startled and we stare at each other, eyes locked. Finally, I put out my hand in a tentative, formal greeting. I can tell he wants to hug me, but despite all the others hugging and touching in the room, I don't want that.

My hand dangles in the air between us and he looks from my hand to my face and back to my extended hand again. Just when I'm sure he won't, he takes it. Our touch is brief and I pull away, suddenly feeling like my knees won't bear my weight. I sink into the nearest chair and he, too, draws himself down to the chair beside me.

I am so grateful for the little orange triangle of table between us. It gives me room to breathe, to actually see him.

He looks the same, same injured eyes, same crooked half smile, same broad shoulders, a little more stooped now, a little less cocky.

"How, how are…?" he starts, but his voice falters and he coughs instead.

"Fine." I don't drop my eyes. "I've come to tell you something."

"Oh." He must know. He starts fidgeting, tapping his fingers on the tabletop. I feel like an executioner, resigned, determined and with such resolve that there is no room for pity. I breathe deeply and look down so he will not see the flash of anger that's still there. There is a moment of awkward silence.

"What do you want to say?"

I look up at him again, into his blue, blue eyes, those earnest, blue eyes. He is afraid of what's coming. I must not delay.

"I have to go away. I won't be coming back. I'm done. I'm done with you."

"What do you mean, done?" His face is a mask. I can't see anger, or misery, or anything. He's gone inside himself.

I continue: "I have to feel again. I have to learn how to feel again. I'm taking myself back, Ian. I don't know if you can understand, but I need to take myself back. And I'm doing it."

"So you won't be coming back here?" He can only see how this will affect him. He doesn't get it. But it doesn't matter if he gets it. This is not about him.

"No. I'm not coming back."

"And afterwards?"

"There is no afterwards."

He can see there is no room in it, no movement, no second chance, so he tries another tack. He leans back in his chair, folds his arms. "I see. So why the hell did you come, eh? Just to tell me I'm cut?"

"Yes, and to tell you what a bastard you were for hurting me. I didn't deserve what you did to me, you know. You chose to do that. I don't know why. That's up to you, but as far as I'm concerned, it's over now. You can't hurt me anymore. You can't touch me. I'm forgiving you. And, you know what? I'm forgiving myself. I am forgiving what happened between us. There."

His eyes close. "You better go."

He leans further back in his chair, away from me, and I study his face for the last time, before standing to leave. There is no malice there, no tenderness either. He is simply a weary man, a person I used to know.

When he feels my weight shift away, however, his eyes fly open and I can still see them pleading.

"Ruthie? Ruth?"

I pause for a moment, standing over him. This time he extends his hand, palm up, and closes his eyes again. I lay my hand briefly on his wrist where his own white scars run brilliant traces across his flesh. There is a moment of warmth, skin on skin, and then I turn and walk away. As the heavy door closes between us, I carry that image in my mind, him sitting alone at the orange table amid all the kissing families, his head back, his eyes closed, his arm slightly raised and his single hand splayed open and harmless.

John Wesley Callis, my dad, died within three years of coming up to the surface. He died without knowing what happened to me and for that I will always be grateful. It would have shattered him to know I was hurt, because I was still his sparkly little tooth child when his heart exploded in the bathroom of the administration block of the Sudbury nickel mine. It's an undignified place to die, perhaps, but because of my significant experience in that other bathroom, it doesn't bother me.

I try to imagine how it happened. He must have felt some discomfort, some buzzing, numbness, or just something strange going on below his carefully pressed shirt. He must have wanted to loosen his collar, or have a drink, I don't know. But by the time Elsie called me, it was over. Over before they loaded him into the ambulance, actually. I am glad he didn't suffer.

We all came back, of course, Claire with her kids, and Theresa with her second husband and his son, and Luke and Jiggs and I. Jiggs came from New York where she lives with another woman and Luke from Japan where he is in some sort of spiritual community. But, hey, who am I to judge? I'm the queen of cults, the silent queen.

The one thing we did talk about was Elsie, about who would look after her now that Dad was gone. The older girls had families, Luke had his Buddhist thing and, according to Jiggs, who was about to shatter the glass ceiling of the New York art scene, I was the likely candidate.

After my silent and brutal trip to Montreal I'd picked up where I'd left off at St. Thomas, trying to raise my marks enough to keep the scholarship fund flowing. Everything felt more difficult, grey and hazy and sadly purposeless. I took some courses over again, the ones I'd blown off in the summer and could not attempt in the fall. I juggled a few electives and even started a couple of classes that would count towards my final degree, but I no longer knew what it was I wanted. I felt like I was driving down an endless gravel road that last semester prior to my final visit with Ian. It would have gone on forever, too, that hopeless road and feeling of moving forward but going nowhere had it not been for the for the unexpected phone call and the devastating news of my father's sudden death.

It was as though Dad's death were part of my destiny, and even though it was the worst possible thing, the most excruciating thing, his death galvanized me. It provided a destination. Dorchester, St. Thomas, any hope of an academic future, I left them all behind and I went back home.

We all know Elsie hasn't long to live, and any move into caregiving has a definite end date. Actually, no one speaks that last part out loud, but it is implied. Elsie had been diagnosed with a neurological disease a year earlier. It was around the same time they had come to visit me in the Maritimes. A farewell trip, I guess, to see all their grown-up children. Was Dad touring Elsie around while she was still well enough to enjoy it? Funny, it was supposed to be her going first, and Dad beat her to it. The race to the finish is close. Elsie's already in a wheelchair, hopping mad and spitting bullets. But her language has started to go, too. We notice slurring around the edges of her words already.

Ama-th-ing Gra-ce, she sings loudly at Dad's funeral, a hunched elderly widow, classically in black, singing from her wheelchair adjacent to the front pew. I wonder if she's claiming it for herself, the Grace, but I don't really know. I know Luke is right, and it won't be long before Elsie joins her beloved John in the great beyond.

"*Ith ik been breed ive.*" It's like being buried alive, she tells me one evening, after the national news, with the long night still ahead of us. And, all I can do is nod, yes, yes, while my glued-together heart cracks open a little more.

But there is mending, too. It's a funny thing, that. The really awful work: the bowel and catheter care, the turning of Elsie's body and the dressing of the inevitable bedsores, become a gift. I am able to take her down that final road slowly, in acts of real service, knowing that she is navigating so much more than I. The transfers to the commode, the terrible feeding tube, the struggle to void, the tears of frustration coursing down her wrinkled old cheeks, the dressings, the home care nurses who come at last and speak to me in whispers, all these terrible things are punctuated by moments of great beauty.

"See the apricot tree, Mom? The one Dad planted when you bought this place? It's blooming. I think this year there might be fruit," and Elsie's eyes smile because her mouth muscles can't do it anymore.

And because she can't speak, I do. About Ian. About God. About everything. Sometimes she vibrates with anger, sometimes her eyes well with pity. Sometimes I wonder if she isn't blaming herself, but I am careful to let her know that it was my decision to remain silent. It was me who chose not to tell.

I brush her hair, and kiss her each night, wondering if I haven't burdened her too much. But she reassures me *No* and the next time she is strong enough, I tell a bit more. Elsie is hungry to hear everything. Towards the end, when she dozes most of the day, I sit beside her and, accompanied by the steady drip and whir of the IV feeding machine, I hold her hand and whisper prayers.

Oh, God of life, we thank You. Sweet Lord, here is Your faithful servant, flawed but ready. Forgive us our shortcomings and gather us under Your trusted wings. Those are my prayers now, simple, heartfelt. I offer them up under my breath while Elsie sleeps in her chair and the sunlight streams in through the windowpanes.

There is some pain, but it is not from the shutting down of her body. Dental care has been difficult and at last I locate a dentist who will come to the house to help my mother with the pools of saliva that form in her mouth, threatening to drown her.

I go for a walk the afternoon the dentist arrives, mostly because I badly need a break and because the home care nurses are coming more often. They come Tuesday and Thursday afternoons, Wednesday morning and at least one night shift on the weekends so I can sleep through the night and ignore the buzzer we have attached to the bed near her feeble bony hand.

That walk is so lovely. It is fall again, seasons away from the autumn of my fall from grace, and the leaves are struggling mightily to stay on the trees. Already a carpet of maples, oak, beech, chestnut and elm leaves line the curbs and flutter across the sidewalks. I stay away longer than I mean to, walking and walking and feeling the sun on my face, thinking about Elsie and Dad and yes, Ian. I wonder about death, where you go, what happens, and I marvel at the fact that I didn't die, that my spirit refused death and that now, like the Dorchester nuns and the Australian thrift shop workers, the Saint Vincent de Paul people, I have this time to give something back to Elsie, who loved me despite it all.

At the house, the strange black Buick reminds me of the dental work and I rush inside, concerned that something has happened. The dentist is there, and the nurses, sitting around the kitchen table speaking softly.

"Is everything all right?" I poke my head into Elsie's room and she looks peaceful, asleep.

"We were waiting for you to get back, Ruth, to have a word."

I sit at the table, pulling the jacket from my shoulders, leaning forward.

"What happened?"

Pam, the day nurse, puts her hand over mine. "It was hard on your mom, Ruthie. Dr. Black didn't feel she should undergo extractions but I'm afraid a lot of her molars were terribly weakened by the constant acidity and, well, they just fell out when he started his examination."

She pushes forward a vial with Elsie's teeth, three of them. It brings back such terrible memories, I want to bolt. But I don't. I just sit, staring at the vial. The dentist speaks.

"I've left some topical cream for pain relief and you can give her painkillers, but, given her state of health, I'm sorry, I don't think your mother needs the trauma of extractions. The nerves are mostly gone due to her condition, so there won't be a lot of pain, very little sensation. It's a great mercy. I'll come again if you need me, but I honestly don't think…" and his voice trails off, the inevitable unmentioned.

"Thank you." I look at the three of them, caring professionals, and I am so grateful for their help. "Thank you."

I show them out and go to sit with Elsie as the day fades into twilight. She looks small and shriveled and there is dried blood at the corner of her mouth.

"Oh, Elsie," I breathe. "Oh, Mom," and I touch my own lips to her mouth, taste that faint saltiness of blood and then I lay my head on her skinny chest, as her barely audible heart flutters in its bone cage.

The buzzer doesn't sound that night and in the morning, I wake with a start, knowing I am too well rested. I force myself to stay under the covers a few extra moments. Even without creeping down the hallway, without poking my head into her room, I already know she has escaped.

I stay in Sudbury. Dad and Elsie's house sells and from the estate I receive a small inheritance. It is enough to buy a small townhouse. I find a part-time job in a used bookstore owned by two gay men, Grant and Alistair. Neither seems to care about making a big profit. They tell me they opened the bookstore because the moonscape of Sudbury drove them to it.

"It's because Sudbury needed books, honey," explains Grant, fixing green tea in the back of the shop amid boxes and boxes of dusty paperbacks. "There wasn't a bookstore in the whole town when we first came. Can you believe that?" And because they sense that I *can* believe it, they hire me three days and two evenings a week. It gives me just enough cash to be able to enroll in classes through distance education. I am determined to finish my degree.

Three and a half years into my new job, something happens.

I am driving across town to a place called Hope Mission. Occupying the front passenger seat of Elsie's old car are three economy-size jars of dill pickles. In the trunk I have boxes and boxes of sandwiches. It is Sunday morning and I am going to downtown Sudbury to serve lunch.

I've never been to the Hope Mission before. I am going as a volunteer. I'm not witnessing, I'm not testifying. I'm doing something useful — handing out sandwiches to people who are hungry.

The Sunday morning streets of the inner city are nearly deserted. There is a *No Knives* sign posted at the entrance to the Cecil Hotel. Below the sign, there is a figure passed out against the building. The parking lot of the XXX Video World is empty, except for a woman working the corner. She looks fortyish, almost twice my age. Her high cheekbones betray her aboriginal heritage. I'd like to think she's out buying milk for her morning coffee or for her kid's Cheerios, but I know that's not the case. I remember the working girls up north, the ones I tried to save. The woman glances at me and turns away.

I find the Hope Mission and slow the car, rolling down the window to speak to a man standing outside.

"I've got food here," I tell him. "Donations. I'm also volunteering. Where should I go?"

He tells me to back down a ramp so others can unpack the trunk. I hit the curb twice trying to maneuver Elsie's big Chrysler down the narrow driveway.

Another group of men carries my boxes of food into the building, and, one of them, a great hulk of a man with squinty eyes, tells me to park around the back of the building and enter on the other side, through a steel door. A skinny guy in a down vest materializes as soon as I enter the building. He has sandy blond hair and an open face. He doesn't look much older then me.

"Hi," he says, thrusting out his hand. "I'm Steve. I'm one of the coordinators. Are you with a group? You are...?"

"I'm Ruth Callis," I tell him. "I'm not with anyone. No organization, that is. I just saw your sign on a community bulletin board and thought maybe I could help."

He looks at me more closely then. "That's great. We hardly ever see people our age around here. It's more church ladies and charity groups. You know, the middle class, middle-age women with lots of time on their hands. It's great to have you."

He leads me inside the building and immediately down an elevator to the basement where the collected food will be distributed. The building feels fortified, the food held under tight security. In a large dining hall in the dimly lit basement, a woman named Monica is herding other volunteers into a corner. Monica introduces herself as the coordinator of today's lunches. She is large and loud and imposing. She barks orders to four or five minions. I look for Steve but he's gone. Monica's face is the colour of borscht, and she is mildly perspiring. She is gentler with the volunteers but I can't help wondering about her blood pressure.

A group of people starts to unwrap the donated sandwiches and place four halves on each paper plate; two meat, one egg and one fish. I follow with a slice of cheese and a chocolate. Steve comes around, and starts stacking the plates five high and carrying them to a holding zone. He pauses in his work when he gets to me. "You doing okay?" I'm touched by his concern and then realize it's probably because it's my first time helping. The other volunteers seem to know what they're doing.

A woman in a white tunic interrupts our work. She calls all the volunteers together. "We will feed 370 people today," she says. "It's the worst week. Welfare cheques don't come out until next weekend. Expect a crowd." She attempts a smile but it is simply lips flattened across teeth. I think she looks tired, stretched.

We continue making the sandwiches plates. Another group of volunteers behind me is cutting raw vegetables, slicing pickles, and arranging huge platters of fruit. Coffee is perking in a 400-cup urn. Juice, too, is being made in enormous vats. Sweets, donated by various bakeries, are displayed in two large cardboard boxes. Sticky buns, muffins, brownies and monster-sized cookies give the cardboard a pleasant oily fragrance. I assume the baking is day-old but nothing looks stale or unappetizing. This is good food.

A commotion at one end of the room breaks my routine. One of the workers is pushing a table around and swearing at Monica, the same broad woman who told me what to do.

"If you can't take it, Marco, just leave," she says, pointing towards a door. "We don't need your griping." Her face is redder still, her voice loud. Marco slinks into the kitchen. The robed woman comes over, the one who told us to expect crowds, and the two women speak to each other in low tones. I keep one eye on the huddled conversation, sort of hoping to see the blond guy appear. He doesn't.

All of us turn back to our business. We're running low on cheese sandwiches and we're out of egg salad. Every time I think we've finished, more empty plates appear.

"You gotta stack the sandwiches flat," says a man with a pocked face and grey, greased-back hair. "And I hope to hell this isn't peanut butter. Don't you know that people are allergic to that shit?" I'm not sure if he's talking to me or not, but he starts pawing the sandwiches, examining them to make sure none are peanut butter.

I see the man Marco muttering to himself as he lays out more plates. I decide to speak: "It's great you do this," I say, by way of encouragement. "This is important work and I'll bet you don't hear too many thank-yous." He looks at me briefly, and then grunts. I can tell he's been on the streets himself and he's only a hair's breadth from walking back to their cold comfort.

"She's a bitch," he says, of Monica. "She's always ordering us around."

I don't say anything. All organizations have personality problems. Why would I expect this street mission to be any different?

There's a flurry of activity, a last-minute rush before we're called to a church service upstairs. The eight or so other volunteers and I file into the clanking elevator. In the small chapel we take our places near the back.

You have to be sober to come to the Sunday morning service but I think some of the people gathered on the folding chairs are still feeling the effects of the night before. There is a strong odour of unwashed bodies, stale pee and cologne. Most of the congregation are First Nations people. The volunteers from churches stand out, pale and neatly dressed.

Our voices, accompanied by a single guitar, sound reedy and thin as the late morning light pours in the large window, barred on the outside. From it I can see a huge group of people milling around outside the Mission, waiting for lunch. We carry on singing. *Blessed are poor in spirit, for theirs is the kingdom of God.*

Back downstairs Monica assigns me a station. My job is to hand out the plates of sandwiches. A woman in a stylish wool jacket next to me introduces herself. "I'm Margaret, a parishioner at St. Faith's," she explains. "My job is to stamp hands." She has short-cropped grey hair. Her eyes are shining. She looks luminous and very, very alive.

"I'm Ruth. I'm not from a church. I just thought I'd give a hand. There seem to be so many more homeless…"

Monica interrupts. She's giving us last-minute instructions: "Give only one plate each. If they come for seconds they can have two half sandwiches, but not on a plate, only on a napkin. And don't let them try and tell you they've got a sick wife or a crippled child or a needy friend waiting outside. Only those who stand in line get food."

Marco's right. Monica is bossy. She jabs her finger in the air for emphasis when she mentions the various ruses employed to get extra food.

"It seems like we have lots," I say, indicating the stacks of hundreds of plates as she brushes past me.

"Have you ever done this before?" she counters.

I fall silent.

The people on juice and coffee detail are getting similar instructions. Monica's voice overrides everything. "Only fill up the mugs a little over halfway. Don't give refills until everyone has been through the line at least once. Ready, people? We're going to open the doors."

A split second later the people come down the stairs, a great tidal wave of humanity. Men, women, and children, hundreds of them, form a line to the left of me and I begin to distribute the sandwiches. At first I murmur a few words with each plate passed out — *Bon Appetit* or *Enjoy* — but I stop after a few people look at me quizzically. *What's that mean?* Some even turn up their lips, scornfully. Do I sound pretentious?

Margaret is the only one ahead of me in the lineup. She is stamping hands and I can tell some of the owners of the hands don't want them stamped. One man, with a nose like a pitted blood orange, is muttering under his breath by the time he gets to me. "Fucking bitch. White trash bitch," he mumbles, grabbing the plate of sandwiches from me. I can't believe he's talking about little Margaret, the church lady, who blithely carries on, smiling up at the people in line, taking their hands, speaking jovially to them like some benevolent Sunday school teacher. She is perfectly oblivious to whatever offence she has caused.

Every third person in the line tells me they are allergic to fish. Monica says the people must accept what they're given, so, even though I want to, I don't switch sandwiches for them. Instead, I watch as they begin pitching their tuna sandwiches into a large trashcan. I'm horrified.

All the sandwiches made of healthy brown breads — the ryes, the multi-grains — are regarded with suspicion. Everyone wants white bread. Plates that hold only half a sandwich in white bread are rejected. "How do you expect us to eat this crap?" one woman mutters, as she drags two children through the food line.

I think of the three loaves of sandwiches I'd made up at home. I'd used twelve-grain bread, good Dijon mustard, low-fat mayonnaise, and lettuce, carefully washed and separated. I'd put two slices of roast beef, and a sprinkling of salt and pepper on each sandwich. But despite my effort, it isn't what is needed at the Hope Mission. I watch as the lettuce is inevitably taken out, the mustard scraped off, the healthy bread left half eaten.

What did I expect? Gratitude? Humility? Did I expect to be thanked?

The line is interminable. The room is hot. Some man is dancing a crazy jig beside the juice urn and I am worried about running out of food. Why did I come here?

Suddenly Steve is beside me, reaching in front of me, taking my place passing out sandwiches. "Let me give you a hand, Ruth," he says softly, as though he somehow knows I'm exasperated. I take a half step back and watch him. He looks every person in the eye, the same way he looked at me when I first came in. He gives them their food gravely, as a simple gift. It seems nothing that the people in the line say or do can lessen the gift of food. The grace, I see, is in the giving. I can see it in this man's face. In the way he passes out the food. There is no judgment. There are no expectations. There is just love.

As I pick up a plate of sandwiches and pass it over the table between us an older Indian woman grabs my hand. I freeze. She won't let go. I see her hair, tangled, and her face, lined. Her eye shadow looks like it's from the night before and most of the lipstick on her mouth is chewed off. The woman is wearing a man's cardigan and a package of smokes stick out of the pocket. Her hands are like claws, clutching my smooth white ones on the edge of the paper plate. "This won't make you good," she hisses, through broken teeth.

I stare. She has read my mind. She knows what I have been thinking. And suddenly I feel my cheeks burn, and humility washes over me, wave upon wave. It's not regret or remorse. What I realize, in that single moment, is that I am no different from the old woman across from me, that we are all poor in spirit. I also realize at the same moment that God is here, in this room, in every last one of us, in the hungry and the fed. We are all part of the great mystery. And I am grateful.

I don't work at Hope Mission again but I do see Steve. He comes to the bookstore one rainy day six months after my brief but powerful encounter with the native woman. He recognizes me right away.

"Hey, I know you. You're the sandwich girl who worked at the Mission," he says, placing a huge cardboard box on the counter.

"Yeah, once. I worked once." I smile ruefully.

"It's not for everyone."

"What about you?" I ask. "Do you still work there?"

"No. It was part of my internship. I'm a social worker now. I just graduated last month. I'm looking for a job right now but meanwhile, I have to sell some books. Your name is Ruth, isn't it?"

I'm surprised he's remembered, and, yes, flattered.

The books he is selling are perfect for our eclectic collection. There are books on meditation, world religion, Gnosticism, Buddhist practice. I turn over a trade book called *Martyrdom in the Early Church*. I'm pretending to look at its condition when in fact I'm terrified it might have my name etched on the inside cover.

"Oh, those," says Steve, by way of apology. "There was a time I thought I'd go into the ministry. It was a bit of a misguided idea, really."

"Really?"

He smiles, half embarrassed. "There's a coffee shop a block away. I don't suppose you'd like to go for a coffee with me?"

I put the book down on the stack of others and look at him again. He's asking me for a date.

"I...I'd like to, really, I would, but I can't leave the shop." I gesture at the books, the shelves, and the fact that I am alone.

But Steve is persistent. "What time do you get off?"

"I'm finished by four. I could meet you then."

It's as simple as that, and as complicated, and as he bangs out the door into the drizzle, I find a small smile playing across my mouth that will not go away.

It's much later, when we decide to move in together, and are sorting through our stuff, that I see the photograph.

I'm not one hundred percent sure that the Ian Bowen person mentioned in Steve's newspaper clipping about the near-drowning is the same man I struggled with those many years ago, but I want to believe it is.

It helps, this discovery, this possible act of mercy, for despite the storm surge of memory, there is some small salvation, for the boy, yes, but also for Ian, and for me, too.

I hunker down beside Steve in the basement and peer at the newspaper article more closely. The photographs beside the item are lovely. There is a younger version of my Steve with his arm around this little tow-headed kid. Both of them are grinning ear to ear. You'd think it was Steve who was the hero. But no, in the paper he gives all the credit to the other guy, to Ian, who may or may not have been there.

I believe it *was* him. The dates on the paper jive. It would have been around the same time as his release, but, of course, there's no telling. Steve gave this man some dry clothes. He gave Ian new clothes. I hope it is so.

There is a second photograph on the yellowed clipping Steve has kept for all these years. It's next to the one of Steve and the little kid who almost drowned. It's a smaller picture of the beach. Nothing but a broad stretch of sand, some dunes in the background and the choppy sea, the place, I suppose, where the rescue happened.

I love this photograph because it is empty. Because of what is not there. I love the brittle print of this faded and bleached black and white photograph in Steve's stash of memorabilia because the sand on the shore bears no marks, no footprints, nothing. It has been swept clean by the wind.

That, to me, is sacred.

Ω